FIGHT

FOR

FREEDOM

FIGHT
FOR
FREEDOM

SIMON SCARROW

Disney • HYPERION BOOKS
NEW YORK

Text © 2011 by Simon Scarrow

First published in Great Britain in 2011 by Puffin Books,
an imprint of the Penguin Group.

For information address Disney • Hyperion Books,
114 Fifth Avenue, New York, New York 10011-5690.

First U.S. edition, 2012

Printed in the United States of America

10 9 8 7 6 5 4 3 2 1

G475-5664-5-12046

Library of Congress Cataloging-in-Publication Data

Scarrow, Simon.
Gladiator : fight for freedom / Simon Scarrow. — 1st U.S. ed.
p. cm.
Summary: After Marcus Cornelius Primus's father is murdered
and his mother kidnapped and enslaved, Marcus is forced to fight
as a gladiator, enduring years of brutal training while he secret
plots to avenge his father's death and rescue his mother.
ISBN 978-1-4231-5101-2 (hardcover)
[1. Gladiators—Fiction. 2. Slavery—Fiction. 3. Revenge—Fiction.
4. Rome—History—Empire, 30 B.C.–476 A.D.—Fiction.] I. Title.
PZ7.S32556Gl 2012
[Fic]—dc22   2011005903

Visit www.disneyhyperionbooks.com

*For Rosemary Sutcliffe, who has inspired
so many of us to love history*

PROLOGUE

CENTURION TITUS CORNELIUS POLLENIUS mopped his brow as he surveyed the battlefield stretching out around him. The hillside was covered with bodies, heaped together in those places where the fighting had been most bitter. His men were searching for injured comrades, or gleaning what little loot they could from their fallen enemies. Here and there the wounded cried out pitifully as they writhed amid the carnage. Among the bodies were Roman legionaries in their red tunics and chain-mail armor, now stained with blood. Titus estimated that thousands of his comrades had been killed in the battle. Even so, the Roman losses were nothing compared to those of the enemy.

He shook his head in wonder at the men, and women, he had faced earlier. Many had only been armed with knives and agricultural tools, and most had no armor, not even shields. Yet they had thrown themselves on Titus and his comrades, shrieking with rage, and eyes blazing with desperate courage. None of which had saved them from defeat against the better-trained and properly equipped soldiers of General Pompeius, the commander of the Roman armies that had pursued and trapped the enemy.

"Slaves," Titus muttered to himself in wonder as he stared at the bodies. "Just slaves."

Who would have thought that the men and women whom most Romans regarded as little more than walking tools would have had so much fight in them? It had been almost three years since the slave revolt began, and since then they had defeated five of the legions that Rome had sent against them. They had also burned many of the villas and pillaged the estates of the most powerful families in Rome. Once, Titus recalled, the slaves had even marched on Rome itself.

Looking down, he saw the body of a boy, little more than ten years old, he guessed. Flaxen-haired and finely featured, the boy's head lolled back over the armor of a dead legionary. His eyes stared into the bright sky, and his mouth hung slightly open as if he was about to speak. Titus felt a dull ache of sorrow in his heart as he gazed upon the child. There was no place for children in a battle, he thought to himself. No honor to be had in defeating them, or killing them.

"Centurion Titus!"

He turned at the shout and saw a small party of officers picking their way across the bodies toward him. At their head stood a large figure, broad-shouldered and wearing a gleaming silver breastplate, across which was tied a thick red ribbon to indicate his status. Unlike the men who had been in the heart of the battle, General Pompeius and his officers were untouched by blood and grime, and some of the younger, fussier officers curled their lips distastefully as they struggled over the dead.

"General." Titus stiffened to attention and bowed his head as his commander approached.

"What a bloody business," General Pompeius observed as he gestured at the battlefield. "Who would have thought that common slaves would put up such a fight, eh?"

"Indeed, sir."

Pompeius pursed his lips briefly and frowned. "Their leader—that Spartacus—he must have been quite a man."

"He was a gladiator, sir," Titus responded. "They're a special breed. The ones that survive in the arena for any length of time, at least."

"Did you know much about him, Centurion? That is, before he became a rebel."

"Just rumors, sir. Seems that he had only made a handful of appearances in the arena before the rebellion broke out."

"And yet he took to command like a duck to water," Pompeius mused. "It is a shame I never had the chance to meet this man, this Spartacus. I might have admired him." He looked up quickly and glanced at his officers. A smile flickered on his lips as he fixed his eyes on one in particular, a tall youth with a narrow face. "Rest easy there, Gaius Julius. I haven't gone over to the enemy. Spartacus is, or was, only a slave when all is said and done. Our enemy. Now he is crushed, and the danger is over."

The young officer shrugged. "We have won the battle, sir. But the fame of some men lives long after they have fallen. If he *has* fallen."

"Then we shall find his body," Pompeius replied tersely. "Once we have that, and display it for all to see, then we will have put an end to any notion of rebellion in the hearts of every damned slave in Italia."

He swung around to face Titus. "Centurion, where might Spartacus have fallen?"

Titus pursed his lips and gestured toward a small hummock a hundred paces away. There the bodies were more thickly heaped than anywhere else on the battlefield. "I saw his standard over there during the fighting, and that's where the last of them fought to the end. That's where we will find him, if anywhere, sir."

"Good; then let's go and see."

General Pompeius strode off, treading over and on the bodies as he made for the mound. Titus and the others hurried after him, and the scattered soldiers ahead of them stood to attention as the small party passed by. When they reached the mound, Pompeius stopped to stare at the terrible scene before him. The fighting there had been fiercest of all, and the bodies were covered with wounds. Titus shuddered, remembering that many of the slaves had fought with bare hands, and even their teeth, until they were cut down. Most of the corpses were so badly mutilated, you could hardly have recognized them as people.

The general let out a frustrated sigh and placed his hands on his hips as he climbed a short way forward over the bodies. "Well, if Spartacus was killed here, then we are going to have a hard time identifying him. I daresay we'll not get any cooperation from the prisoners in finding him." He nodded toward the cluster of figures surrounded by watchful legionaries a short distance from the edge of the battlefield. "Damn it. We need his body. . . ."

Titus watched as his commander stepped over the twisted limbs and bodies of the dead at the top of the mound. Pompeius was halfway up when a movement caught Titus's eye. A head rose slightly among the bodies, then an instant later a blood-spattered figure that Titus had thought dead sprang

4

up behind the general. The slave had lank dark hair and a thin beard, and his lips parted to reveal crooked teeth as he snarled. A short sword was clenched in his hand, and he rushed awkwardly across the heaped bodies toward the Roman general.

"Sir!" Gaius Julius shouted. "Look out!"

Titus was already moving as Pompeius turned to look back. The general's eyes widened as he saw the slave running at him, sword point leveled. Titus tore his blade free of the scabbard and raced up the mound of bodies, the flesh giving under his nailed boots. The slave thrust his sword at Pompeius's throat, and the general stumbled back to avoid the blow, his heel snagging on a body. He fell back heavily, crying out in alarm. The slave clambered forward and stood over the general as he raised his sword to strike.

Titus gritted his teeth and desperately sprinted forward. At the last moment, the slave sensed the danger and snatched a glance over his shoulder. Just then, Titus crashed into him with his full weight, and the slave's sword jerked from his hand. Both men tumbled to the ground, narrowly missing General Pompeius.

Titus tried to move his sword, but the handle barely budged, so he released his grip and groped for the slave's throat. The other man's body bucked under Titus, and his hands clawed at Titus's arms as he growled with an almost animal fury. The centurion tightened his grip, choking off the slave's noises. As he felt the pressure on his windpipe, the slave renewed his struggling. One of his hands grabbed Titus's wrist and tried to pry his fingers loose, while the other felt for his face, broken fingernails scratching at Titus's cheek as they moved up. Titus clenched his eyes shut as tightly as he could and clenched his hands just as tightly. The slave kicked up with his knees in response, and his own eyes bulged as he clawed at Titus's. The centurion turned his head and pressed it into his shoulder.

The slave's movements became frantic, then suddenly faded in strength, until his hands fell away and his head dropped back. Titus hung on for a moment longer, just to be certain, and then opened his eyes to see the dead man's tongue protruding through his teeth. Releasing his grip, Titus rolled away and scrambled back onto his feet, breathing hard. He looked down and saw that his sword had plunged into the man's ribs—that's why he had been unable to move it. The slave would have died anyway.

Beside him, the general, weighed down by his elaborately decorated breastplate, was struggling to his feet. He looked over and saw the dead slave, and Titus stooping over the body, as the centurion ripped his blade free.

"By the Gods, that was a close escape!" Pompeius looked down at the slave's body. "He would have killed me but for you, Centurion Titus."

Titus did not reply as he used the slave's grimy tunic to wipe the blood from his sword blade. Then he sheathed the weapon and stood erect again. The general smiled faintly at him. "I owe you my life. I shall not forget that."

Titus nodded his thanks.

"You should have a reward." The general stroked his chin and then gestured toward the slaves that had been taken prisoner. "Help yourself to one of them, in my name. That is a fitting prize for saving my life; but know this also, Centurion. If you ever need my help again, then you have my word that I will do what I can for you."

"You are too kind, my general."

"No. You saved my life. There is no reward too great for such an act. Now choose a prisoner to be your slave—a good woman, perhaps."

"Yes, sir. What of the rest? Are they to be shared among the men?"

General Pompeius shook his head. "Normally, I would be glad to do so. But every slave throughout the empire needs to be taught a lesson. They need to be shown what awaits those who rise up against their masters." He paused, and his expression hardened. "Once you have made your choice, give the order for the rest to be crucified. They will be nailed up along the road from Rome to Capua, where the revolt began."

Titus felt a cold chill down his spine at the general's brutal command. For a moment he felt the urge to object. The slaves were beaten. Their revolt was crushed. What need was there for such barbaric punishment? But then his training and discipline took over, and Titus saluted his general, before turning to pick his way across the battlefield toward the prisoners to choose the one who would be spared before the rest were led away to a long, painful death.

ONE

The island of Leucas, ten years later

MARCUS KNEW THERE WOULD BE TROUBLE the moment old Aristides came running into the courtyard early one summer morning. Marcus had been playing happily with Cerberus, trying to train the coarse-haired hunting dog to sit and then lay down at his command. But Cerberus had just cocked his head to one side, tongue hanging out, and stared blankly at his young master. As soon as he saw Aristides, he bounded over to the old man and wagged his tail.

The goatherd was gasping for breath, and leaned on his staff and swallowed until he had recovered enough to speak.

"Three men." He pointed a trembling finger toward the track that climbed the hill from Nydri. "Big men . . . soldiers, I think."

Marcus's father was sitting at the long weathered table in the shade of a trellis entwined with grapevines as thick as his wrist. Titus Cornelius had been busy working on the accounts of the farm, and now he lowered his stylus onto the waxed slates and rose from his bench to stride across the small courtyard.

"Soldiers, you say?"

"Yes, master."

"I see." Titus smiled faintly before he continued in a mild tone. "And what would you know about soldiers, old man? Animals, yes. But soldiers?"

Aristides straightened up and stared directly at his master. "Two of them have spears, and they're all carrying swords."

Marcus glanced at his father, noting a brief flicker of anxiety cross his face. Marcus had never seen his father look worried before. His craggy face was marked by several scars, relics of his service in the legions of General Pompeius. He had been a centurion—a battle-hardened officer—when he had taken his discharge and left the eagles. He had bought the farm on the island of Leucas and settled down with Marcus's mother, who had given birth to him a few months earlier. Since then, Titus had made a steady income from a small herd of goats tended by Aristides, and the grapevines that covered his land. Marcus remembered happier times when he was a small boy—but for the last three years the rains hadn't come—and drought and blight had ruined the crops. Titus had been forced to borrow money. Marcus knew it was a lot—he'd heard his parents whispering about it at night when they thought he was asleep, and he continued to worry about it long after they had fallen silent.

The soft shuffle of feet made Marcus turn to see his mother emerging from her room overlooking the courtyard. She had been weaving a new tunic for him, but had abandoned her loom as soon as Aristides had spoken.

"They have spears," she muttered, then stared at Titus. "Perhaps they're going into the hills to hunt boar."

"I don't think so." The old centurion shook his head.

"If they're hunting boar, then why carry swords? No, this is something else. They're coming to the farm." He took a pace forward and patted Aristides on the shoulder. "You did well to warn me, old friend."

"Old?" The goatherd's eyes twinkled briefly. "Why, I am less than ten years older than you, master."

Titus laughed, a deep hearty laugh that Marcus had known all his life and always found reassuring. Despite a hard life in the legions, his father had always been good-humored. At times he had been tough with Marcus, insisting that he fight his own battles with some of the children down in Nydri, but there had been no doubting his affection.

"Why are they coming here?" his mother asked. "What do they want with us?"

Marcus saw his father's smile fade. "Trouble," he growled. "That's what they want with us. Decimus must have sent them."

"Decimus?" Marcus saw his mother raise a hand to her mouth in horror. "I told you we should have had nothing to do with him."

"Well, it's too late for that now, Livia. I'll have to deal with him."

Marcus was scared by his mother's reaction. He cleared his throat. "Who is Decimus, Father?"

"Decimus?" Titus sneered and spat on the ground. "Just some bloodsucking swine who someone should have taught a lesson to years ago."

Marcus stared back blankly and Titus chuckled, reaching forward to fondly ruffle his son's dark curls. "He's quite a piece of work, our Decimus. The richest moneylender on

Leucas, and thanks to his influence with the Roman governor, he's now the tax collector as well."

"An unfortunate combination of businesses," Livia added quietly. "He's ruined several of the farmers around Nydri already."

"Well, he won't ruin this one!" Titus growled. "Aristides, bring me my sword."

The goatherd raised his eyebrows anxiously and then hurried inside the house as Cerberus stared after him for a moment and then trotted back to Marcus's side. He stroked the dog's head affectionately. Livia moved to grasp his father's thick arm.

"What are you thinking, Titus? You heard Aristides. There are three of them, armed. Soldiers, he said. You cannot fight them. Don't even think about it."

Titus shook his head. "I've faced tougher odds, and won. As you know well enough."

Marcus's mother's expression hardened. "That was a long time ago. You haven't been in any kind of fight for over ten years now."

"I won't fight them if I don't have to. But Decimus will have sent them to collect money. They will not leave without it."

"How much money?"

Titus looked down and scratched the back of his neck. "Nine hundred sestertii."

"Nine hundred!"

"I am behind three payments," Titus explained. "I've been expecting this."

"Can you pay them?" she asked anxiously.

"No. I have almost nothing in the strongbox. Enough to see us through to the winter, and then..." He shook his head.

Livia frowned angrily. "You had better explain everything to me later. Marcus!" She turned to her son. "Go and fetch the money chest from beneath the shrine in the atrium. *Now.*"

Marcus nodded and made to run into the house.

"Stay where you are, boy!" Titus called out, loud enough to be heard for a hundred paces in every direction. "Leave the chest where it is. I'll not be forced to pay a single coin before I am ready to."

"Are you mad?" asked Livia. "You can't fight armed men alone."

"We'll see," Titus responded gravely. "Now, take the boy and go indoors. I'll deal with it."

"You'll get yourself hurt, or killed, Titus. Then what will become of Marcus and me? Answer me that."

"Go indoors," Titus commanded.

Marcus saw his mother open her mouth to protest, but both of them knew the steely look in Titus's eyes. She shook her head crossly and held out a hand toward Marcus. "Come with me."

Marcus stared at her, then at his father, and stood his ground, determined to prove his worth to his father.

"Marcus, come with me. Now!"

"No. I'm staying here." He drew himself up and placed his hands on his hips. "Cerberus and I can stand at Father's side, if it comes to a fight." He wanted the words to sound brave, but his voice quavered slightly.

"What's this? Stay?" Titus asked, bemused. "You are not

yet ready to take your place in the battle line, my boy. Go with your mother."

Marcus shook his head. "You need me. Us." He nodded at Cerberus, and the dog's ears pricked up, and he wagged his bushy tail.

Before Titus could protest, Aristides came out of the house. In one hand he clutched his staff. In the other he held a sword scabbard, from which a leather strap dangled. Titus took the weapon and looped the strap over his head, shifting his shoulder until he was satisfied that the sword hung well and the hilt was within easy reach. Aristides went over to the gate and kept watch on the road that led down the slope toward Nydri. Suddenly, Titus snatched at the sword handle and ripped the blade out in one motion, so swiftly that Marcus flinched. He let out a small cry. Cerberus growled.

His father glanced at him with a smile, and sheathed the sword. "Easy there; I was just checking that the sword drew swiftly. It's why I keep the scabbard and blade oiled—just in case."

Marcus swallowed nervously. "In case of what, Father?"

"In case of moments like this. Now, you leave this to me. Go into the house until I call for you."

Marcus stared back defiantly. "My place is at your side, Father. I can fight." He grasped the leather pouch and the thongs of the sling tucked into the belt fastened around his waist. "I can hit a hare at fifty paces with this."

His mother had been watching the two of them. Now she called out, "For pity's sake, Marcus! Come inside, now!"

"Livia," her husband cut in. "You go. Take shelter in the kitchen. I'll speak to Marcus. He'll come to you directly."

She made to protest, then saw the fiery light in his eyes

and turned away, her sandal scuffling over the flagstones. Titus turned back to Marcus and smiled fondly. "My boy, you are still too young to fight my battles. Please, go with your mother."

But it was too late. Before Titus had finished speaking, there was a sharp hiss from Aristides. The goatherd cupped a hand to his mouth and called out as loudly as he dared, "Master! They're coming!"

TWO

His father gestured toward the entrance to the house. "Marcus—stand over there, and don't move."

Marcus nodded and clicked his fingers to catch the dog's attention. "Follow!"

They took up position in the shaded side of the small entrance hall leading into the modest atrium of the farm-house, out of sight of the gate. Aristides took a firm grasp of his crook and stood ready, to one side of the gate.

All was still for a moment. Marcus's heart was thudding inside his chest, and his mouth was dry. Then he heard them, the muted voices of the three men walking up the lane toward the gate. One of them made some comment, and the others laughed. It was a harsh, unpleasant sound, and Marcus cursed himself. He had said he could help his father but he had no shot for his sling, and in any case, he needed space and time to make the weapon ready.

Marcus knew he had a good eye, and Aristides had taught him well—well enough to kill one of the wild dogs that had been preying on the younger goats earlier, in the spring. But in the present situation the weapon was as good as useless.

Just then he saw one of his father's vine canes leaning

in the corner of the entrance. He snatched it up and held it ready, determined to strike hard with the gnarled end if there was a fight.

The men's voices died away as they neared the gate. Their boots crunched over the gravel, and they entered the farm. Marcus peered around the corner of the entrance hall and glanced over at the unwelcome visitors. A tall, muscular man led the way. He had straggly hair streaked with gray and held back by a leather headband. Marcus guessed the man was not many years younger than his father. He looked solid enough, and the scar stretching diagonally across his face was proof that he was used to fighting. On either side of him, and a pace behind their leader, the other two were equally tough-looking, and each carried a spear in addition to the swords that hung from their belts.

Titus looked them up and down before he cleared his throat and spoke directly. "Who are you? State your business and then be on your way."

The leader's hard expression creased into a smile, and he raised his hands to placate Titus. "Easy there, sir! There's no need to act the hard centurion with us. We're just here to bring you a message. From Decimus." The smile faded.

"First, tell me your name."

"Why?"

"I like to know who I'm dealing with," Titus replied evenly as his hand slid up and rested over the pommel of his sword hilt.

"Very well, I am Thermon. I deal with my master's more difficult customers."

"Speak your piece, Thermon, and go."

"Now then, now then, there's no call for such an inhospitable attitude, sir. The reason we're here is simple enough. You owe our master some money. A thousand and fifty sestertii, to be precise. He has sent us to collect the debt."

"Nine hundred," Titus replied evenly.

"Pardon, sir?"

"I owe nine hundred sestertii. Not a thousand and fifty."

The leader folded his hands together and cracked his knuckles. "Ah, you see, there's the question of additional interest to be paid on the debt. You now owe Decimus one thousand and fifty, like I said. . . . My master wants the money. Now."

Titus sighed wearily. "I haven't got it. Decimus knows this. I've told his agent that I will pay him next year, as soon as I have had a good harvest. Now, you'd better turn around and go back to Decimus and explain it to him carefully, so that there's no misunderstanding this time. Tell him he will have his money as soon as I can afford to pay it." Titus paused briefly. "And there will be no extra interest. He will have what I owe him, and no more. Now, I will tell you one last time. Leave my property."

The leader puffed his cheeks and shook his head. "Sorry, Centurion, that simply won't do. We either leave with the money, or with valuables sufficient to cover the amount—the full amount—you owe Decimus. That's how it is."

Titus stared back at him, and the other men tightened the grip on their spears and inclined the tips slightly toward the former centurion. Marcus could sense that the confrontation would explode into violence at any moment. He clenched his fists around the vine cane. He knew the dog sensed the danger too. The hackles began to rise along Cerberus's spine, and the dog snarled, revealing gleaming white fangs.

Before either Titus or his visitors could act, there was a sudden movement to the side of the gate as Aristides stepped forward, clutching his staff in his frail hands.

"The master told you to leave!" His voice was thin and reedy, but there was no mistaking the determination in his deep-set eyes below the thick white tufts of hair lining his brow. "Get out."

Thermon blinked in surprise and then let out a roar of laughter. His two men followed suit, laughing nervously as they glanced from Aristides to Titus.

"Centurion, where on earth did you find this relic?" Thermon shook his head and quickly sized up Aristides. "I doubt we'll need to count him into the inventory. He's not worth anything—you'd have to give him away."

Marcus felt a fiery anger in his heart as the men insulted Aristides. He saw his father's expression darken. Titus gritted his teeth and growled. "My slave is not for sale. And you will do as he says and get off my land."

Thermon's humor instantly faded. He drew his sword and turned to nod at his men, and they lowered the points of their spears. Thermon faced Titus again. "Your choice, Centurion. Pay up, or else."

Titus sneered as he drew his sword and settled into a fighting crouch. "I think I'll choose 'or else.'"

Marcus stared anxiously at his father. His limbs trembled. There was no way Titus could win alone against three men. Marcus had to do something.

Just then, Aristides launched himself at the nearest of Thermon's men with a shrill cry, swinging his staff around in an arc. The man turned and held out his spear, blocking the blow with a sharp crack of wood on wood. The goatherd pressed forward, groaning with the effort. Thermon's man was younger, stronger, and used to handling a weapon, and he easily absorbed the charge. He thrust back, sending Aristides flying. With a pained grunt, the goatherd fell on his back. At once his opponent stood over him and drew back his spear, as if to strike.

"Cerberus! Catch!" Marcus yelled, and he hurled his vine cane at the man. There was a blur of fur and teeth as the dog leaped forward and jumped for the stick. The dog's body slammed into the man, bowling him over and making him drop his spear. Aristides rolled aside and staggered to his feet, desperately trying to scramble out of reach before the man could recover.

Meanwhile, Titus swept forward with a roar, violently knocking aside a spear thrust from Thermon's other companion, and smashing the heavy brass guard of his sword into the man's face. His head snapped back and he dropped, out cold.

But before Titus could turn on Thermon, the intruder was already making his attack. His sword thrust straight at Titus's chest. The centurion swung his own sword around, just parrying the blow in time. The point cut through the air inches from his scalp. At once, Thermon pulled his sword arm back and thrust again. This time Titus was not quite quick enough, and the blade sliced through his sword arm.

"Ahh!" Titus cried out, instinctively slackening his grip. Thermon seized the advantage, and with a ringing blow, knocked the sword from Titus's hands.

Marcus felt an icy fist of terror clench his heart. Snatching a deep breath, he charged out from the entrance and jumped onto Thermon's back, wrapping his thin arms around the man's throat.

"What in Hades?" Thermon snarled. But Marcus held on as tight as he could—terrified but determined not to let go. He heard an excited bark, then Cerberus sprang forward, sinking his teeth into Thermon's sword arm. Caught between the dog and the boy trying to throttle him, Thermon cursed them both furiously through his gritted teeth. He released his grip on the sword, and it clattered to the ground.

"Good boy!" Titus shouted as he snatched up his sword and went for the man facing Aristides.

"Look out!" Thermon grunted.

His companion's attention was still focused on the old goatherd, and so he barely had time to take heed of the warning before Titus swung a cut at his arm, slicing through to the bone. With a shrill cry of agony, the man dropped the spear and clutched his arm to his chest. Titus kicked the spear toward Aristides.

"Take it. If he tries anything, run him through."

"Yes, master!" The goatherd grinned. "It'd be a pleasure."

Titus turned and raised his sword to Thermon's throat. "Let him go, Marcus, and call off the dog."

Marcus loosened his grip and dropped to the ground, heart beating wildly. He caught his breath and snapped his fingers. "Cerberus! Drop!"

Reluctantly, the dog loosened his jaws and padded around Thermon with a parting snarl, before he trotted to Marcus's side. Marcus was proud of his dog—he patted Cerberus on the head. "Good boy."

Thermon rubbed his throat with his hand. Blood oozed from the teeth marks on his other arm. He stared at Titus with a look of bitter hatred.

Titus smiled. "I think you'd better take your men and report back to Decimus. Tell him he'll have his money in good time. Tell him that if he tries to send any more of his lackeys to harass me, they'll get the same treatment you have."

Titus gestured to the man lying on the ground. "Now pick him up and get off my land."

Thermon and the man with the wounded arm picked their comrade up, with some difficulty. His arms over their shoulders, they made their way to the entrance. Thermon paused briefly to glance over his shoulder. "Centurion, this isn't over. Be warned—I'll be back, with more men. You'll pay dearly for defying Decimus."

"Pah!" Titus spat on the ground.

Then the unwelcome visitors were gone, and there was only the sound of their boots scraping up the path.

Marcus looked at his father and Aristides. All three of them were breathing heavily. Then Titus let out a cheer and Marcus joined in, his heart filled with relief that they were all unhurt, and also pride that they had beaten their foes. Titus slapped his hand down on Marcus's shoulder.

"Well, you're a chip off your old man's block, and no mistake!"

Marcus looked up at him and beamed with happiness at the praise. "And Cerberus too, Father. He helped."

"He did indeed!" Titus fondly stroked the dog's head.

Aristides tossed the spear aside and joined them. Even

though the old man was a slave, Titus put his spare arm around him and patted him on the shoulder. "As fine a victory as any I've known. Well done, men!"

Marcus and Aristides laughed happily, and Titus joined in, until he noticed a figure standing in the entrance to the house, watching them coldly.

"I hope you're happy with yourself," Livia said.

Titus drew himself up defiantly. "That I am."

"Really? Do you think this is over? I heard him. He says he will be back, with more men."

Titus waved a hand dismissively. "I doubt it. We've taught him, and Decimus, a lesson. You'll see. If he tries anything against a Roman citizen, and a decorated centurion at that, then he knows he'll catch it in the neck. But if it makes you feel more comfortable, we'll keep a watch out for them."

Marcus saw his mother shake her head. She turned away and walked back into the house. Even though his heart burned with pride at having fought at his father's side, he could not help wondering if she was right. What if Decimus did send more men? They would surely be better prepared to take on his father next time.

"Well, that was fun!" Titus grinned. "Something worthy of a celebration. Aristides!"

"Master?"

"Slaughter your best goat. Tonight we celebrate our victory with a feast!"

Marcus looked up and exchanged a smile with his father. Titus patted his cheek and nodded with satisfaction.

"My little soldier. You'll make quite a fighter one day. You'll see."

THREE

Several days after Decimus's men had been driven off, Marcus and Aristides were sitting on a slab of rock, watching over the goats.

"Cerberus served you well the other day." Aristides smiled, then his expression grew more serious. "However, you still have some way to go before that dog is fully trained."

Marcus looked down at Cerberus. The dog sensed his attention and looked up with a devoted expression, and wagged his tail happily. "He seems tame enough."

"He's tame, but he's not trained," Aristides said firmly. "It was quick thinking to throw that stick for him, but you can't rely on that working next time."

"Next time? You really think those men will come back?"

"It's possible." Aristides forced himself to smile dismissively. "Even if they don't, that's no reason not to finish training Cerberus. He's done well since you found him, Master Marcus."

Marcus nodded. It was over a year since the peddler had come by the house with his cart filled with old pots, knives, cups, and other wares. Cerberus had been chained to the back of the wagon to guard its contents. He had been starved and beaten to make him as vicious as possible, to deter anyone attempting to take anything from the wagon. Marcus's mother had taken one look at the contents of the cart and was about to send the peddler on his way when Marcus intervened. The sight of the dog had broken his young heart.

"Let me buy him, Mother," he had whispered to her.

"Buy him?" Livia looked amused. "What with? You have no money."

"Then you buy him. Please."

She shook her head. "He's a worthless wild animal, Marcus. No good for anything."

Marcus looked at the animal and saw through the matted hair and bared teeth—saw the tormented and frightened creature within. "He's been badly treated. He needs care. Let me have him, and I promise I can train him and make him useful on the farm. Please." He caught the sleeve of her tunic and stared up at her. "If that man is allowed to own him for much longer, the poor dog will die."

His mother stared back at him, and then frowned, as if a memory had been reawakened. She looked up at the peddler and asked curtly, "How much for the dog?"

The peddler's eyes narrowed shrewdly. "Twenty sestertii, seeing as it's for the young lad there."

"Ten. And no more."

"Ten?" The peddler pretended to look surprised. "But he's a first-class hunting dog. Good lineage and all that. Worth a fortune, he is."

"Ten," Livia said firmly.

The peddler paused, as if weighing up the offer. Then he nodded. "All right, then, but I'm robbing myself."

He untied the dog from the cart and offered the rope to Marcus. Livia held him back as she spoke to the peddler. "No. You tie him to that post, there behind the barn."

Once the dog was secured, she went inside for the money and counted the coins out into the peddler's hand. He closed his fingers at once and scurried back to his cart.

"Good luck with him. You'll need it."

Then he cracked his whip and the cart trundled away, leaving Marcus staring at the dog as it backed against the wall of the barn and watched its new owners suspiciously.

Aristides had a peculiar talent for taming animals, and he spent his spare time trying to pass on his skills to Marcus. Together, they had worked on Cerberus in a barred store-room behind the olive press. Marcus remembered that first night—the old man had fed Cerberus a sleeping potion, then the two crept in and bathed the dog's wounds. Afterward, he was fed a diet of gruel made up of scrap meat from the kitchen and ground barley. Weeks passed, and the dog soon recovered its health, and fur grew back over the bald patches, covering his bruises and scars. Coached by Aristides, Marcus began to offer the dog pieces of meat. At first he offered the meat through the bars, and Cerberus approached warily before snatching it away and rushing to the back of the store-room, where he gulped it down. Then Aristides and Marcus entered the room, and Aristides gently urged Marcus to offer the meat by hand. It took all of Marcus's courage to step forward and hold his hand out.

"Don't flinch," the goatherd urged him. "You must not let him know you are afraid."

The first few times, Cerberus snatched the meat and ran, but after a few days he took the meat and ate it where he stood. Then, one day, after he had gulped the meat down, he stepped cautiously forward and sniffed Marcus. The puffs of warm breath on his skin made Marcus nervous, but he held his hand still until he suddenly felt the dog's tongue lick his fingers. His breast filled with a warm pride and love for the animal, and he glanced at Aristides with a delighted smile. "Did you see?"

The old goatherd nodded and returned the smile, patting the boy on the head. "There, I told you if you were patient we would win him over."

Soon, Cerberus was happy to let Marcus stroke him, and a month after he arrived they led him out of the room and took him for a walk around the farm. The dog was wary at first, before the delight of every scent took hold, and he trotted to and fro, sniffing the ground but always staying close to Marcus and Aristides. It wasn't long before Marcus was walking the dog by himself and starting the first simple lessons in obedience. Three months after Cerberus had arrived at the farm, Marcus presented the dog to his mother and father in the courtyard.

"Well! He's much improved," Livia said with a surprised expression. "The coat looks in good condition, and he's put on some weight."

"True," Titus mused, squatting down to look closely at the dog. He felt its muscles and lifted the jowls to check the teeth, all without any reaction from Cerberus. Titus looked at his son. "You've done well, boy."

Marcus smiled with pride, then he gestured to the goatherd. "Aristides helped me, Father. I couldn't have done it without him."

"Yes, he is good with animals. Always has been. Now then, the question is, what use can this one be put to? Can he be trained, I wonder?"

Marcus smiled. "Watch."

He clicked his fingers and pointed to the ground at his side. "Sit!"

Cerberus pulled away from Titus, trotted to Marcus's side, and sat. Marcus opened his hand so the palm was parallel to the ground. "Lie!"

Cerberus shuffled his front legs forward and sank onto the ground. Marcus paused and then circled his hand around. "Die for Rome."

Cerberus rolled over onto his back, legs flopping loosely. Marcus's mother clapped her hands in delight.

"What a clever dog!"

"Clever?" Titus frowned. "It's a simple trick. Besides, a clever dog wouldn't die for anyone. If you can teach him something useful to help on the farm, then he's yours to keep, boy. Otherwise, he must go."

Marcus and Aristides tried to teach Cerberus how to help herd the goats, but the dog always treated the lessons as a game, and ran barking at the goats until he was called off and placed back on his leash. They had better success with hunting. Cerberus had a fine nose for prey, and more often than not he could chase down any hares before they reached the safety of their burrows. Titus, grudgingly, allowed the dog to stay.

Now, after the visit of Decimus's men, Marcus was

determined to complete Cerberus's training with a more dangerous set of skills. When he explained his ideas to Aristides, the goatherd puffed his cheeks and scratched his head.

"I'm not so sure that is a wise idea, Marcus. At the moment, the dog has a good nature. He loves people. If I do as you ask and we train him to attack, then you may lose that side of him. He will become a very different animal indeed."

Marcus had already made his mind up. If, or more likely when, Decimus sent more men to the farm, then his father would need all the help he could get. He looked steadily into Aristides's eyes and nodded. "We must do it."

Aristides sighed and looked down at the dog, and sadly caressed its ear. "Very well, then. We'll start today."

While they trained the dog, Titus told every member of the household to keep an eye open for any men approaching the farm. He organized a rota for himself and Aristides to keep watch during the nights. He took the first and last turns. Each night as Marcus made his way to his bed, he saw his father seated on a stool just inside the courtyard gate, his drawn sword resting across his thighs, and a large copper dish propped up beside him to be beaten if he had to sound the alarm. Marcus worried about it constantly, but no one came in the days that followed, and then the days stretched into a month, and still Decimus sent no men, or even any message.

Life on the farm continued with its usual routines, and after Marcus had carried out his daily duties, he devoted his time to training Cerberus. Just as Aristides had warned him, the dog became tense, seemingly wary of everyone except Marcus and the goatherd.

One night he was dropping off to sleep—the pale yellow glow of an oil lamp flickering on the simple chest that was the only furniture in his room—when his mother came and sat on his bed.

"I haven't seen much of Cerberus lately," she said, stroking his hair. "He's never around the house. There was a time when I had to watch him carefully to make sure the scamp didn't sneak anything from the kitchen."

"I'm keeping him in the storeroom again."

"Why? He's no trouble to have in the house."

"It's to do with his training," Marcus explained. "Aristides said it would be best if he was kept away from other people for a while."

His mother raised her eyebrows, and then shrugged. "Well, the old man must be right. He knows his animals well enough."

Marcus nodded, then smiled at his mother. She stared back at him, and her hand froze on his head. A momentary look of pain crossed her face, and Marcus felt a stab of alarm. "Mother, what is it?"

She withdrew her hand quickly. "Nothing. Really. Just that you reminded me of your father for a moment. That's all." She patted his cheek and leaned forward to kiss him. She got up to leave, but before she could, Marcus put a hand on her arm. "Will we be all right?" he asked softly.

"Pardon?"

"Will the men come back?"

She was silent a moment before she nodded. "Don't worry, Titus will protect us. He always has."

Marcus was comforted by that, and for a moment his mind wandered. Then he asked, "Was Father a good soldier?"

"Oh, yes. One of the very best." She closed her eyes. "I knew that as soon as I saw him."

"When did you meet him?"

Her eyes opened again, and she paused a moment before responding. "I met Titus soon after the revolt was put down."

"The slave revolt? The one that was led by the gladiator?"

"Yes. Spartacus."

"Father told me about that once. He said that Spartacus and his rebels were the greatest threat that ever faced Rome. He said they were the toughest and bravest men he had ever fought. He was there at the final battle with the slaves." Marcus recalled the story that his father had told him. "He said that it was the hardest battle he had ever been in. The slaves did not have much armor, and hardly any weapons, but they fought to the end. Only a handful surrendered."

"Yes..."

"If father could defeat Spartacus and the slaves, then he must be able to beat Decimus's men."

"That was over ten years ago," she said. "Titus is an older man now. He is not a centurion any longer."

"But he will protect us, won't he?"

She smiled faintly and stroked his cheek. "Yes. Of course. Now get to sleep, my darling boy."

"Yes, Mother," he replied sleepily, and rolled onto his side, nestling his head down into the bolster. She continued stroking his hair for a while, until his eyes closed and his breathing became even. Then she rose up and crossed quietly to the door. She stood there a while, and Marcus drowsily opened his eyes a fraction to look at her, wondering at her strange expression when he'd spoken of Spartacus. By the wan glow of the lamp, he could see that her eyes were glistening, and a tear began to roll down her cheek. She sniffed and abruptly cuffed the tear away before turning to the oil lamp and puffing out the flame. The room was plunged into darkness, as Marcus heard her feet padding softly away down the corridor.

He lay there, restless. Why had his mother been crying? Was she scared like him? He had always thought of his father as a tough, strong man. Titus was never ill, and worked his farm in the cold wind and rain of winter and the blazing heat of summer without a word of complaint or any sign of discomfort. Marcus knew his father was older than his mother. Much older. His face was battered and creased, and his thinning hair was streaked with gray. By contrast, she was slender, dark-haired, and quite beautiful, Marcus thought. How had she come to marry him? The more he thought about it, the more questions formed in his head. It was funny, he reflected, just how little he knew about his parents. They had always been there, always together, and he had taken them for granted. Yet now that he thought about it, they seemed an unlikely couple. He felt an itch on his back, on his right shoulder blade, and he reached around to scratch. His fingertips traced their way over the strangely shaped scar tissue that had been there as long as he could remember. He lightly dug his nails in, and rubbed until the itch had gone.

He rolled onto his back and stared into the darkness of the rafters above. He resolved that from now on he would put every spare hour into training Cerberus. If those men came back, from what his mother had said, there was no guarantee that his father could beat them again. Marcus would have to stand by his side. He was big enough to handle a meat cleaver, or one of his father's light hunting javelins. And he would have Cerberus with him. He half smiled at the thought, reassured by the idea that Cerberus would protect them. Then he drifted off into a troubled sleep, haunted by vague images of dark figures stealing through the night toward the farm.

FOUR

THE NEXT MORNING WAS HOT, although the sky was hazy enough to hide the mountains on the mainland across the narrow strip of sea from Leucas. The air was still and, apart from the light rhythmic sawing sound of the cicadas, all was quiet. Hundreds of crows were swooping from one patch of trees to the next, like swirling scraps of black material.

"There'll be rain," Aristides remarked, squinting up into the sky. "I can feel it."

Marcus nodded. He had been helping Aristides select ten of the younger goats to be sold in the market in Nydri. It had not been easy, as the animals were skittish for some reason, and the two of them had to move very carefully in order not to alarm the kids. Once a noose had been dropped over their necks, it had been easy enough to lead them to join the others in the stock pen a short distance from the farm. Marcus and Aristides had just caught the last one, and now they were resting in the shade of an olive grove.

"Cerberus will need a walk soon," Aristides continued. "He's been shut up in the storeroom all morning."

Marcus nodded again. He had had to make sure that the

dog was out of the way while they rounded up the goats. "I'll see to it in a moment."

He looked out down the slope. A mile away, the cluster of red roofs and white walls of Nydri lay by the sea, a metallic blue today, with lighter and darker patches where the faint breeze rippled the surface. He wiped a bead of sweat from his brow.

"It's beautiful here, isn't it?"

Aristides looked at him with a surprised expression. "Why, yes, I suppose it is."

"Sometimes I think I would like to live here forever. On the farm, with my family. That includes you, Aristides."

The old man smiled. "That's a kind thing to say. But you will be a young man in a few years, keen to leave home and see the world for yourself. Have you thought of what you might like to do?"

Marcus nodded once more. "I'd like to be an animal trainer. Like you."

Aristides chuckled. "I am just a slave, Marcus. I was born a slave. All my life I have been the property of other men and never had the chance to do what I want, or go where I willed. I was theirs to treat as *they* willed. Not all masters are as kind or fair as your father. Trust me. You would not want to be a slave."

"I suppose not." Marcus stared out to sea again for a moment. "Father wants me to be a soldier. He says he still has some influence with General Pompeius and can get me enrolled in a legion. If I am a good soldier, and prove my courage, then I could become a centurion like him."

"I see." Aristides nodded. "And would you like that?"

"I think so. I've heard him tell stories of his years in

the legion. I would be proud if I could be like him. And he would be proud of me."

"Yes, I imagine so. What does your mother think?"

Marcus frowned. "I don't know. Whenever I talk about it, she goes very quiet. I don't understand why. I thought she'd want me to be like him."

He felt something lightly tap his shoulder, and looked up. "Here's the rain."

More drops fell, and they saw that the overcast sky had darkened over the mountains behind the farm, and a veil of rain was coming down the slope toward them.

"You go back to the house," said Aristides. "I'll stay here and watch the goats. We don't want them panicking and trying to escape from the pen."

Marcus nodded and quickly rose to his feet. The rain was now falling steadily, pattering through the leaves on the trees. Marcus hurried across to the storeroom, slipped the latch, and ducked inside. At once there was a clicking of toenails across the paved floor as Cerberus bounded over to him, jumping up to lick his face.

"Enough, boy!" Marcus laughed, then remembered what Aristides told him about being firm. He hardened his tone. "Sit!"

Cerberus instantly sat down, and his bushy tail swished once and then was still as he looked up at Marcus, waiting for the next instruction.

"Good boy." He stroked the dog's head, and the tail started wagging again. Outside, the rain was now coming down hard, drumming on the roof tiles, and dripping through wherever it found a crack. A dazzling burst of light lit up the gap in the door. Marcus stared outside. The rain slashed down like thousands of silver rods, and with the dark clouds overhead, it was hard to see beyond a hundred paces. A terrible crash of thunder shook the air, and Cerberus flinched, then let out a frightened whine.

Marcus knelt down and put an arm over the dog's back. He was trembling. "Easy, boy. It'll soon pass."

But some time later, the rain had still not eased at all. Marcus stood in the storeroom and watched as it continued to pound down on the farm. Every now and then, lightning would freeze the world in garish white, and the thunder would rip through the heavens. Marcus found it impossible to avoid the thin trickles of rain coming through the old roof, and all the time Cerberus became more afraid. At length, Marcus decided it would be better to shelter in the house. The kitchen would be warm, and there might be some scraps he could use to comfort Cerberus.

"Come on, boy." He patted the dog's side. "Come!"

Easing the door open, Marcus braced himself and ran down the side of the storeroom toward the gate, with Cerberus at his heels. He dashed through the courtyard to the entrance of the house. It had taken him no more than ten heartbeats to reach shelter, but his tunic was drenched and Cerberus's flanks were streaked with matted fur. At once Marcus knew what was about to happen.

"Cerberus, no!"

But it was too late—the dog shook himself, spraying the entrance corridor with drops of water, just as Marcus's mother emerged from her room to see who had entered the house.

"What on earth!" She held up her hands to shield her face from the muddy spray.

Cerberus finished shaking and looked around at his master, with his tongue lolling out.

Livia lowered her hands and glared down at her son as she hissed, "What is that wet dog doing in my house?"

Another figure emerged from the far end of the corridor, and Titus laughed as he took in the scene. "No shelter from the rain indoors or out, it would seem!"

His wife turned her glare toward him. "I'm glad you think it's funny."

"Well, yes, it is." Titus scratched his head. "Very funny, actually."

He winked at his son, and both of them laughed. Livia scowled. "Men and boys, I don't know which are worse. If I had my way—"

She was interrupted by a panicked cry from the gateway. The laughter died in Marcus's and his father's throats.

"Master!" Aristides shrieked.

Livia clutched her hand to her face.

Titus ran down the corridor into the courtyard, and Marcus followed him. Over by the gate, the goatherd was slumped against the wall. An arrow protruded from his chest. Blood spread down his tunic. He leaned his head back and groaned as the rain splashed down on his face and straggly beard. As Marcus and Titus reached him and knelt at his side, his eyes flickered open. He raised a hand and grasped Titus's sleeve.

"Master, they've come back!"

He coughed, and frothy blood hung from his lips. He groaned again as he dropped Titus's sleeve and shuddered. Looking up through the gate, Marcus stared along the track, now running with tiny rivulets. He saw movement under the olive trees. With a blinding flash of white, another bolt of lightning lit up the sky, and there, frozen like statues, he saw several men armed with spears and swords. One had a bow, which he was holding up, ready to loose an arrow toward the house. Marcus saw the arrow fly, even as the lightning vanished, and just before the thunder crashed, he heard a thud. He looked down, and Aristides stared back, wide-eyed. The arrow had struck him in the neck. The bloodied arrowhead had burst out the far side, a hand's breadth from the skin. The goatherd opened his mouth, but there were no words, just a gush of blood before he slumped to one side.

Titus reacted instantly. "Get my sword!"

Marcus ran back toward the hall, where the weapon hung from a peg. He glanced back to see his father heaving the solid wooden gate around on its hinges to close it. Through the narrowing gap, Marcus could dimly see the men bursting from the cover of the olive trees and sprinting across the narrow strip of open ground toward the gateway. He turned away and ran into the hall, slipping on the flagstones. His mother grabbed his arm.

"What's happening?" She saw the goatherd lying on the ground. "Aristides?"

"He's dead," Marcus replied flatly, then pulled free as he reached up and grabbed his father's sword by the hilt, wrenching it free of the scabbard.

"What are you doing?" Livia asked in alarm.

Marcus did not reply, but clapped a hand to his thigh as he glanced at Cerberus. "Come!"

The two of them rushed out of the hall into the rain. On the other side of the courtyard, Marcus could see that his father had almost managed to shut the gate. But by the time

Marcus reached him, the first of the attackers was squeezing through the gap.

"Father! Your sword!" Marcus held it out, hilt first. Titus snatched it, threw his left shoulder into the gate, and thrust his blade around the edge. There was a howl of pain, and the pressure on the gate eased momentarily, allowing Titus to push it back several more inches. Marcus braced his feet and added his weight against the door.

"Marcus! Get out of here," his father growled through gritted teeth. "Run. Take your mother and run. Don't stop for anything."

"NO!" Marcus shook his head, his heart torn. "I'm not leaving you."

"By the Gods! Do as I say!" Titus's angry expression crumpled into fear and anxiety. "I beg you. Run. Save yourselves."

Marcus shook his head, his feet scrambling on the wet ground as he tried to help his father. On the other side, the attackers were steadily forcing their way in. Cerberus stood behind his master, barking wildly. Inch by inch, Marcus and his father were being forced back. Titus tried the same trick as before, stabbing around the edge of the gate, but this time they were ready, and his blade was parried away with a sharp ring of metal on metal. He hurriedly drew his arm back and looked down at Marcus.

"We can't stop them. We have to fall back. Grab Aristides's staff, then be ready to fight when I step away from the gate."

"Yes, Father." Marcus felt his heart beating wildly. Despite the rain coursing down his face, his mouth felt dry. Was this how soldiers felt in battle? he wondered briefly.

Then he ducked down, scurried around his father, and snatched up the staff lying beside the body of Aristides. His eyes met those of the nearest attacker outside. The man's lips parted in a sneer, and he reached a hand toward Marcus.

"Cerberus! Take him!"

The dog responded to the command at once, pouncing through the gap and jumping up to seize the man's hand in his powerful jaws. He bit down hard, and bone and flesh were crushed between his teeth. The man screamed and tried to snatch his hand back, but he could not break free. Marcus called out again.

"Cerberus! Leave!"

The dog released its grip and backed away, snarling. With a last fruitless thrust of the gate, Titus paced backward to his son's side and went into a crouch, sword held ready. "Hold the staff like a spear," he said hurriedly. "Strike at their faces."

Marcus nodded and tightened his grip as the gate, with no resistance from the inside, suddenly flew open. Two of the men fell sprawling into the courtyard. Titus leaped forward, striking one with a vicious cut to his shoulder. The bone cracked as the blade bit in. Then he yanked it free and slashed to the side, slicing into the face of the other man, who toppled to his side, hands clutched to his head as he howled in agony. More men spilled through the gap, and one of them thrust his sword at Titus. The veteran just managed to parry it in time, but was caught off-balance and had to fall back a pace.

Marcus stepped up and thrust the staff into the face of the man who had tried to strike a blow. He felt the impact jar his arms, right up to the shoulder. The man's head snapped back, and he fell to the ground, unconscious, his nose crushed by the end of the staff.

"Good work!" Titus yelled, his lips drawn back in a frightening grin.

For a moment, the other attackers hesitated, and then Thermon's voice sounded from the back. "What are you cowards waiting for? Get them!"

As the attackers rushed forward, Marcus yelled, "Cerberus! Take 'em!"

There was a blur of drenched fur as the dog jumped in, snapping at legs and hands. But there were too many of them. They came forward in a mass. Titus managed to strike once more, thrusting deep into a man's belly, before he took a spear thrust in his shoulder. He stumbled back, then another man hacked at his sword arm, and the blade cut through, shattering the bone. The sword dropped from his fingers. Another blow caught him in the knee, and with a grunt he slumped down.

"Father!" Marcus glanced around, lowering the staff a little. He stared at his father in terrible anguish.

"Keep your weapon up!" Titus bellowed. "Face front!"

His booming voice caused the attackers to pause, and they stood back, in an arc around him, weapons poised. Marcus was at his father's side, staff raised once again, daring them to take him on. Cerberus had sunk his teeth into another man and was savaging his arm, until the man, who was wielding a long club, swung it down and smashed it onto the dog's head. Cerberus dropped to the ground and lay on his side, his head in a puddle as the rain splashed around his muzzle.

"Cerberus!" Marcus called out in horror—but the dog lay still. Marcus wanted to go to him, but just then, Thermon pushed his way through his men and stood in front of Titus.

He smiled cruelly as he patted the flat of his sword against the palm of his spare hand. "Well now, Centurion, it seems the situation is reversed. How does it feel to be beaten? To lose your final battle?"

Titus looked up, blinking away the rain. "You can't get away with this. Once the governor hears what you've done, he'll have you crucified. You, your men here, *and* Decimus."

Thermon shook his head. "Only if someone is left to *tell* the governor what happened."

Titus stared at him for a moment and then muttered, "You wouldn't dare."

"Really?" Thermon pretended to look surprised. Suddenly he swept his sword arm out and thrust with all his strength. The tip of the blade punched into Titus's chest, burst through his heart, and crunched against the ribs in his back. He let out a gasp and then a deep sigh. Thermon braced his boot against Titus's shoulder and yanked his blade free.

"Father!" Marcus looked down in disbelief as his father's body slumped against his leg, and he toppled face-first onto the ground. "Father!" he cried shrilly. "Don't die! Don't leave me! Please...please don't die."

At once, someone snatched his staff away. Rough hands grabbed him by the arms and pinned them to his sides.

There was a scream. Marcus turned and saw his mother, hands clasped at either side of her head as if she were trying to shut out a bad sound. She screamed again. "Titus! Oh my Gods! Titus..."

"Take her!" Thermon ordered. "Put 'em both in chains. Then search the place for any valuables. Decimus wants anything that can be sold."

Marcus looked down at his father's body, numbed by what he saw. But then, as one of Thermon's men strode toward his mother, he felt something snap inside. He bit down on the arm of the man holding him. The man cried out and loosened his grip, and Marcus snarled as he clamped down with his jaws and lashed out with his feet.

Thermon turned toward him. "Someone, deal with that little brat."

The man with the club, the one who had struck down Cerberus, nodded and turned toward Marcus. Without a moment's hesitation, he raised the club and swung it at the boy's head. Marcus never felt the blow. His world suddenly exploded into white, and then there was nothing.

FIVE

At first, Marcus was aware of a dull pounding pain in his skull. Then there was an uneven jolting and a regular shrill squeal of an axle. He became aware of light and warmth on his face, and he slowly stirred, blinking his eyes open. The world was blurry, and juddered about, and he felt sick, so he closed them again.

"Marcus."

A hand cupped his cheek gently.

"Marcus, can you hear me?"

He recognized the voice as his mother's, and there was anxiety in her tone. Marcus opened his mouth, but his tongue and lips felt too dry to speak.

"Just a moment," she said, and then something pressed lightly to his mouth, and he tasted water. He took a few swallows before he turned his face aside and licked his lips.

"Mother, I'm all right," he managed to croak. Marcus opened his eyes again and forced them to focus. He was staring up at a metal grille. Raising himself up on his elbows, he looked around and saw that he was in a large cage on the back of a wagon drawn by a team of mules. A dirty leather covering was tied over the cage, providing shade for the occupants. Besides him and his mother, there were four others, two of whom—tall, thin men—had skins as black as charred wood. The others were teenage boys, perhaps five or six years older than Marcus.

"Don't try to stir so quickly," his mother cautioned. "You had quite a crack on the head."

Marcus raised a hand to feel for the place where his skull was hurting, and winced as his fingertips discovered a large, solid lump. He struggled to remember what had happened to him. Then it all came flooding back in a terrible rush of images. Aristides, Cerberus . . . and his father. He looked at his mother, eyes wide with pain.

"Father."

She gathered him up in her arms and held him to her breast, stroking the back of his head.

"Yes, Titus is gone. Murdered."

Marcus felt a dreadful pain course through his body, as if his heart had been torn out of him. He wanted his father as never before. Wanted him right here and now. Wanted to feel safe in his strong arms, to hear his hearty laugh once more. His pain was unbearable, and he buried his face in the folds of his mother's cloak and sobbed.

"Hush, child," his mother said after a while. "There's nothing you can do. He's gone. His shade has joined his comrades in the underworld. Titus is at peace. He is watching us now. You must show him that you are strong. So dry your eyes." She paused a moment and continued. "Make your father proud of you. You must honor his memory, even if you don't yet know . . ." She stopped and eased him gently back.

Marcus's eyes were sore from his crying, and his head felt worse than ever, pounding away inside his skull. She stared directly at him, and he nodded.

With great difficulty he controlled his grief and looked around the cage again. "Where are we going?"

"They're taking us to Stratos."

Marcus frowned. He had never heard of the place. "Is that far from home?"

She nodded.

He looked out through the bars. The wagon was rumbling along a broad road. On one side, hills rose up, covered in dense forests of pine and oak. On the other, olive groves stretched out. Through the gaps, Marcus occasionally caught sight of the sea sparkling in the distance. He did not recognize the landscape.

"How long have we been in this . . . cage?"

"Three days. You were unconscious most of the time, and delirious when you stirred."

Three days! Marcus shook his head at the thought. They must already be farther from his home on the farm than he had ever gone. He felt afraid.

"Marcus, listen—we're being taken to the slave market," his mother explained as gently as she could. "Decimus has ordered that we be sold as slaves to cover the debt. I think Decimus is trying to take us far enough from Leucas so that there's less chance anyone will discover precisely what he has done to get his money back."

Marcus listened to her words with difficulty. The thought of being sold into slavery hit him like a blow. Of all the fates that could befall a person, slavery was one of the worst. A slave was no longer a person, but a mere object. He looked up at his mother. "They can't sell us; we're free. We're citizens."

"Not if we can't pay Decimus his money," she replied sadly. "He is acting within the law, but he knows if word got out that he had killed one of Pompeius's veterans and enslaved his family, then life might become very difficult for him if Pompeius took offense." She lifted his chin with her hand and stared directly into his eyes. "We must be careful, Marcus. Thermon said that he would have us beaten if we uttered one word about the situation to anyone. You understand?"

Marcus nodded. "What can we do?"

"Do? Nothing, for the moment." She turned her head away, and her voice continued, broken and despairing. "The Gods have forsaken me. They must have. After all that has happened, to return me to slavery is a cruel blow. So cruel."

Marcus felt a chill in his heart. What could his mother mean? Return her to slavery? "You were a slave, mother?"

She kept her face turned from him as she replied. "Yes."

"When?"

"When I was a child, Marcus."

"No."

She nodded. "I was born into a household in Campania, south of Rome. I was a slave for over sixteen years, until Spartacus and his rebels came to the estate and set us all free."

"You joined Spartacus?" Marcus's mind filled with memories of the stories his father had told him about the great slave revolt. And all the time, his mother had kept her silence. He cleared his throat. "Did Father know?"

She turned her face back to him with an expression of

bitter amusement. "Of course Titus knew. He was there at the end. At the final battle. He found me in the slave camp when the legions sacked it after the battle. He claimed me as spoils of war." Her tone had turned bitter. She swallowed and continued more calmly, "That's how we met, Marcus. I was his slave. His woman. For the first two years, until he gave me my freedom on condition that I become his wife."

Marcus was silent as he reflected on what she had told him. It had never occurred to him that his parents could have met in such a way. They had always been there, constant and unchanging, and the idea that they might have led quite different lives before was something he had never really considered. True, his father had told him tales of his life in the legions, but in Marcus's eyes the hero of such stories was not a young man, a different man. Marcus always imagined his father as he was now. He felt a stab of grief as he corrected himself—as his father had been when he was alive.

Then something else struck him, and he looked up at his mother again. "The slave revolt was ten years ago, wasn't it?"

"Yes."

"And I'm ten. If you married father after two years, then that means I must have been born a slave."

She shook her head. "Titus had it declared that you were his son, and therefore free, the moment you were born."

"I see." Marcus was not certain how he felt. This was all painfully new to him, in addition to what had happened since the men arrived at the farm. His thoughts were interrupted by a bitter laugh from his mother. He looked at her in concern. There was a slightly mad look in her dark eyes.

"Mother? Mother, what's so funny?"

"Funny? Nothing's funny." Her lips quivered. "It's just that I was born free, in Thrace, then enslaved when I was your age. Then Spartacus freed me, then I was a slave again until your father freed me. And now? A slave once again." She lowered her head and was still for a moment. Then Marcus saw a tear drip down onto her thigh. He shuffled around so that he could put a hand on her shoulder.

"Mother?" He swallowed nervously. "I'll look after you. I swear it. On my life."

"You're a boy. My little boy," she muttered. "I should be looking after you. Yet, what can I do? I am a slave. . . . There's nothing I can do." She raised her head, and he saw the grief in her eyes. "After all that the Gods have done to me, I thought they had finally given me some peace on that farm. Peace where I could grow old with Titus and raise a fine son who would never know the terrible burden of slavery."

"We won't be slaves for long, Mother. Decimus can't do this to us." He frowned with determination. "I won't let him get away with it."

She stared into his eyes with pity, then gently pulled him into her arms and held him tightly. "Marcus. You are all that I have left."

Her tears began to flow again, and Marcus felt his own eyes burn with a similar urge to cry. He gritted his teeth as he looked over her shoulder at the other slaves in the cage, fighting his tears. They looked back with blank faces, too weary or despairing to react. Marcus silently swore a sacred oath that he would never accept slavery. Never.

SIX

IT TOOK ANOTHER FOUR LONG DAYS before the wagon reached its destination, but finally at dusk on the last day, they entered the town of Stratos.

Set astride one of the main trade routes across the mountainous interior of Graecia, the town had long outgrown the walls that dated back to the days of the small city-states almost constantly at war with one another. Nowadays, the walls of the old city were a maze of narrow streets where the wealthier families lived and did their business. Beyond the walls sprawled the ramshackle buildings of the poor.

During the journey, Marcus and his mother had little to do with the others inside the cage. Their fellow slaves knew only a handful of words in Greek, had no understanding of Latin, and spoke in some unknown barbarian tongue.

The wagon rattled down the main road leading into the town, pausing at the arched gateway to pay the toll, and then continued toward the slave market.

For Marcus, who had been raised on a farm for all his life, and who had only ever known the fishing village at Nydri, the town was unnerving. The shrill cries of street vendors and beggars assaulted his ears, while the stench of rubbish and sewage filled the air. He wrinkled his nose as he breathed in.

"Ughh! Do all towns stink like this?"

"As far as I know," his mother replied with an equal look of distaste.

The wagon entered a large market square in the center of Stratos and then turned through a gate into a narrow courtyard. Two burly guards stood just inside, armed with cudgels. The place had been a stable once, but now there were iron grilles across the entrance to each stall, and Marcus could see the ragged forms of men, women, and children of all ages huddled behind the bars. Beneath them was a thin spread of filthy straw.

"Whoa!" the driver of the wagon called out as he pulled sharply on the reins. The mules clopped to a halt. A large man in a plain brown tunic waddled out of a doorway and approached the wagon. He nodded a greeting to the driver, who climbed stiffly down from his bench and stretched his back.

"What's this lot, then?" The man jerked his thumb at the prisoners in the cage.

"Slaves." The driver yawned. "Property of Decimus. Wants them put into the next auction."

Marcus grabbed the bars and pulled himself up. "We're not slaves!"

"Shut it, you!" The driver whirled around and slashed his coiled whip at Marcus's knuckles. Marcus fell back with a cry of pain. "One more word out of turn, and I'll beat you black and blue."

The driver turned back to the other man with a laugh. "The boy's a born liar. Like all slaves. Just ignore him and his mother there. They go into the auction, as I said. All right?"

The auctioneer nodded and pointed to the only remaining empty cell. "Put 'em in there. I'll add them to the sale inventory for tomorrow."

"Right."

As the auctioneer waddled back to his office, the driver made his way to the end of the wagon and loosened the coils of his whip. Reaching for the key that hung around his neck, he unlocked the door and backed off a pace as he swung it open.

"Get out!" He gestured to the ground to make sure that the other prisoners understood his meaning.

One by one they climbed out, Marcus and his mother last of all. The driver pointed to the cell and pushed one of the others toward it. They were all hungry and stiff after living in the cramped confines of the cage for so many days, and slowly made their way into the cell. The driver thrust Marcus inside, so that he stumbled against his mother, and then slammed the door shut and turned the key in the lock before striding off to join the auctioneer.

Inside the cell, Marcus and his mother sat down on the straw and leaned against the dirty plaster wall. While his mother stared at the opposite wall, Marcus's mind was filled with frightening thoughts about the next day's auction. What if they were bought by a mine owner? He had heard terrifying stories about the conditions slaves endured in the mines. It was little more than a living death. Then the worst of all possibilities occurred to him. He turned to his mother with a horrified expression.

"What happens if we are sold to different owners tomorrow?"

His mother stirred, as if from a troubled sleep, and looked at him. "Sorry, Marcus, what did you say?"

"What happens if we are split up, at the auction?"

She stared at him and forced a smile. "I don't think that will happen. The auctioneers don't like to separate families. It makes for discontent."

"But what if they do?" Marcus felt a stab of fear. "I don't want to leave you."

She took his hand and squeezed it. "We'll stay together. You'll see. Now try to sleep. Here, put your head in my lap."

He wriggled around and lowered his head into the folds of her long tunic, and she began to gently run her fingers through his dark curls. She had comforted him this way for as long as he could remember, and once remarked that he had his father's hair. Marcus recalled that he had laughed at the time, since his father's scalp only had a thin crop of wiry hair. As she stroked him now, his body began to relax, and for a while his mind drifted back to dreamy memories of the farm, Aristides, and Cerberus, as if they were still alive. Most of all, he thought of his father, strong and proud. Marcus wished his father was there to protect him and his mother. An image of his father, lying dead in the rain, filled his mind, and it was a long time before he finally fell into a troubled sleep.

During the night he was awakened by a loud outburst. Shouts and yells came from another cell as a fight broke out. The auctioneer and his guards turned up with torches and clubs, and then all Marcus could hear was them beating the prisoners back into silence. He tried to get back to sleep, but he was unsettled by the violence, and his thoughts once again turned to the grim situation he and his mother were in. What would become of them?

There was a deafening clatter as the guard ran his club along the iron bars, and Marcus was startled into wakefulness.

"On your feet, slaves!" the guard bellowed, then moved on to the next cell. "Wakey, wakey!"

Starting with the cells nearest the main gate, the prisoners were chained together by their ankles and escorted out of the courtyard into the market. Marcus estimated that there were at least a hundred people waiting to be sold, and the morning dragged on as they were taken out in batches to be auctioned off. All the time, he felt his guts knot with anxiety over the terrible prospect of being parted from his mother.

At last, a guard came to the cell with a club in one hand and a heavy length of chain with ankle irons in the other. He let them out one at a time, clamping the iron collars around each prisoner's ankle and then hammering home the locking pin. When Marcus and his mother had joined the short line, the final six were led out of the yard. The market square was crowded, and people pressed around Marcus and the others as they shuffled a short distance toward the stage, where the auctioneer stood waiting. Marcus felt hands squeeze his arms as he passed, and one man forced his mouth open to look at his teeth, before being thrust back by the guard.

"You'll get to examine the goods soon enough, once you've bought 'em."

They were led up a short flight of steps and made to stand

in a line at the rear of the stage. The guard took his small hammer and knocked out the pin on the ankle shackle of the first prisoner, one of the black men. He dragged him forward, to the side of the auctioneer. It had been a busy morning and the sun was high in the sky. Sweat rolled down the fat man's cheeks, and his hair was plastered to his skull. Drawing a deep breath, he raised his arms to attract the attention of the crowd, and called out.

"I have the honor to be selling six slaves on behalf of Decimus, a town father of Stratos. The first two are Nubians, fresh spoils from a punitive raid. Both are young, healthy, and strong." He grasped one of each man's arms and held them up. "Look at those muscles! With a bit of training, they'll make exotic house slaves. Or, if you want to make full use of those muscles, perhaps field hands, or boxers. Perhaps even gladiators! Bound to be a fine investment all around. So, come now! What am I bid for the first?"

"Two hundred sestertii!" a voice cried out.

"Two hundred?" The auctioneer turned toward the voice. "Is that you there, sir? Yes. Two hundred, then!"

"Two fifty!" another voice cried out.

"Three!" came the reply.

The bidding continued in a frenzy, one shouted price after another, with the auctioneer hard put to keep up with the pace. Then finally the bidding stopped, at twelve hundred sestertii.

"Twelve hundred... Is that the final offer? Twelve hundred? Honored ladies and gentlemen, fine specimens like this rarely come on the market. Come now, surely someone with a good eye for a bargain must be prepared to raise the bid?" He looked around hopefully, but there was no response. The auctioneer waited a moment longer and then clapped his hands together. "Sold!"

The man was led off the stage to a small pen where a scribe noted the details of the sale on a waxed tablet and collected payment from the buyer. The second Nubian went for a similar price, and then the two teenage boys were bought for much less by a tall thin man with neatly oiled hair and kohl around his eyes. The auctioneer mopped his brow with a rag and then indicated Marcus and his mother.

"The final lot in this morning's sale, honored ladies and gentlemen. A mother and son. The woman is not yet thirty. She can cook and weave and should be fertile enough to breed for some years yet. The boy is ten and in good health. He has been taught to read, write, and count. With a little training he could be useful in a trade."

Marcus lowered his head in shame. To hear himself and his mother described in this way made him feel no better than an animal.

"I am sure you'll agree, they make a fine deal together," the auctioneer continued. "Of course, any buyer with a shrewd eye for a bargain might consider selling the boy on when he is a little older. And if the woman is productive, who knows what profits she might yield from breeding?"

"No!" Marcus yelled out. "You can't do this! We were kidnapped!"

The auctioneer nodded quickly to the guard, who slapped Marcus hard about the face, knocking him down onto the stage. The crowd roared with laughter. The guard clenched his fist in Marcus's hair and pulled him back to his feet, hissing into his ear, "One more word from you, and it'll be your mother I hurt, not you. Understand?"

Marcus nodded, trying not to cry as his scalp burned with pain. The guard held him by the hair a moment longer before releasing him.

"The boy just needs a firm hand, as you can see." The auctioneer grinned falsely. "So who will open the bidding?"

There was a brief pause as the audience considered the two desperate-looking figures, and then a large man with a cruel face started to raise his hand. Before he could speak, there was a shout from near the back of the crowd.

"Stop there! They are not for sale!"

The auctioneer and the crowd turned toward the voice. Marcus, too, tried to see who had spoken, as a faint hope kindled in his breast. Perhaps this was it. The moment he had prayed for. Perhaps they were saved.

A figure pushed through the crowd, and as the man approached the stage, Marcus recognized him, and his heart sank like a stone.

Thermon.

He climbed onto the stage as the auctioneer regarded him crossly, hands on his fleshy hips. "What is the meaning of this? What do you mean, they're not for sale?"

"I speak for Decimus. I am his steward," Thermon replied haughtily. "My master says that these two will not be sold after all."

"Not sold?" The auctioneer raised his eyebrows. "Why-ever not?"

"I don't need to explain the reason to you. It is the will of my master. Understand?"

The auctioneer nodded. "As you wish." He turned to the guard. "Remove them. Back to the cell."

As the crowd fell to mumbling at the surprising turn of events, Thermon approached Marcus and his mother.

"Decimus has changed his mind." He smiled coldly, and Marcus felt the hairs tingle on the back of his neck as Thermon continued. "He's got other plans for you two."

SEVEN

SOON AFTER THEY WERE RETURNED TO their cell, a man entered the courtyard. He was slightly built and tall, and his narrow face made him look taller still. Except for a fringe of silvery hair, he was completely bald, and his scalp gleamed as if it had been polished. Marcus noticed that he walked with a limp, which he tried to conceal by walking slowly. He wore a silk tunic with pale leather boots, and there was a gold bracelet around each of his wrists.

The man smiled thinly as he approached the bars of the cell. "The delightful wife of Centurion Titus, and his young boy, if I am not mistaken. I imagine that you have guessed who I am."

Marcus's mother kept her expression fixed as she regarded the man. He shrugged and tilted his head slightly to one side. "Well, I am disappointed. I had hoped that the wife of one of General Pompeius's finest centurions would be more polite. Never mind. So then, I am Decimus. Town father of Stratos and a duly appointed tax collector of Graecia." He bowed his head in a mock greeting. He regarded them for a moment in silence before his expression turned into a sneer. "Not so high and mighty now, are you? Neither you, nor that fool Titus. Arrogant as ever, thinking that he could ignore his debt and send my men packing. It's been a long time coming, but now I have paid him back in his own coin, as it were."

He suddenly pretended to look surprised and clicked his fingers. "Oh! But I imagine that you didn't know that your husband and I were old friends. Perhaps not *friends*, but certainly comrades."

Marcus looked up at his mother, but she still refused to speak.

"We served in the glorious Sixteenth Legion in Spain. Under Pompeius. We were optios. Do you know what that means? We were the men waiting for the chance to be promoted to centurion. Then the chance came. One of the centurions was killed in a skirmish, and good old Titus and I were waiting to see which of us would get the promotion. It should have been me. I was the better soldier, without a doubt. Everyone knew it. Anyway, the day before the general made his choice, Titus and I had a little drink. Then another, and one thing led to the next, and he suggested we have a little mock swordplay, to prove who was the better swordsman. Just for fun, you understand. Only it wasn't just for fun. Titus wasn't even drunk; he was pretending to be. We feinted and parried, and he seemed to slip, tripping forward, and his sword tore through my thigh."

Decimus moved closer to the bars. He seemed to have forgotten Marcus's mother and was now looking intensely at Marcus. "An accident, you see?" Decimus smiled bitterly. "The wound was bad enough for the legion to discharge me. So there I was, out on my ear, and Titus got the promotion.

He always claimed it was an accident, of course. Wait, I'll show you."

Decimus lifted the corner of his tunic and raised it to reveal his right thigh. Marcus sucked in his breath as he saw a thick, white, knotted length of scar tissue stretching up from the knee.

"Quite a scar, isn't it, my boy?" Decimus lowered the tunic. "I suppose your father did me a favor, in a way. If I had stayed in the army, I would have ended up on a miserable little farm on the side of some obscure island, just like him. As it was, I made my fortune in supplying grain to the legions. I bribed the right people and won the contract for tax collection in this province. You can imagine my surprise, and then my joy, when Titus approached me for a loan. I expect he thought that 'time was a great healer.' Not for me it wasn't. So I loaned him some money on easy terms—easy enough to encourage him to borrow more, and before too long he was deeply in debt, and I had a legal right to take my revenge." He held up his hands. "You know the rest of the story."

Marcus's mother cleared her throat and spoke firmly. "You may have had the legal right to recover your debt, but not to murder Titus and enslave his family."

"Really? I merely sent my men to collect what was owed to me. The fact that your husband resisted violently and unfortunately died as a consequence is not my fault. As any court in this town would agree."

"I wonder if General Pompeius will agree when he hears of this outrage?"

"General Pompeius will never find out. I am not a fool, Livia. If word ever got to Pompeius that one of his veterans had suffered such a fate, he would visit his anger on the man responsible, sure enough. That's why you were pulled out of the auction." Decimus smiled. "That was just a little performance for my benefit, so that I could wring another drop of revenge out of the situation. I could never afford to let you be bought by someone who might well listen to your story and believe that you had been wronged."

"So what will you do with us?" Marcus asked anxiously.

Decimus looked down through the bars. "I could have you and your mother killed, young man. Quietly strangled and thrown off a cliff into the sea. I could do that." He paused to let his words take effect. Marcus recoiled in terror.

"However, as I live with the memory of the wrong your father did to me, so you both will live with the memory of how you were made to pay for his deed." Decimus stroked his pointed chin. "I have a farming estate in the Peloponnese. It is in a small valley surrounded by hills. It is hot in summer and bitterly cold in winter, and I spend as little time there as possible. But the soil is good for barley, and the slaves of the estate are worked hard to add to my fortune. That's where I will send you, to live out your days working, under the whip, as a slave in my fields. There you will die, forgotten and unmissed. General Pompeius will never, ever learn of your fate, or that of Titus."

He took a deep breath and smiled faintly. "A fitting revenge, don't you think?"

Marcus felt a brief moment of dread, but then he was seized by rage and a desire to clamp his hands around the throat of the tax collector. With a shrill, animal cry, he lunged at the bars, clawing at the man's tunic.

"Marcus!" his mother shouted. "It won't help us!"

She pulled him back and held his arms tightly as Decimus chuckled. "Quite a temper on him. But there is courage too. He is a soldier's son and no mistake."

Livia's eyes blazed. "He is ... my son."

Decimus looked puzzled by her response, but before he could say anything, Livia looked at him pleadingly.

"Whatever happened between you and Titus happened years ago. He is dead and you have had your revenge. There is no need to inflict this on me and the boy."

"Ah, if only that were true. You must understand this from my perspective, my dear. If I let you both go now, with Titus dead, it would only be a matter of time before the boy sought to avenge his father. Isn't that right?" He smiled at Marcus.

Marcus glared back and nodded slowly. "One day I will find you, and I will kill you."

His mother's shoulders sank in despair. "Decimus, he is only ten. He doesn't know what he's saying. Show him mercy and he will remember mercy."

"If I show him mercy, I will merely be signing my own death warrant. He must disappear like his father, as must you."

Livia thought quickly. "Let him go. Send *me* to your estate. As long as I am your hostage, he will do you no harm. Isn't that right, Marcus?"

Marcus looked into her eyes and understood that she was begging him to agree. But there was never a moment's doubt in his sense of determination to do his duty and see that justice was done to the memory of his father. Of course he was afraid, scared out of his wits by the terrible fate Decimus had prepared for them, but there was a cold, hard fury—stronger than the fear, stronger even than his grief or his concern for his mother. He shook his head.

"I'm sorry, Mother. But this man is right. While I live I will think only of paying him back for what he did."

"You see?" Decimus raised his hands in a helpless gesture. "What is a man to do? I'm sorry, but there it is. You will both go to the estate, and there you will work until you die. Farewell." He nodded solemnly, and before he turned away, he stared a moment into Marcus's hate-filled eyes. "You would have grown into a fine man, Marcus. It is a shame it ends this way. I respect you and would be proud to have a boy like you for a son. Such a pity..."

Then he walked away, at the same slow pace, with a slight rolling gait. Livia watched until he had disappeared out of the gate before turning on her son.

"You little fool!" She grabbed Marcus's arm and held him in a tight grip, making him wince. "Are you trying to get yourself killed? You're just like your father, all fine principles and no common sense. I told him he could never win. I told him..." She stopped abruptly and clenched her teeth.

"Mother, you're hurting me," Marcus said, glancing at his arm. Her gaze dropped, and then she let go of him and covered her face with her hands.

"I'm sorry, my darling. So sorry. Forgive me." She started to cry.

"Mother, don't," Marcus said. He felt as if his heart were being torn apart. He touched her cheek gently. "I love you. I'm sorry."

She lowered her hands and kissed him on the forehead. "Oh, Marcus, my little boy. What is to become of us?"

At first light, the driver of the wagon came to collect them, holding a club and watching them warily as he ordered them to climb back into the cage. As soon as the door was closed and locked, the driver clambered up onto his bench, picked up his whip, and cracked it over the heads of his mules. The wagon lurched forward and rumbled out of the slave auctioneer's holding pens. Marcus shuddered as the wagon passed the stage where he had stood the day before. For an instant he relived the terror he had felt at the thought of being parted from his mother. The market square was empty, apart from a handful of beggars sleeping in the arches under the aqueduct.

As they passed through the gates and down a broad street lined with small houses, Marcus felt his mother nudge him.

"We must escape," she whispered with a nervous glance toward the driver. "We have to find a way to get out of here."

"How can we?"

His mother smiled faintly. "There is a weak spot." She nodded toward the driver. Marcus looked up at the broad shoulders of the man sitting on the bench, slightly hunched forward as he held the reins and occasionally clicked his tongue to encourage the mules to keep up the pace.

"Him?" Marcus raised his eyebrows in surprise. "He's too big for us to manage. We're not strong enough."

"There is a way, Marcus, but you must do exactly as I say."

EIGHT

THE WAGON SOON PASSED OUT OF the sprawling slum that surrounded the town, and emerged into open countryside. Stratos stood on the bank of a river that flowed out toward the Adriatic Sea. On either side of the lazily flowing current, the land was covered with fields of wheat, as far as the slopes of the forested hills that rose steeply from the plain. Soon the wagon was laboring up the narrow zigzagging track that had been cut into the slope of a hill. The tall pines on either side created a pleasant shade, and the warm air was filled with the scent of the trees. The slope was thickly carpeted with soft brown pine needles, broken up by clusters of ferns and the odd outcrop of rock. There was no one else in sight, and the wagon had not passed anyone along the route so far. Marcus and his mother were far from relaxed, however.

"This spot will do," Livia muttered. "Marcus, I'm going to pretend to be ill. I'll do what I can to make it look convincing, but you must do your part. You have to make him believe that you think I'm dying. Can you do that?"

Marcus nodded. "I'll do my best."

"Then let's hope your best is good enough." She smiled encouragingly. "He'll stop and come to have a closer look.

You have to persuade him to open the cage. I watched him do it when we arrived in Stratos. I don't think his eyes are good. He leaned forward to see as he fitted the key to the lock. That's the moment we must strike. When I say 'now,' we kick the door of the cage back into his face, as hard as we can. If we take him by surprise, we can get out of here before he recovers."

"Then what, Mother?"

"Then we run, like lightning."

"No, I meant where do we go?"

She frowned briefly. "We'll think that through later. Best to find General Pompeius, I should think. If anyone can see that we have justice, and have Decimus punished, then it must be Pompeius. He has great power, and besides, he owes Titus a favor."

"What favor?" asked Marcus.

"Titus saved the general's life in the final battle against Spartacus. Pompeius has to honor that debt." Livia eased herself away from the side of the cage and lowered herself into the soiled straw lining the bottom. "Ready?"

Marcus nodded, but he wasn't sure; his heart beat more quickly.

His mother worked up some spit and then began to force it out of her mouth in a sticky, foaming dribble. She curled into a ball, clutching her hands to her stomach. She winked at Marcus, then rolled her eyes up and began to shudder as she let out a low, animal groan. The effect was quite startling, and even though he knew she was acting, Marcus could not help becoming alarmed. He gripped her shoulder and cried out in a concerned tone. "Mother . . . Mother?" Then his voice rose to an anguished pitch. "Mother!"

The driver glanced around. "Keep yer mouth shut, you."

"My mother's sick!" Marcus cried out. "She's really sick. You must help her!"

His mother started to shake violently and roll from side to side as she groaned in apparent agony.

The driver sighed with frustration and pulled back on the reins. "Whoa! Whoa there, blast you!"

The mules clopped to a halt and stood patiently in their traces. The driver lowered the reins and twisted around to look down into the cage. "What's wrong with 'er, then?"

"She's sick." Marcus swallowed nervously and made a frightened face. "I think she's dying. Please, help her!"

"Dying?" The driver squinted. "She ain't dying. She'll have to get over it when we stop for the night."

"That's too long," Marcus replied desperately. "She needs help now."

"Help? Well, what can I do? I'm just a bloody wagon driver."

Marcus thought quickly. "If she dies, then you'll have to answer to Decimus. I'll tell him you just sat there and watched it happen."

The driver scowled at him and then climbed down from the bench and walked along the side of the wagon. There was a faint rustle of straw as Marcus's mother braced her sandals against the iron bars of the cage door. The driver paused as he reached the back of the wagon.

"So what's wrong with 'er?"

"I don't know," Marcus replied anxiously. "She needs shade and water."

"Hmmm." The driver scratched his head doubtfully.

Livia started to make retching noises.

"Don't go and be sick!" the driver growled. "You go and puke your guts up in this heat, and we'll be stuck with the stink of it for the rest of the journey."

"Then let her out," Marcus snapped. "Before she throws up."

The driver thought a moment. "All right, then. But just her. You stay in the cage, and I'll get her out."

Marcus nodded.

The driver groped for the cord around his neck and brought the key out. He squinted and leaned forward to fit the key into the lock. Marcus tensed his muscles as his heart beat wildly. At the same time, he forced himself to look as though his only concern was for his mother, and held her hand in both of his. There was a metallic rattle as the key started to turn, then a loud click as the bolt slipped back.

"Now!" Livia screamed. As she kicked her legs out, Marcus threw himself toward the door of the cage, crashing into it hard. The iron bars of the door leaped back, smashing into the driver's startled face. He cried out in pain and surprise and fell onto the road. Marcus scrambled out of the cage and jumped to one side, away from the driver, who sat on his backside in the road as blood streamed from his broken nose. Livia grabbed the edges of the cage door and thrust herself out, landing heavily beside Marcus. She grabbed his hand.

"Run!"

They sprinted to the side of the track. Behind them the driver heaved himself up onto his feet and bellowed, "Stop!"

It was a foolish reaction, and one that allowed Marcus and his mother to gain a few more paces before the driver started after them, heavy sandals scrabbling in the grit lying

69

on the road. Livia had started toward the downhill side of the road, and now they were slithering and sliding through the soft heaps of pine needles as they scrambled down the slope.

"Stop!" the driver shouted after them. "Stop right now, or I'll beat the living daylights out of you when I catch yer!"

Marcus risked a glance back and saw that the driver was perhaps thirty feet behind them. He was slightly ahead of his mother, and pulled her hand. "Come on!"

She grimaced, struggling to keep up over the difficult ground. Around them the slope was dappled by shafts of sunlight passing between the branches of the pine trees, the contrast between light and shadow making it hard to concentrate on the ground ahead.

That was when it happened.

With a sudden cry, Marcus's mother pitched forward as her foot stubbed up against a rock buried in the soft pine needles. She hit the ground hard, driving the breath from her lungs as she rolled down the slope. Marcus dropped to his knees at her side.

"My ankle!" she hissed through clenched teeth. "Ohhh, my ankle."

Marcus glanced down and saw that the flesh was torn along the side of her foot, and blood was pulsing out of it. She squeezed his hand tightly as she tried to stand. At once she let out a scream of agony and collapsed back onto the ground. Biting back on her pain, she stared at her son. "Run, Marcus. Run!"

He shook his head frantically. "No! I can't leave you."

She released his hand and thrust him away. "Run!"

The driver was only a short distance away now, a

triumphant look in his eyes. Marcus returned his mother's gaze. "I can't leave you. I can't."

"Run!" she shouted. "Save yourself. Find Pompeius. Go!"

She pushed him away again and struggled up onto her knees as she turned to face the driver. Marcus backed away a few paces, then turned and ran. His heart filled with fear for his mother, but at the same time he knew that she was right. If he stayed, they would both be taken. If he escaped, then he might find some way to rescue her. He took one last look back and saw his mother throw herself at the legs of the driver. She wrapped her arms around the man's knees and cried out, "Run, Marcus!"

Then her voice was cut short as the driver angrily tried to thrust her aside. Marcus ran on, down the slope, heading for a place where the pine trees grew more closely together and would make it harder for the driver to follow him. His mother cried out again, her voice growing more distant and deadened by the forest. "Run!"

"Stop, you little bugger!" the driver shouted.

Marcus reached the thicket and rushed on, thrusting the slender branches aside and ignoring the scratches to his hands and arms. The shouts behind him gradually became more faint, and then there were only the sounds of his feet scuffling through the pine needles, the swish of the branches and the deep sobs of despair that were wrenched from him as he fled, farther and farther away from his mother.

NINE

MARCUS RAN ON FOR A MILE or more, his eyes brimming with tears. His heart was beating wildly, and the heat of the morning sun beneath the boughs of the pine trees had caused him to break out in a sweat. The run through the trees had left his face and hands scratched and bleeding, and his muscles ached from the effort. Yet the pain on his skin and in his limbs was nothing compared to the agony that engulfed his heart. He stopped and leaned forward, resting his hands on his knees as he struggled for breath. He strained to listen for any sounds of pursuit above the noise of the blood pounding through his head, but there was nothing except for the faint caws of crows swirling across the forest.

As he recovered his breath, Marcus tried to think about his situation, but it was impossible to concentrate while images of his mother, injured and at the mercy of the driver, flooded through his mind. Her shouts to him to run still echoed in his head. Marcus straightened up and turned back to stare uphill toward the road. He felt like a coward. He also felt more afraid of being alone than he did of the driver, or of the punishment that the driver had threatened him with. With a sharp intake of breath, Marcus decided what he must do. He turned around, searching the ground until he saw what he was looking for. A short distance away was a fallen tree. He ran over and snapped off the largest branch that he could handle. Hurriedly stripping off some of the small twigs, Marcus gripped the end of the branch and swung it around, one way and the other, then he whacked it on the tree trunk. The blow jarred his arms, but the branch did not snap.

"That'll do," he muttered to himself, then set off up the slope, climbing back in the direction he had fled. He knew that he had little chance against the burly driver unless he could find some way to surprise him. If Marcus could do that, then he might be able to knock him unconscious, even kill him. Then he could rescue his mother and take the wagon somewhere to find help. His thoughts stilled for a moment. Could he really kill the driver if he had the chance?

"Yes," he growled. He would do it, if he had to.

As Marcus emerged from the thicket of pine trees he had used to escape from the driver, he crouched low and picked his way over the carpet of pine needles, making no noise. His eyes and ears strained to pick up any signs of life ahead. There was no movement, apart from the faint shimmer of light and shadows on the ground. When he reached the place where he had left his mother, Marcus knelt down. The needles were disturbed and there was a smear of blood on a rock. He stared at the blood for a moment as a wave of anxiety gripped his body. Then he swallowed, grasped his makeshift club more tightly, and crept up toward the road. As his eyes drew level with the rutted surface, Marcus paused and glanced cautiously from side to side. The road was empty.

There was no sign of the wagon.

He climbed onto the road and stood in silence, staring in the direction the wagon had been headed. He did not know what to do. No idea at all. His first instinct was to run after the wagon and see through his plan to attack the driver and rescue his mother. But the panic and fear that had seized him earlier had begun to recede, and he was able to think more clearly. He could follow the wagon and wait for the chance to strike, but having been tricked once, the driver would be on his guard. If Marcus was caught, then it would all have been for nothing, and he and his mother would be condemned to the living death of working in a slave gang on Decimus's estate. And there was little doubt that the driver would give him a severe beating, as well, before throwing him back into the cage.

His mother was right. He must find help. Find someone who would listen to what he had to say and give Marcus and his mother justice, and punish Decimus. A spark of anger ignited in his chest at the thought of the man who had taken away his happy life and stolen his parents from him. Punishment would not be enough for Decimus. He must pay with *his* life.

With a heavy heart, Marcus turned around and started to walk back in the direction of Stratos. There was no question of entering the town again. If he was recognized, he would be caught and thrown into the auctioneer's cells while a message was sent to Decimus informing him that the runaway slave was recaptured. Instead, Marcus decided to make his way to the river and follow it to the sea, where he could find a port. Then he would find some way to get on board a ship bound for Italia, where he would find General Pompeius and tell him everything. But even as he resolved to make this his plan, Marcus knew that the path ahead of him was difficult and dangerous.

He rested the club on his shoulder and increased his pace as he strode along the rough track. Overhead, the sun had risen to its zenith, and the heat was scorching, rippling off the baked hard earth of the road a short distance ahead. Once he was clear of the pine trees, Marcus could see Stratos down in the valley below, and the broad silvery ribbon of the river snaking across the valley floor before it passed through some hills in the distance. He left the road and made his way cross-country toward the river, cautiously passing through several olive groves and a vineyard on his way. Occasionally he saw people but kept well clear of them. Marcus was not sure if he could risk encountering anyone who lived close enough to Stratos. They might know of Decimus and hope to claim a reward for returning a runaway slave to him.

By the time he reached the river, Marcus's throat was parched. He found a quiet spot where reeds grew along the riverbank and squatted down to drink, cupping his hands into the cool water. When he was refreshed, he removed his boots and waded into the river. There he removed his tunic and washed it in the gentle current, rubbing out the dirt that had soiled the cloth during the days he had been locked in the cage. When that was done, he lay the tunic out on the riverbank to dry in the sun. He settled nearby, in the shade of a stunted bush, and rested. The strain of the previous days had been eased a little by bathing in the river, and Marcus gradually drifted off into a deep sleep.

When he awoke, night had fallen. Around him, the shrill sound of cicadas filled the darkness. The air was cool, and he reached across for his tunic. It was dry, and once he had pulled it over his head, Marcus felt more comfortable. As he slipped his boots on and tied the laces, he glanced up. A half moon hung in the sky, bathing the landscape in the faintest of blue hues. Marcus felt hungry and realized that he hadn't had anything to eat since the previous evening. He squatted down by the river to cup some water into his hands and drink his fill before setting off.

Marcus stayed as close to the river as he could, following it downstream. At first he found it unnerving, and every sudden rustle in the grass or crackle of a twig caused him to duck down and keep still. His heart beat quickly, and he strained his eyes and ears for any sign that he was being hunted. Only when he was satisfied that the noise had been made by some animal did Marcus warily continue on his way.

Twice during the night he came across small villages nestled on the riverbank. He crept carefully around the dark masses of the small houses and hovels, but no oil lamps glimmered in the darkness, and no one stirred except for a dog in the second village, which barked briefly and let out a long, low howl before falling silent. As the first pale glow of dawn crept over the horizon, Marcus came across a third village. There was a gnawing ache in the pit of his stomach, and he reluctantly decided that he must risk finding something to eat. He had no idea how the people of the village would react to finding a young Roman boy on their doorstep. He would have to try to steal some food. The thought of stealing concerned him for a moment. It had been drummed into him by his father that theft was dishonorable, and that a man who stole from his comrades should be severely disciplined. Yet now Marcus was hungry, so hungry that it was painful and distracting. A year ago he had been ill and unable to keep any food down and hadn't eaten for days, so he knew that if he did not eat soon he would feel light-headed, faint, and weak. There was no avoiding it. He must have food, however he came by it.

Marcus carefully approached a large house on the edge of the village. Outside the entrance, a small flame flickered in a brazier. By its light, Marcus could see a man curled up on the ground. He paused long enough to satisfy himself that the man was asleep, and then crept closer. There were two long, low buildings extending on either side of the house, and the acrid smell of goats wafted on the night air. Marcus guessed that these were the sheds where the livestock and other food-stuffs were kept. He reached the end of the nearest shed and flattened himself against the roughly plastered wall.

He was still for a moment, listening for any movement, but there was nothing, apart from the shuffling of one of the goats on its straw bedding, then silence. Marcus felt his way along the wall until he came to a door. He eased the latch up slowly, wincing as it grated. The door was mounted on heavy wooden hinges, and creaked as he opened it just enough for him to squeeze inside. A thin shaft of moonlight fell across the floor of the shed. By its light he could see another door on the far wall. Next to it stood racks filled with stoppered jars. Marcus moved farther inside and came to some shelves. His fingers lightly felt across the objects stored there. There were some root vegetables and bags filled with grain. Then he found some hard-surfaced objects the size of large stones. He picked one up. He pressed hard on one and it yielded. It was light, and as he raised it to his nose, he smiled. Bread. He quickly picked up a few more of the small loaves, and carried on searching. The next shelf had some cheeses, and he took the largest one that he could manage, and then helped himself to an empty waterskin lying next to the shelves. He could fill it from the river, he decided as he started back toward the door, happy with his finds.

But as he walked quickly away, his foot caught on something heavy. There was a grating sound, and an instant later a heavy jar smashed onto the flagstones. Liquid splashed up against his legs, and the air was filled with the aroma of olive oil. An icy jolt of fear shot down his neck. The sound had been enough to alert the farmhands—he was sure of it.

He made to run to the door, but the spilled oil made the flagstones slippery, and he was forced to tread carefully. Marcus heard a shout from the main farm building, and he emerged from the shed into the moonlight to see that the man by the fire had risen to his feet and was sounding the alarm. Marcus ducked down behind a pile of firewood beside the shed, to keep out of sight. Even though it was night, the moonlight would provide enough illumination for the man to spot him in the open. A door crashed open just inside the entrance, and a moment later two more men joined the first.

"What's going on?" one of them asked.

"Heard something break in one of the storerooms."

"Animal?"

"We'll soon find out! Come on." The first man lowered a torch into the brazier, and the flames quickly carried to the oil-soaked rag binding the end of the torch together. The three of them started toward the shed, lit by a wavering pool of orange light from the flame of the torch. Marcus realized that they would see him in a matter of moments. He would not be able to outrun them laden down with the food he had taken, but he was starving and he knew that he would not be able to go on without something to eat. He glanced around desperately, until his eyes fixed on the oil gleaming in the entrance to the storeroom.

Rising up from behind the logs, he ran back to the door.

"There!" The man with the torch thrust out his arm. "That boy!"

"Little thief! Let's have him."

They burst into a run. Marcus glanced around and then ducked back into the shed.

"Ha! He's trapped now," one of the men shouted with glee. "We've got him."

Marcus carefully made his way across the pool of oil to the door on the far side. It was fastened with a simple bolt, but it was stiff and squealed faintly as he struggled to draw it back. There was a glow in the room as the man with the torch reached the entrance. Trying not to panic, Marcus struggled again with the bolt. His heart pounded with terror at the thought of being captured. Just then it shot back, and he thrust the door open.

"Stand still, you!" the man shouted across the room.

Marcus glanced back. "Make me."

Then he ran off into the night. Behind him he heard the men enter the shed, and there was a cry of alarm and a soft thud, then another, as they slipped and lost their footing in the slick of olive oil.

"Watch that torch, you fool!" a voice cried.

Marcus ran on, away from the village, making for the safety of the shadows under the nearest olive grove a hundred paces away. He did not dare look back as his pursuers shouted in panic. Only when he reached the trees did Marcus pause and glance over his shoulder. The door was clear to see, lit by a strengthening glow of red and orange from inside the shed. One of the men came stumbling out, silhouetted by the glare within. The torch must have set fire to something in the shed, and now the flames were spreading quickly. The shouts of the men had roused more people from the house. Marcus's chest heaved as he caught his breath and watched for a moment, content that no one was pursuing him. He tore at one of the loaves and chewed quickly. The first of the flames licked through the roof of the shed as several figures began to throw buckets of water onto the fire.

Marcus felt a surge of guilt at the sight. He had only wanted to eat, and was shocked by the growing blaze. Once the fire was put out, the people who owned the farm would be sure to send men to look for the culprit. He had to move on quickly and get as far away from there as possible before daylight. Biting off some more bread, Marcus turned away and hurried through the olive grove. He strode as quickly as he could, not daring to run, for fear of tripping and twisting his ankle in the dark. After he had put a mile between himself and the farm, Marcus turned back toward the river and continued following it downstream.

At first light he saw that the river was flowing through a narrow gorge, and he was forced to follow a steep path leading up the hill to the side. When Marcus reached the crest, puffing from the effort, he stopped dead. On the far side of the hill, the ground fell away to a narrow strip of coastal plain. Below, a large port lay in the shadow of the hill. Beyond the thick stone walls lay a confusing maze of dull red-tiled roofs, stretching out toward the coast, where there was a wide bay. Twenty or thirty ships were moored beside the wharf, and many more lay at anchor.

For the first time, Marcus felt his spirits rising as he stared down at the ships. Some of them were bound to be sailing to Italia, and he would find a way to get aboard one. He would work his passage, or, if necessary, he would stow away and jump over the side as soon as the ship dropped anchor off the coast of Italia. Then he must get to Rome and find General Pompeius. Marcus knew that a long road lay ahead of him, and he must travel it alone and overcome the dangers he encountered on the way by himself. If only his father were here. He would know what to do and he would be strong enough to see it through. For a brief moment Marcus doubted whether he could do it, and then he remembered his mother, and his heart filled with renewed determination to rescue her.

Marcus ate half of a loaf, and some of his cheese, and set off down the hill toward the port.

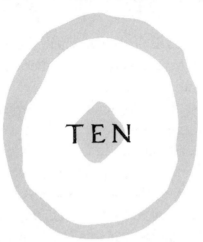

TEN

"**Y**OU WANT TO JOIN MY CREW?" The captain of the *Fair Wind* smiled as he looked down at Marcus. They were standing on the deck of his ship in the harbor of Dyrrhacium, and around them the crew glanced with amused expressions at the small figure of Marcus. He swallowed nervously before he replied to the captain.

"Yes, sir."

"I see. So, what experience do you have?" asked the captain as he rested his hands on his hips.

"Experience?"

"Of sailing ships. Like this one." The captain gestured around the deck. At the moment, cargo was being loaded into the ship. A steady stream of porters came up the gangway, laden with bales of richly patterned material. The crew of the ship took the bales and lowered them to some sailors in the hold, who carefully stowed them away. Above them towered the mast, with a furled sail hanging at a slight angle. Ropes stretched down in all directions from the mast and sail.

Marcus drew a breath and tried to sound confident as

he replied, "I've been on a ship before, sir. I'm sure it will all come back to me."

The captain scratched his jaw and stepped to the mast, plucked one of the ropes out, and cocked his head at Marcus. "Well, then, my young sailor, what's this one called?"

Marcus looked at the rope, then traced its path up the mast until he lost sight of it among the other ropes and pulleys. He felt his heart sink as he turned his gaze back toward the captain. "I can't remember, sir."

"Rubbish! You're no sailor. That's clear enough. You don't know one end of a ship from the other."

"But I have to get to Rome!" Marcus protested. "I don't eat much and I can work hard."

"Maybe, but not on my ship." The captain shook his head. "I've no use for you, lad. Not until you get some sailing experience. Now get off my ship before I give you a good hiding."

Marcus nodded as he backed away cautiously and then turned to hurry back down the gangway onto the wharf. It was past noon and the paving stones were blistering hot underfoot. He hurried across toward the shade of one of the warehouses. A faint smell of spices struggled to compete with the odor of fish, sweat, and sewage. Despite the heat, the wharf teemed with life as sailors, porters, merchants, hawkers, and fishermen mingled along the broad thoroughfare beside the water. Marcus watched them for a moment, and looked out over the mass of masts and rigging that towered over the heads of the crowd. There was no shortage of ships. The only problem was finding a way to get a free passage to Italia. If that proved impossible, Marcus decided he must stow away.

He had spent most of the morning going from ship to ship to see which ones were headed across the Adriatic sea, and asking if he could travel with them and pay his fare by working on the ship. But no one had any use for a ten-year-old boy. While some had refused him harshly, others had been suspicious, and one captain had asked him straight out if he was a runaway slave. Marcus had denied it, made his excuses, and left the ship at once. He decided he must be more careful. Decimus would be posting rewards for the return of an escaped slave, and the farmers would be equally keen to find the thief who had caused their storeroom to go up in flames.

He had half a loaf of bread and some of the cheese left, and he took them out of his tunic and began to chew without much enthusiasm. When the food was gone, he would have nothing left, and unless he could find a way to earn some money or join the crew of a ship, he would be forced to steal once again. Marcus felt guilty as he considered the prospect. Not for the first time, he cursed Decimus for being the cause of all his suffering. Once he had finished eating, Marcus filled his waterskin at the public fountain and then settled down in the doorway of a boarded-up shop to let his food go down and to rest for a while.

The afternoon heat became oppressive, and the wharf began to get less busy as people drifted off to rest for an hour or two. The teams of porters retreated into the shade inside the warehouses, where some of them settled to playing dice, while others ate or slept. On board the ships, the crews also sat down to rest, sprawled out on the deck wherever they could find shade. Soon all was quiet and only a handful of people still went about their business along the length of the wharf. Marcus realized that this might be the best chance he had to get aboard a ship, while the crews were dozing. He brushed the crumbs from his tunic and rose to his feet. Opposite him, the deck of the *Fair Wind* looked deserted, and Marcus strolled casually along the wharf, looking over the ship out of the corner of his eye. He had discovered that the ship was bound for Brundisium, a busy port directly opposite the coast of Graecia. An ideal choice for Marcus.

As he slowly passed by, he could see that most of the crew were lying under an awning spread out over the aft deck, where the shaft of the steersman's tiller hung over the side. There was only one man in the bow of the ship. A wineskin was clasped to his chest and he was snoring loudly. The cargo hatch lay open, right next to the gangway. With a quick look around to make sure that none of the crew was watching him, Marcus walked back to the gangway and crossed it confidently, as if he were one of the crew returning aboard—in case anyone on the wharf was paying attention to him. When he reached the break in the ship's rail, Marcus eased himself down and crept onto the deck. He paused, looking both ways. The drunk was still asleep, his snoring so loud that Marcus swore he could feel vibrations through the wooden planking beneath his feet. Looking the other way, he saw that no one had stirred under the awning.

"So far, so good," he muttered to himself. The raised wooden coaming of the cargo hatch was less than six feet away. He cautiously approached it on hands and knees, wincing at the heat of the deck. When he reached the hatch, he warily looked over the edge and down into the hold. The ship's cargo seemed to consist mainly of bales of fabric, which had been carefully piled toward the rear of the hold. The front had been packed with planks of a dark wood, almost black. There was little available space, and Marcus realized that the *Fair Wind* would finish its loading soon and then set sail. Perfect, he thought.

Easing himself over the worn edge of the coaming, Marcus dropped onto a large bale of woolen cloth, with a soft thud. He paused a moment to listen for any sign that he had been detected, and then climbed over the bales toward the rear of the hold. He picked a spot near the top, midway across the beam of the ship. There, he eased one of the bales out and, straining against the weight, pulled it onto the rest of the pile under the hatch. Climbing up into the gap he had created, Marcus pulled out another bale and placed it carefully below the gap. Then, sliding in, he tugged a third bale forward and thrust it around to conceal the space he had created on top of the bales of material. There was a small slot to one side, just big enough for him to squeeze through. From the far side he could see out into the hold, and once the cargo-hatch grating was in place, he would get some light and air on the voyage across the sea.

It was hot in the hold, and as he lay there and waited for the loading to continue, Marcus felt sweat prick out all over his body. Very soon he felt thirsty, but fought the temptation to take a drink from his waterskin. He must make the water last. If it ran out, or he began to starve and his situation became too uncomfortable, he decided that he would just have to give himself up to the crew and hope that they did not return him to Graecia or, worse still, hand him back to Decimus once they discovered his identity.

After the best part of an hour, as far as he could guess the passage of time, Marcus heard the thud of feet on the deck above as the crew rose to continue their duties.

"Back to work!" the captain bellowed. "And you there! You porters, get the last of the cargo aboard. The ship has to sail before dusk. Move yourselves!"

A short time later, Marcus watched through the narrow gap he had left himself as two of the crewmen climbed down into the hold and began to pack the last bales of material into position. Overhead, he heard the steady thud of feet. A few wooden cases and several crates of large amphorae were lowered into the hold, completing the loading, and then the men climbed up to the deck. There was a deep rumble as the grid was heaved over the cargo hatch. Marcus breathed a sigh of relief that he had not been discovered, and stretched out in the small hiding space he had made for himself. At least with the fine material surrounding him, he would have a comfortable surface to rest on. The main problem was going to be the discomfort of the heat in the hold and the thirst that was already building up in his throat.

Once the *Fair Wind* was loaded, the captain bellowed orders for his crew to prepare to sail. The gangway was hauled aboard, the sail lowered, and then the oars were thrust over the side to push the ship away from the wharf. With a regular creak and splash, the long oars propelled the ship out into the harbor, through the waiting shipping, and then out into the open sea. Marcus felt the sudden shift in the ship's motion as it encountered the light swell in the unprotected waters outside the harbor. At once, his stomach lurched, and he felt a horrible dizziness sweep through his body. He clapped a hand to his mouth and tried not to be sick. The last thing he wanted was to spend the voyage surrounded by his own vomit.

Outside his hiding place, he could hear the muffled shouts as the captain ordered his crew to brace up the sail and settle the ship on her course across the expanse of sea that separated Graecia from Italia. As the *Fair Wind* began to ride the swell in long swooping motions, Marcus curled into a ball and groaned. His stomach felt very unsettled, and he had to use every bit of his self-control to stop himself from throwing up. At length, he could resist the urge no longer. He eased the bale of wool aside, leaned out into the hold, and was sick. The nausea came again and again, and soon Marcus had nothing left inside him. Yet still he retched, his stomach clenching painfully, until the urge passed and left him sweating. Marcus knew that the vomit was bound to be seen when the ship pulled into port, but he hoped that it would be put down to one of the crew who had not been able to make it to the side of the vessel in time.

As dusk fell, he took a sip of water, rinsed his mouth, and spat it out before taking a fresh mouthful to drink. Then, after making sure he had covered the entrance to his hiding place, Marcus curled up again and tried to take his mind off his sickness by planning out his next moves. Once the ship reached Brundisium, he would need to find his way off the vessel without being spotted. Then he would have to make his way to Rome and find the house of General Pompeius.

For a moment he was seized by the horrible fear that he had set himself an impossible task. After all, he was only a small boy, entirely on his own. He had been born and raised on his father's farm, and had never traveled any farther than twenty miles from his home. He still had a long way to go before he reached Rome, and even then he would need to find some way to speak to General Pompeius. If the general was as great and powerful as his father had said, then it would not be easy. As these doubts and fears worked their way into his mind, the image of his mother suddenly burned into his thoughts. Marcus clenched his fists and angrily shook off his worries, and told himself that he was being a coward. His father would have been ashamed of him. He edged himself into the corner of his hiding place, closed his eyes, and tried to fight off the anxieties over his future and the nausea that rose and subsided along with the motion of the ship.

He spent the night and the whole of the next day in his hiding place, only emerging to empty his bladder into the bilge, while taking care not to be seen through the grating that covered the hold. By the following night, Marcus had begun to get over the worst of his seasickness, but his waterskin was empty and his stomach grumbled with hunger. He lay on the wool bale for some hours in the darkness, unable to sleep, and then in the early hours he heard the captain's voice as he stood by the mast, just in front of the cargo hatch.

"Damn this foul wind. . . . First mate!"

Footsteps padded over the deck, and then the crewman replied, "Yes, sir?"

"The wind's veered again. Rouse the watch. I want the sail sheeted tight in. Tell the steersman to keep as near to the wind as he can hold the ship. Unless this wind changes, we're going to lose a day, maybe two, before we reach port."

"Aye, sir. I think so."

"Carry on."

The mate turned away to summon the watch, and Marcus

heard shouting and the thud of feet on the deck. A short while later, the ship heeled a little more. The motion became less settled as the bow slammed into the waves. Marcus felt his heart sink as he thought over the brief exchange he had heard. The ship was delayed. If the captain was right, then it might be some days before they reached port. Marcus knew that he must have some water and food before then, if he was going to survive and have the strength to continue his quest for General Pompeius. There was only one thing for it. He must leave the hold and try to find something to eat and drink. Better to do it now while it was dark and there was less chancc of being seen.

He waited a while to give the crew time to settle back down, and then wriggled out of his hiding place. The hold was filled with the sounds of creaking timbers and the slosh of water in the bilge. Above him, Marcus could just make out the thick crossed lines of the grating that covered the hold, except for one corner where there was a square gap. It was just large enough for a man to climb through, and Marcus guessed it was there in case the crew needed to check the hold without having to remove the grating. Creeping carefully across the wool bales and crates packed tightly together, Marcus approached the gap. The hold was sufficiently full for him to reach it without any difficulty. He reached up and gripped the edge of the hatch, and then, muscles tensed and straining, he lifted himself up. As his eyes came level with the rim of the hatch, Marcus looked around the deck.

The first glimmer of dawn was filtering across the horizon. At the stern of the ship, there stood a man clasping the tiller that controlled the huge steering oar. A handful of men lay on the deck in front of him. Closer to the hatch, some more figures sat hunched together against the ship's side. One of them shifted, and Marcus heard the clink of a chain. They must be slaves, he realized. Part of the ship's cargo. No one seemed to have seen him, and Marcus let out a long, low breath of relief. Then his eyes fixed on some baskets and a barrel at the base of the mast.

Marcus eased himself up over the edge of the hatch and onto the deck. Then, staying low, he slid across the weathered and worn planks until he reached the foot of the mast. His fingers groped over the edge of the nearest basket and came across some hard, round objects. Apples. He smiled and helped himself to four, tucking them inside his tunic. Even though he was pleased with his find, Marcus knew that apples alone would not satisfy his hunger.

A sudden snore made him jump, and he glanced around in terror. Only a few feet away, curled up on the deck, was one of the crew. The man muttered something and then grunted before he began to breathe deeply. Marcus was about to turn his attention back to the baskets when he saw a half-eaten loaf of bread and some sausage beside the man. He licked his lips at the thought of making a meal of the crewman's spare food. With a quick look around to satisfy himself that no one was paying him any attention, Marcus edged toward the snoring sailor. He paused a short distance away and then stealthily reached out a hand to pick up the bread and sausage. With a slight smile of relief that the man was still asleep, Marcus turned back toward the cargo hatch. He was keen to return to his hiding place, and feast, before the light got any stronger and gave him away. He had almost reached the hatch when the steersman's deep voice boomed out across the deck.

"Change the watch! Change the watch! Morning watch, unreef the mainsail."

The crew began to stir, and the man whose food Marcus had helped himself to snorted and began to sit up wearily, his hand groping toward where the food had been. He opened his eyes and looked straight at Marcus. He blinked and frowned, saw the sausage and bread in Marcus's hand, and his eyes widened in surprise.

"Thief!" he cried out, scrambling across the deck toward Marcus.

ELEVEN

Marcus lashed out with his boot, the nailed leather striking the sailor in the face. The man cried out and clasped his hands to his nose as the blood began to run. The sound alerted others nearby, who turned to look.

"Who's that boy?" someone called out.

"Well, he's no passenger!" another voice responded, and some of the men on deck laughed. "Seems we have ourselves a stowaway, lads."

Marcus backed away from the man he had kicked, then went into a crouch. He bit a chunk off the sausage and chewed furiously. Watching the men on the deck carefully, he backed against the opposite side of the ship. More of the crew and passengers edged forward curiously, while at the rear of the vessel the captain emerged from the hatch leading to the handful of small cabins at the stern. He was followed by a large man in a red tunic, who climbed up beside the steersman for a better view.

"What is all this nonsense?" the captain bellowed. "What's going on here?"

"Stowaway, Captain," one of the sailors replied, pointing

toward Marcus. "Must have been in the hold and got hungry, like. That's why he's gone and nicked Spiro's food."

The man Marcus had kicked wiped the blood from his face and rose to his feet with a growl.

"Right then, boy," he hissed. "You are going to pay for that. Thought you could take Spiro's ration and get away with it, eh?"

He reached to his side and drew out a dagger from his wide leather belt. Marcus quickly weighed him up. The sailor was not quite as old as his father had been, with unkempt dark hair hanging loosely around his face. His lips parted in a cruel sneer, revealing a handful of crooked teeth. As he raised his knife, he swayed slightly, and Marcus guessed that he must have had rather more to drink than was wise. Marcus took another bite at the sausage as he watched the sailor closely.

The man's sneer turned into a snarl of rage. "Thief!"

He ran at Marcus, his knife gleaming dully in the pale dawn light. At the last moment, Marcus ducked to the left, and the sailor stumbled into the rail along the ship's side. Some of the men laughed, and Spiro glared around the deck before he fixed his eyes on Marcus again.

"Think you're clever, boy? Well, I'm going to cut you good for that."

From the tone of the man's voice, Marcus knew that he was in grave danger. The man might even kill him if he had the chance. For a moment it felt as if an icy hand had clamped around the back of his neck. Marcus was more afraid than he had ever been in his life. He let the bread and the sausage drop from his fingers and crouched low, ready to spring aside. Already he was thinking about his next moves, his wits quickened by the knowledge that he was engaged in a fight to survive.

"Go on, Spiro!" a sailor called out. "Show the boy what a man you are."

There was more laughter, but Marcus saw that the comment had caused the sailor to become even more enraged. He sprang toward Marcus, slashing out with his blade as he did so. Marcus leaped to the side, hearing a faint hiss close to his ear as the blade cut through the cool dawn air. He ran to the middle of the deck and turned back to face Spiro as the sailor strode toward him, hunched forward.

"Keep running, boy. I'll corner you. Sooner or later."

Marcus glanced to the side and saw the dark lines of the mast's shrouds sweeping down toward a series of heavy wooden pins. He glanced back just in time to see Spiro make another attack, leaning forward and thrusting the point of his blade out. Marcus dodged aside, then was forced to back away again as Spiro slashed at his face. The small crowd of onlookers melted away on either side as the sailor pursued his prey toward the stern.

"Here, young 'un!" a voice cried out, and there was a clatter on the deck close by Marcus as a knife landed on the planking. "Take it!"

Marcus snatched the knife up and scrambled away from yet another attack. This time some of the sailors cheered him on, admiring the agile way he was avoiding Spiro's attacks. But Marcus knew that time was on the sailor's side. He would find a way to corner Marcus, and then it would be over. The sailor would cut him down where he stood and dump his body over the side into the sea.

Marcus ducked around the man and sprinted back toward

the side of the vessel where the shrouds curved down, and there he turned to face the man again. Spiro paced steadily toward him, breathing heavily from the strain of his exertions. He shook his head mockingly, flicking aside a thick strand of hair that had fallen over one eye.

"You've got a knife, but do you know how to use it?"

Marcus swallowed nervously. "Why don't you come closer and find out?"

Spiro feinted with his blade. Marcus thrust out the knife with both hands, to parry the attack, and stepped back against the ship's side. Shifting the knife to his left hand, he let his right hand drop, felt behind him for one of the pins, and lifted it out of its hole.

The sailor stood before him, an arm's length away. He held his arms wide, as if to catch Marcus whichever way he tried to run.

"Time to pay old Spiro the price for stealing," the sailor leered.

Marcus swallowed nervously. The time had come to strike, yet he knew he must divert the sailor's attention at the critical moment. He lowered his left hand.

"Please, don't hurt me," he pleaded softly. "I give in."

He tossed the knife onto the deck, just behind the sailor. The man instinctively glanced around and down, his hair flopping across his face like a curtain. Marcus snatched out the pin, jumped forward, and smashed its heavy wooden bulk against the side of Spiro's head. The sailor dropped to his knees with a groan, head rolling back as his mouth sagged open. His blade fell from his hands, and he fixed Marcus with a dazed expression before he collapsed unconscious at his feet.

There was a brief silence before one of the crew let out a low whistle. Then another man cheered, and more joined him in a ragged chorus of shouts of approval. Marcus looked around at their faces and saw the amused admiration in their expressions. Many of them were smiling at him, and he felt a surge of elation and triumph flood his heart and mind. Then he looked down at the man lying at his feet. A moment ago, the sailor had been set on killing Marcus, without mercy. Marcus regarded him with a cold hatred. Then he leaned down and picked up the knife that had been tossed toward him.

For a moment, he paused, not sure what to do. From somewhere inside him, a dark urge to seek revenge seeped out. It was not just revenge against this sailor, but a desire for vengeance against all those who had caused Marcus to be at this point, separated from his mother, his home, and the warm, loving embrace of the idyllic life he had lived on the farm. He took a sharp breath and raised the knife, ready to plunge it down into the sailor's heart.

"No you don't!" a voice growled, and a hand seized his wrist in a powerful grip. "Drop the knife."

Marcus twisted around to see the captain towering over him. He tried to pull his arm free, but the man was far too strong for him. The captain let him struggle for a moment, and then, with a look of contempt, he lifted Marcus off his feet so that he was dangling above the deck. He felt a burning pain in his shoulder as the joint and muscles stretched, and could not help letting out a sharp cry of agony.

The captain leaned forward so that his face was close to Marcus's. There was no pity in the man's eyes as he growled, "I said, drop the knife. Last warning, boy."

Marcus knew that his position seemed hopeless, but the captain had made a mistake lifting him off the deck. Swinging his leg back, Marcus kicked out with his boot, striking the captain's knee. His foot connected with a solid blow, and the captain winced and bent forward as he let out a groan. At once, Marcus tried to pull himself free again, but the man kept his grip, even as he shut his eyes briefly to fight off the pain. When he had caught his breath and opened his eyes, there was no mistaking the captain's fury.

"Little git..." the captain spat. "You've had your fun. Now it's my turn."

He strode toward the side of the ship, holding Marcus off the deck at arm's length.

"You can swim the rest of the way." He sneered at Marcus as they reached the side-rail. The captain lifted him up in both hands and held Marcus over the water. He glanced down and saw the milky blue sea churning along the side of the hull with a soft hiss. There was no sign of land anywhere, and the prospect of being abandoned in the sea to die terrified Marcus. He clamped his spare hand into the folds of the captain's tunic and clung on for his life.

"Wait!" a deep voice called out. "Captain, listen to me!"

Marcus looked over the captain's shoulder and saw the man in the red tunic. The captain turned his head toward his passenger. "What? What is it?"

"Spare the boy," the man said calmly. "You cannot leave him to drown."

"No?" The captain smiled cruelly. "Why not? He's a stowaway. A thief, and violent with it. I should have seen that when I first clapped eyes on him back in Dyrrhacium. Typical wharf rat. Those scum don't deserve to live." He turned back toward Marcus and braced his muscles to hurl the boy out into the waves.

"Let him live and I'll buy him," the man added.

The captain paused, torn between the desire to avenge himself for the blow Marcus had inflicted on his pride, and the chance to make some money. He cleared his throat. "How much?"

"What's your price?"

"Huh?" The captain frowned, not quite sure what to ask for. After a brief pause, he edged back and dumped Marcus on the deck between himself and the man in the red tunic. Marcus gasped with relief to feel the solid deck beneath his back. For the moment, he had been spared, and he felt a surge of hope as he stared up at the passenger who had offered to buy him. The man was powerfully built with neatly cut dark hair. He wore leather armguards around each of his hairy wrists. He stood with his hands on his hips and waited for the captain's response.

"Why do you want to buy the boy, Lucius Porcino? He's just a little runt." The captain gestured toward the men in chains, sitting silently on the deck. "You trade in gladiators."

The man looked down at Marcus and shrugged. "He shows spirit. Looks fit enough to last a few years. But I doubt he'll ever amount to much more than a common kitchen slave. So, name your price. I'll pay a fair sum."

The captain's eyes narrowed. "Three hundred denarii."

"Three hundred?" Porcino's eyebrows rose in surprise. "I could buy a full-grown man for that. It'll be years before this one can earn his keep. Three hundred indeed!" He shook his head and jerked his thumb over the side. "You'd better throw him in, then. I'm certainly not paying three hundred."

He turned away and began to make his way back toward the hatch at the stern leading down to the cabins. Marcus stared after him in despair, his heart heavy in his breast, like a rock. The captain bit his lip and called after the man.

"Two hundred!"

Porcino paused, mid-stride, and turned around slowly. He looked at Marcus again and rubbed his bristly chin thoughtfully. "I'll give you one hundred. And I'm robbing myself at that price."

The captain decided on one last try. "A hundred and fifty, then."

"Done." Porcino strode back to the captain, spat in his own hand, and held it out. The captain took his hand and they shook to seal the deal. Marcus felt a surge of relief—he was almost grateful to the man who had saved his life. He smiled faintly as Porcino looked down at him, but there was no friendship in his expression. No sense that he had saved Marcus out of some impulse to help another human being. Just the hard stare of a professional businessman.

"Piso!" He clicked his fingers. A wiry man in a brown tunic pushed through the loose ring of sailors who had gathered to watch. Porcino turned to him. "Take the boy. Chain him up with the rest of them."

"Yes, master." Piso bowed his head.

The captain, meanwhile, turned to bellow at his men, ordering them to break up the crowd and for those on watch to get back to their duties. As the men dispersed, he turned to Porcino. "I'll have that money before we reach port, eh?"

Porcino nodded, and with a last cold look at Marcus, the captain turned and made his way aft, limping. Porcino could not help a brief grin at the man's discomfort. But his face hardened as he turned back to Piso. "Make sure you chain him well. Don't want him trying to give us the slip once we reach Brundisium."

"No, master."

Porcino glanced at Marcus. "And find him something to eat and drink."

"Yes, master."

Porcino puffed out his cheeks. "I hope you're worth the money, boy."

Marcus swallowed and responded quietly. "Thank you."

"Thank you?" Porcino laughed. "I've made you into a slave, boy, not a friend. Never forget it."

Piso leaned down and plucked Marcus off the deck. As he was led toward the silent figures of the chained slaves, Marcus realized he had cheated death only to end up a slave yet again.

TWELVE

THE *FAIR WIND* REACHED BRUNDISIUM at first light two days later. As the sun slanted across the deck, the captain gave the order to reduce sail, and the ship ghosted between the vessels lying at anchor. The steersman carefully set a course toward an empty berth alongside the wharf as several sailors stood by with mooring ropes, ready to sling the tarred loops to some of the men waiting on the wharf.

Marcus struggled to his feet and leaned against the side rail as he looked around. Brundisium was much bigger than the port they had left back in Graecia. A huge citadel, built on a rock that jutted into the harbor, was linked to the mainland by a narrow causeway. Shipping crowded the water on either side of the citadel, and a squadron of sleek warships rode at anchor near the harbor entrance. Ashore, the warehouses, temples, civic buildings, and crowded tenement blocks sprawled inland, oppressed by a haze of smoke that hung over the port.

The urban stench of sewage, sweat, and decaying food that had assaulted Marcus's nose at Dyrrhacium was even more potent here. Looking down into the calm water of the harbor, Marcus saw that it was covered with rubbish and dead fish, and the bloated corpse of a dog bobbed near the surface close to the ship. His nose wrinkled in disgust, and he wondered how anyone could bear living in the towns and ports that he had seen since leaving the farm. He felt a pang as he recalled the clean, pine-scented air of the mountains of home.

Marcus turned his mind away from such memories, and instead he considered his new companions. As well as himself, there were six men chained together. They were young and fit, and all of them bought by Porcino in slave markets across Graecia. Three of the men were from Thrace, and they kept to themselves, adopting a haughty attitude toward the other slaves. Two of the others were from Athens, and the last man was from Sparta.

At first they had ignored Marcus, as Piso had fastened the shackles around his ankles and run the end of the chain through the ring bolt on Marcus's right ankle. But once Piso had finished his work and sauntered off to have his morning meal of bread dipped in fish sauce, the nearest man, an Athenian with a flattened nose, nudged Marcus.

"You showed that sailor up nicely. The captain, too." He smiled at Marcus. "I'm Pelleneus, from Athens." He nodded toward the man next to him, a heavily bearded giant. "This is Phyrus. He's from Athens as well."

"Rhodes," the giant mumbled. "Told you, I was from Rhodes. Until I was sold to that damned Athenian woman." He cast his eyes down and continued mumbling, but Marcus could not catch any of the words.

Pelleneus winked. "Don't mind him. He has his happy moments. Which is more than I can say for some." He leaned closer to Marcus and continued quietly. "The Spartan doesn't speak a word, though Piso reckons his name is Patroclus. As for the Thracians..." He shrugged. "They keep to themselves. Won't even talk to me or Phyrus. What about you, boy? What's your name?"

"Marcus Cornelius Primus."

"A Roman name?"

Marcus nodded. "My father was a centurion."

"I see," Pelleneus nodded archly. "So what is the son of a Roman centurion doing skulking in the bottom of a cargo ship?"

Marcus wondered how much he should say. He was not sure what would happen if it was discovered that Decimus had claimed him as his property. Until he knew better, it would be best to be tight-lipped about some details of his past, he decided. "My father was killed—murdered—by a moneylender. My mother was kidnapped. I escaped. Now I'm looking for my father's old commander to see if he can help my mother and me get justice."

Pelleneus nodded sympathetically. "And who might this commander be?"

"General Pompeius."

"Pompeius?" Pelleneus raised his eyebrows. "As in Pompeius the Great?"

"Yes, that's what father called him. You know of him, then?"

"How can you *not* know of him?" The Athenian smiled, and then shook his head. "Well, young Marcus, if you really think someone like Pompeius the Great would stir himself to come to the rescue of the family of one of his former junior officers... then you have a lot more faith in Roman justice than I have."

"Father was one of his bravest men." Marcus frowned, his pride hurt. "One of his most trusted soldiers. Pompeius even gave him a special sword as a gift when he retired from the legions. Of course Pompeius will help us." Marcus looked down at his feet. "All I have to do is find him."

"Huh." Phyrus interrupted without looking around. "And how you going to do that, young 'un?" He shuffled his foot so that the chain clattered on the deck. "You're a slave now."

"No," Marcus said fiercely. "Your master, Porcino, had no right to buy me. I'll wait until we're off this ship, then explain everything to him. Maybe there could be a reward in it for him if he helps me find Pompeius," Marcus added hopefully.

Pelleneus laughed. "You'd better get to know Porcino before you get your hopes up. Somehow, I'm not sure he will be very interested in your story."

"I'm a Roman citizen," Marcus replied. "This can't happen to me."

The Athenian looked at him with pity in his eyes. "It already has. You'd better get used to it, lad."

Marcus fell into a sullen silence for a while before he spoke again. "This man, Porcino. Is he a slave dealer?"

Pelleneus shook his head. "No, he's not a dealer. Porcino is a lanista."

"Lanista?" Marcus wondered.

"A gladiator trainer," Pelleneus explained. "He runs a school for gladiators near Capua. According to Piso, he is one of the best trainers in the business. For that, I suppose you should be grateful, at least."

"Grateful?" Marcus could hardly believe his ears. He had heard of gladiators from his father and knew of the terrible danger they faced every time they stepped in front of a crowd to entertain them with a bloody fight to the death. "Why should I be grateful? I've been saved from drowning only to be enslaved in a gladiator school. I don't want to die on the sand of some arena." He shuddered at the thought.

"Look at it this way: if you have to be trained as a gladiator, then you might as well be trained by the best. It could give a man the advantage when the time comes for him to fight."

The Athenian might have a point, but Marcus had no intention of being owned by the lanista long enough to find out. He would have to speak to Porcino as soon as he could, and explain the injustices that had been heaped on him and his family. But before he spoke with the lanista, it would be wise to see what kind of a man Porcino was.

"What's he like?" Marcus asked.

"Porcino?" Pelleneus pursed his lips. "He's a hard man. Bound to be, after having survived in the arena long enough to win his freedom. But he's fair enough. If you do as you are told and do it quickly, he'll treat you well."

A shadow fell over them, and Marcus looked up to see Piso. The man dropped a stale loaf and a hunk of dried meat onto Marcus's lap.

"Eat," he said simply, then turned and walked away.

Marcus hurriedly tore into the bread, desperate to feed his hunger. As he chewed, he glanced sideways at his companions and prayed that Pelleneus was wrong. He had to convince Porcino to set him free. His mother's life depended on it. Only he could save her from a lingering death on Decimus's slave estate.

Once the ship had been securely moored alongside the wharf, the captain gave the order for the gangway to be lowered and for the cargo hold to be opened up. While the captain made a deal with one of the port's gang masters to unload the cargo, Piso came and changed the slave's shackles, swapping their ankle rings for large iron hoops that fastened around the neck. The collar felt heavy and uncomfortable on Marcus's shoulders, but he knew better than to complain while Piso stood over them with a heavy wooden club. Porcino had already gone ashore to make arrangements for the provisions needed for the journey to Capua. When he returned, Piso gestured to the chained prisoners. "On your feet! Move yourselves!"

Marcus responded quickly and obediently, and the others shuffled onto their feet behind him. Once they were all up, Piso shoved Marcus toward the gangway, causing him to stumble as the chain became taut between him and the others. Pelleneus stepped forward just in time to save Marcus from falling headlong. With a steady *chink, chinkle, chink* from the chains, the seven prisoners shuffled across the gangway and onto the wharf. Porcino was waiting for them. He sat in the saddle of a small horse and was leading a string of three mules loaded down with nets of bread and crudely cut chunks of salted meat. He had a sword belt fastened around his middle, and a club hung from his saddle horn.

With Porcino leading the way and Piso bringing up the rear, the small column of prisoners wound its way along the wharf to the main street leading through the port. No one spared Marcus a second look as he passed by, and he felt his heart sink as he realized no one was going to see that he had been wronged. To their eyes, he was just another slave, one of the vast number who landed in Brundisium over the course of a year. He wondered if he should call out for help—if he should shout about all the wrongs that had been done to him. The moment he slowed down, however, steeling himself to cry out that he had been kidnapped, Piso strode along the line and prodded him with the end of his club.

"Keep the pace up, boy! No slacking."

Marcus stumbled on for a short distance and then settled into the rhythm of the other prisoners as they passed through the city gates. After leaving Brundisium, Porcino followed the coast road, heading north. To their right, the sea sparkled invitingly, now that they were safely ashore. To the left, the landscape rolled gently toward a distant line of hills. Farms and some large agricultural estates lined the road. Close to the port, there was a constant stream of traffic: carts large and small carrying goods to be exported, or piled high with imports from across the empire.

By the time evening came, they had passed fifteen of the milestones, and Marcus was exhausted. His feet burned from the steady pace he had been forced to endure on the hard surface of the road. Porcino led them a short distance to the edge of a small pine forest.

"We'll stay here for the night. Piso, settle them down and feed 'em."

"Yes, master."

Marcus and the others slumped to the ground. Unlacing his boots, Marcus examined his feet and winced as his fingers found a burst blister. If they marched the same distance tomorrow, and the day after, he knew he was going to be in agony. Pelleneus and the other slaves stretched out on the ground and rested briefly, until Piso approached them with a basket he had taken off the back of one of the mules. In his other hand he carried a waterskin. He moved down the line, giving each of them some bread, a lump of cheese, and some dried meat. Marcus was the last to be fed, and he nodded a brief thanks before he spoke to Piso in a low voice.

"I want to speak to Porcino."

Piso glanced at him in surprise. "You what?"

"I said I want to talk to Porcino."

"Slaves don't give orders. So you keep quiet and eat up, eh?"

Marcus shook his head. "I'm not a slave. I shouldn't be here. I have to speak to Porcino and explain the situation."

Piso looked around at his master. The lanista was building a fire a short distance away, his powerful frame hunched over the kindling he was breaking up and arranging into a compact bundle. Piso smiled to himself and turned back to Marcus.

"Well, if you insist, I'll fetch him."

"Thank you." Marcus smiled. He sat and watched as Piso approached his master, bowed his head, and mumbled a few words that Marcus did not catch. Porcino looked past Piso toward Marcus and nodded. Then he stood up, stretched his back, and strolled over to the chained prisoners.

"You, boy. On your feet," Porcino said evenly. "Piso tells me you want a word."

"That's right." Marcus nodded, his hopes rising at the chance to explain his predicament finally. "You see, I was kidnapped and—"

Porcino's hand whipped out and slapped Marcus hard on the side of the head. His vision exploded into a brilliant white cloud of sparks. He staggered back, reeling from the blow. Porcino hit him again, and Marcus collapsed onto his backside with a grunt. A fist clenched into his hair and shook him painfully.

"When you speak to me," Porcino growled in his ear, "you call me *master*. If you fail to do that next time, I'll knock your teeth out. Understand?"

"Yes," Marcus replied, dazed by the blows.

The hand twisted his hair violently. "Say that again!"

"Yes, master."

"Louder, boy!"

"YES, MASTER!"

At once, Marcus was released and fell onto his back, gasping at the pain in his head. Porcino loomed over him, hands bunched into fists as he glared at Marcus.

"That'll be the last time I show you any mercy. Whatever you were before, now you are my slave. My property, to do with as I want. You will call me master, and you will do whatever I say *at once*, without question. Is that clear?"

"Yes, master."

Porcino narrowed his eyes for a moment, then straightened up, relaxing his hands. "Then I'll have no more of your nonsense. If I, or Piso, hear one more word of any ridiculous story about being kidnapped again, I'll beat you so badly your mother would never recognize you."

He turned away and strolled back to make his fire. Marcus stared after him, terrified. He felt a hand pluck his sleeve.

"Here." Pelleneus spoke in a kindly tone as he handed Marcus his food. "Eat up. You need all your strength. We've a long journey ahead of us."

THIRTEEN

They continued marching up the coast in the following days. Each night they stopped, Porcino took turns with Piso keeping watch over the prisoners. When he got the chance, Marcus carefully examined his neck collar and the link through which the chain fastened him to the others. The iron was strong, and the pin that fastened the collar had been firmly seated so that he could not make it budge at all. At length, Marcus realized that he would not be able to get out of the collar while he was chained to the others. He would have to bide his time and wait until they reached their destination. When the collar came off, he could turn his mind to thinking about escape again.

The one consolation of the situation that kept him from sinking into complete despair was the knowledge that each step took him closer toward Rome and General Pompeius. From what he could glean from Piso, the lanista's gladiator school was just outside a town called Capua, in the region of Campania, just over a hundred miles south of Rome. If the chance to escape came, then Marcus felt confident that he could at least reach the great city by himself.

On the fifth day after leaving the port, they reached the

small town of Ventulus, where Porcino left the coast road and took them onto a route heading inland. The gently rolling farmland soon gave way to hills and then mountains as they headed west. Summer was coming to an end, and the evenings turned so cool that Marcus found it hard to sleep, curled up on the ground, his teeth chattering. It took some time before the effects of exhaustion and an increasingly numbing despair allowed him to finally drift off for a few hours.

All the time, he harbored a simmering rage against Porcino, and vowed to all the Gods that there would be a reckoning one day. Meanwhile, he avoided the lanista's gaze and never dared to address him directly. On the coldest nights, when the road crossed the highest points of the mountains that ran down the spine of Italia, Piso lit them a fire.

As the prisoners sat in the warming glow of the flames, Marcus thought for the first time about how the rest of his companions had come to be here. Maybe they all had stories as unjust as his own. He turned to Pelleneus.

"How did you end up one of Porcino's slaves?" he asked.

Pelleneus gave a bitter laugh. "You want to know more about the life of a slave, boy . . . ? Unlike you, Roman citizen, I was born into slavery, in an inn in the slums of Athens. I was raised with a handful of other children whose mothers worked there. As soon as we were old enough, the slave who ran the establishment on behalf of the owner had us out on the streets stealing for him. Jewelry and other valuables from market stalls. We also picked the purses of the wealthier citizens of the city as they strolled through the crowded streets." The Athenian smiled at the memory, but his expression hardened as he continued. "Then one day my mother rejected the advances of the head slave. As a result, the slave took his revenge and bullied me relentlessly.

"In the end, I snapped. I was fourteen when I finally turned on the slave and used my fists. It was a short fight, in the inn's kitchen, with the women screaming in panic all around us, as customers ran for cover. I won the fight, beating the man to a bloody pulp. Beating him so badly he died from his injuries a few days later."

"You killed him with your hands?" asked Marcus in astonishment.

Pelleneus nodded. "Not the smartest thing I ever did. Once the owner heard, he wanted to make an example of me. He demanded that I be put to death. However, it turned out that one of the customers who had witnessed the fight owned a team of boxers and decided that I had potential. So, he bought me and trained me until I had grown to manhood, and since then I've been fighting in bouts across southern Graecia, losing only a handful of fights in ten years. It was at a fight staged at the party of a wealthy merchant that Porcino saw me and decided my talents might be more profitably used in the arena. He paid a high price," Pelleneus said with evident pride in himself. "Now I'm looking forward to fighting before the crowds in Rome."

Marcus looked at him curiously. "You mean you actually *want* to become a gladiator?"

"Why not?"

Marcus could not help a surprised smile. "Because you'll be putting your life at risk every time you fight."

"I've been in fights before."

"And, as you say, you haven't won them all."

"True," Pelleneus conceded.

"If you lose a fight in the arena, it could well be your last," Marcus suggested. "Seems to me that it's more dangerous than boxing."

"Then the trick of it is not to lose," Pelleneus replied. "If I train hard and learn all I can, then I will have every chance of winning in the arena."

"Unless you meet a better gladiator."

Pelleneus pursed his lips. "Then it will be a case of putting up a good fight. If a man does that, the crowd will want him spared. If I live long enough, and win enough fights, there will be rewards." He stared into the fire and smiled longingly. "I might even win my freedom one day and have enough money put aside to buy a farm, or a small business, and live out the rest of my life in comfort."

Marcus did not know much about the lives of gladiators, and what Pelleneus had just told him sparked a thought. If he could not escape his current position and was condemned to life as a gladiator, then what if he lived long enough to make his fortune? He could return to Graecia, buy his mother's freedom, take her back to the farm, and return to the way things had been before Decimus's thugs had destroyed their lives. If the chance came, then he would be a good enough fighter to take on and defeat those who had killed his father. Best of all, he would find—and kill—Decimus. He dwelled on the prospect for a while, until he became aware that the iron collar was chafing his collarbone, and he shifted the neckline of his tunic to cushion his skin.

It brought him back to reality. Whatever ambitions Pelleneus might have, the truth of the moment was that they were all slaves. The property of the lanista, Porcino, to do with as he wished. As he thought about it, Marcus decided that it would be better to continue with his first plan. However difficult, he must try to escape and find General Pompeius, rather than spend years preparing to become a gladiator, and then more years risking his life in the arena in order to win liberty and riches so that he could rescue his mother, if she survived until then.

The fire was starting to die down. The Thracians and the Spartan had already lain down to try to sleep, close to the fire. With a deep sigh, Phyrus followed suit, curling up on his side like a child. Before long, the air reverberated with his deep snores, but his sleep was troubled and he frequently twitched and mumbled snatches of sentences that made little sense to Marcus.

"What about him?" Marcus nodded to the slumbering giant. "What's his story?"

Pelleneus looked at their companion with a pitying expression. "Poor Phyrus shouldn't be here. He may be as strong as a bear, but he does not have the heart of a fighter. I fear for him once we reach Capua and enter the gladiator school."

"Porcino must think he has potential," Marcus reflected. "Otherwise, why buy him?"

Pelleneus glanced around to make sure that neither their master nor Piso was within earshot, but he lowered his voice anyway. "Porcino just sees his size, his strength. He does not see the man within. Well, more of a child than a man, I think."

"How did Phyrus come to be bought by Porcino?"

Pelleneus drew up his knees and wrapped his long, muscled arms around them. "From what he's told me since we were chained together, Phyrus was little more than an infant when he was brought to Athens. He was owned by a Greek merchant and raised as a household slave, until the merchant and his wife had a child. A boy. Phyrus was made his body servant. He virtually raised the boy, and loved him like a brother. However, as the child grew and began to return Phyrus's affection, the mother became jealous and demanded that Phyrus be sold. The father would have none of it. He saw how much Phyrus meant to his son and knew it would break the boy's heart. So, from what I can gather, the mother claimed one day that her most precious bracelet had been stolen. She insisted that the entire house be searched from top to bottom." Pelleneus looked at Marcus and smiled sadly. "You can guess what happened."

Marcus thought briefly, then nodded. "They found the bracelet in Phyrus's quarters?"

"Yes. Under his bedroll. The mother convinced her husband to sell Phyrus. It broke his heart to leave their boy. He was auctioned in the slave market at Athens. Phyrus stood out among the other slaves on sale, as you can imagine. Porcino was impressed enough to buy him." He looked down at Phyrus. "He wouldn't hurt a fly if he could help it. I am afraid for him. I doubt he will survive for long once we reach the gladiator school, unless he learns to fight."

Marcus thought for a moment as he hugged his knees. Since being taken from the farm, he had been consumed by his own problems. Only the injustice done to him and his family mattered. It seemed that the rest of the world was an uncaring place filled with people who knew nothing of his grief. He had thought that his suffering was the worst thing that could happen to a person. If others would only listen to his tale, then they would think so too, and do what they could to help to correct such a monstrous injustice.

Now Marcus understood that the world was filled with injustices, and that others, like Phyrus, suffered too. Marcus was not a special case, singled out by the Gods to endure the harshest cruelty and grief. There were others with similar tales, carrying similar burdens. Marcus was not quite sure how he felt about it. The thought of so many more people suffering as he did struck him with a kind of numbing horror. Yet, at the same time, for the first occasion since he had been seized by Decimus's henchmen, he felt that he was not alone. There was some comfort in that.

He raised his head and spoke softly. "What about the others? The Thracians and the Spartan?"

Pelleneus scratched his chin. "I hardly know anything about them. Only what Piso has told me, and that's no more than a few comments. The Thracians were part of a gang of outlaws that were hunted down and destroyed by a Roman column. The Spartan—well, he's something of a mystery. Piso says he is an outcast. He disgraced himself among his people, and they condemned him to slavery."

"Disgraced himself? How?"

"Who knows?" Pelleneus shrugged, and glanced warily at the sleeping Spartan before he continued. "They're not as civilized as us Athenians. They're a prickly people, the Spartans. Still think they are the toughest nation in Graecia. Even today they raise their young as if the only thing in life that mattered was being tough and going to war. Chances are that he just looked at someone's wife the wrong way. Or maybe he couldn't face fighting a pack of wolves with his hands tied behind his back, and they branded him a coward." Pelleneus smiled quickly to show that he was joking. "Anyway, he doesn't talk about it. Doesn't talk about anything, come to that. Only speaks when spoken to by Porcino or Piso, and even then only in sentences of one word. Seems that Spartans are somewhat lacking in small talk."

"But they know how to fight," Marcus responded. "My father told me that. He said that when he was serving with Pompeius's army, they had some Spartan mercenaries fighting with them. The toughest men he had ever seen." Marcus recalled the admiration in his father's voice as he'd spoken of them. "And the most fearless."

"Well, our Spartan friend is going to need those qualities if he is to survive in the arena," Pelleneus mused. "Of course, he'll need other qualities too. Fast reflexes and quick thinking. And thinking doesn't come easily to a Spartan."

"Nor does sleep," a deep voice growled. "Not when some Athenian keeps you awake all night with his prattle."

Pelleneus started, and he and Marcus looked across the sinking flames of the fire, to where the Spartan lay, eyes open. He closed them again, without another word, and lay quite still. They watched him for a moment, not sure if he was awake or asleep. At length, Pelleneus muttered, "Better get some rest. Bound to be another long day's march tomorrow."

Marcus nodded, still watching the Spartan. Then he eased himself down onto his side, with the curve of his back as close to the fire as he could bear. For a while he thought about his companions. Most of them were hard men with experience of fighting. There was much he could learn from them. And he was beginning to realize that he would need to learn quickly in order to survive, if he had to begin a new life in Porcino's gladiator school.

FOURTEEN

THE NEXT DAY, THEY LEFT THE mountains behind and descended onto the plain of Campania. A vast expanse of farmland sprawled out before them, and Marcus was astonished by the number of large farming estates and grand villas that he could see from the foothills. The Romans of Italia were clearly as wealthy as he had heard they were when his father had told him of his travels through the heart of the empire.

The view quickened the heart of Piso as well, and he raised his club and pointed out into the plain. "There's Capua. Home for us all now, boys!"

Marcus tried to follow the direction Piso had indicated, but he could see several towns on the plain, and in the distance, the looming mass of a great mountain appeared as a vague outline against the horizon.

"What's that?" he asked, pointing.

"The mountain? That's old father Vesuvius. Some of the best wines in all Italia are made from the grapes that grow on his slopes. Quite a sight, ain't it, boy? You'll grow used to it. You can see the mountain clearly from the gladiator school."

Piso's tone was light, and Marcus realized it was the first

time he had seen the slave in a cheerful mood. He turned and raised an eyebrow at Pelleneus. The Athenian smiled back as he spoke out.

"You're cheerful this morning, Piso."

"Of course. I'm coming home. Haven't seen my wife and the girls for over four months."

"You have a wife?"

"Yes." Piso scowled at Pelleneus. "So?"

"Nothing, just a side of you I haven't seen before. That's all."

Piso's expression assumed its customary surliness. "Pick up the pace there, no dawdling! The master wants to reach the school before dark. Move it!"

The shackled slaves lengthened their stride while Porcino rode some twenty paces ahead of them, casually munching on an apple.

The well-worn earth and gravel of the road gave way to a paved surface as they descended from the hills, and the road stretched out across the plain in a straight line. The air was warm for most of the day, but toward the end of the afternoon, the sky clouded over, the atmosphere grew hot and cloying, and the prisoners sweated freely as they were driven on by Piso to keep up the pace. As dusk crept across the landscape, there was a flicker of lightning in the distance, in the direction of Vesuvius, and a puff of breeze stirred Marcus's hair and cooled his face. Just after they passed a milestone a short distance outside Capua, Porcino turned off the main road and led them down a narrow lane lined with poplar trees. The first drops of rain began to fall as they came to the end of the lane. It descended gently into a vale. Before them, in the gloom, Marcus saw the gladiator school.

A plastered brick wall ten feet high surrounded a large complex of buildings, pens, and training areas. Immediately outside the wall stood an oval wooden arena, perhaps a hundred feet across, linked to the school by a covered way. Beyond the arena stood some stables and large cages, and in the nearest of them, Marcus could see the gray shape of a wolf, ceaselessly trotting back and forth behind the bars. A short distance away sprawled a large villa with a courtyard garden, which, Marcus guessed, must be where Porcino lived. At each corner of the walled enclosure stood a solid tower, where guards watched over the gladiator school and its inmates.

Porcino led his small column down into the vale and up to the main gate of the gladiator school. A heavy wooden door, barred on the outside, filled an arch wide enough to take a large covered wagon. As the lanista approached, six guards emerged from a door in the side of the gatehouse. Marcus saw that each man wore a helmet and scale armor, with a sword belt hanging from the shoulder. They looked like soldiers to him. It was clear that Porcino guarded his gladiators closely. Marcus thought his training school would probably better be described as a prison.

The guards heaved the heavy timber bar through the iron holders fastened to the door, and slid it into the slot in the gatehouse before hauling the door open. Then they stood to the side and bowed their heads at their master as he rode by. As soon as the last of the column of prisoners had passed inside, the gate was closed, and there was a deep grating sound as the timber bar was hauled back into place, locking the gate.

Marcus glanced around and saw that they were passing

between low buildings. An enticing odor of food wafted from an open door, and inside, he could see a handful of slaves laboring over steaming cauldrons as they poured in some diced vegetables and chunks of meat. On the other side was a storage area protected by stout iron bars. Inside, on shelves and pegs, hung a wide variety of weapons: swords, spears, tridents, daggers, axes, and maces, with wooden versions of the same weapons hanging nearby. The sight of so many deadly weapons made Marcus flinch as he imagined what damage they might do to his flesh and bones. The next storeroom contained armor: helmets, shields, armguards, shin armor, and breastplates, neatly arranged on shelves.

Porcino led them out from between the buildings into an open training area where the ground had been beaten hard and covered with fine gravel. He reined his horse in and turned it to face the prisoners, who shuffled to a halt and stood chained in a line, while the lanista surveyed them for a moment. The rain began to fall in earnest, and Marcus and the others were quickly drenched to the skin as they stood in silence and waited to be addressed.

Porcino sat straight-backed in his saddle, drew a breath, and then spoke loudly so that he could be heard above the patter of the rain.

"This is your new home," he announced with a wave of his arm. "This is the only home you have from now on. Where you came from is no more than a memory, and it will go easier with you if you try to forget your past lives. That is all dead to you now. All that remains is to learn how to fight and survive. If you master those skills, you may live for many years, and some of you may earn your freedom one day. I won't pretend that the odds are on your side. They aren't.

Most of those who pass through the gates of my gladiator school will find death in the arena. A few will die here, while they are being trained. It is a hard life. You will be driven to exhaustion. You will be taught to withstand pain. You will learn how to fight with all the skills of an elite warrior. Needless to say, it will be a long, difficult process. If you survive and succeed, you will fight, and maybe die, like real men. If you fail here, then there is only death on the sand, or the living death of a broken, pathetic cripple for those lucky enough to be sold on to a new master."

Porcino paused to let his words sink in and then continued in the same harsh tone. "Your life here will be governed by strict rules. You break them at your peril. You will be whipped for minor breaches of the rules. If you raise your fist against any of the trainers, or if you attempt to escape, or if you are overheard making a plot against me or my trainers, then you will be beaten to death by your fellow students. Obey us and work hard and you will be rewarded from time to time. Learn all you can and put it to good use, and ultimately you may be rewarded with fame, glory, and riches that you could never have earned as free men. Think on that tonight, and in the morning your training will begin."

Marcus shuddered. This was it. And there would be no escape.

Turning to Piso, Porcino nodded. "Remove the shackles. Take 'em to the cell for the night. Feed them and issue them fresh tunics."

"Yes, master." Piso bowed his head as Porcino turned his horse around and walked it back toward the gatehouse. Piso strode up to the line of prisoners and took out the pin hammer from his haversack. He started at the far end of the line, and Marcus was forced to watch as the rain slashed down. The last light had faded from the sky, and now there was only the faint loom of the moon, appearing fitfully through the clouds scudding across the heavens. In the watchtowers and around the buildings, slaves were busy kindling the torches and braziers that would provide some illumination for the compound during the night.

Marcus was soaked through and shivering while he stood listening to the sharp ringing blows as Piso knocked out the pins that fastened each of the prisoners' collars. One after another they stood rubbing their necks and shoulders where the iron rings had weighed on their flesh. At last Piso finished with Pelleneus and moved on to Marcus.

"Tilt your head to one side," Piso ordered.

Marcus did as he was told, flinching slightly as Piso roughly grasped the collar, feeling for the head of the pin in the gloom. He raised his hammer and took careful aim. The first blow sounded so close to Marcus's ear that the ringing impact felt like it was inside his head. He could not help jerking his head and shoulders to one side.

"Hold still!" Piso growled, yanking on the collar to pull Marcus back into position.

"Oww!"

"Silence, boy."

There was a tense pause as Piso relocated the pin and readied the next blow. This time, Marcus was expecting the impact and the deafening clamor in his ear. He still winced but managed to keep his body and head still as Piso hammered the pin out.

"There." Piso stepped back, hammer in one hand and the collar in the other.

Marcus had grown accustomed to the weight of the iron collar, and now relished the sudden feeling of lightness. He reached up and gently rubbed the skin where the metal had rested.

"Thank you."

Piso gathered up the collars and the chain, and nodded toward Marcus and the others standing in the rain. "Right, follow me!"

He turned and marched across the training ground toward two long, low buildings. The nearer was the bigger of the two and was fronted by a colonnaded shelter. Doors opened at regular intervals along the length of the building. The new arrivals passed a handful of burly men gathered around a table where they shared a jug of wine. One of them raised a cup to Piso.

"New boys, eh?"

Piso did not reply, and passed on by with a scowl as the man continued.

"They who are about to die salute us!"

His companions burst into good-natured laughter.

Marcus looked the men over as he walked by. They were in superb condition, with well-muscled arms. Some bore livid scars on their faces, and one was heavily bandaged around his bicep. Marcus's heart quickened as he realized these must be gladiators, the fighting elite of the Roman world.

"Marcus!" Piso snapped. "Don't drag your feet, boy, or I'll have you standing in the rain all night."

Marcus hurried to catch up with the others. Some of the rooms were lit by oil lamps, and he caught glimpses of simple but comfortable-looking rooms.

"Doesn't seem quite so hard a life to me," Phyrus muttered

to Pelleneus. "I thought gladiators were supposed to have it tough."

"So did I," his fellow Athenian replied in a puzzled voice.

Piso chuckled unpleasantly as he overheard the brief exchange. "That's the barracks for the gladiators who have completed their training. They've earned their privileges. You lot are starting at the bottom with the rest of the trainees. This way, come on!"

He led them past the barracks to the second building. It was a much simpler structure with no doors along the sides, no colonnaded shelter, and only a handful of windows. There was a large door at one end manned by two guards in full armor, like those on the main gate. Beside the door were rows of pegs from which chains and shackles hung. Piso dropped his burdens by the door and nodded to one of the guards.

"Open up. Then fetch some food."

The guard nodded and took a brief glance in through a small grille before he fitted his key into the lock and turned it. Opening the door just wide enough to admit Piso and the others, he stood to one side as they shuffled into the building, then closed the door behind them. The interior was one long hall, with stalls along each wall. A torch burned in a high bracket at each end of the building, providing a gloomy light that was enough for Marcus to see that there were no beds or bedrolls in the stalls, just straw. In the walkway between the stalls was a large tub of water and a latrine with six seats over an open drain that ran out through the far wall. Dimly visible figures stirred along the length of the building to inspect the new arrivals.

Piso pointed out two of the empty stalls near the door.

"Thracians in the first stall. The Spartan, Athenians, and the boy in the second." He pointed to the water-butt and the latrines. "You have all the necessaries here, and two meals a day. This is your home until—or if—you pass basic fitness and weapons training. Better get as much sleep as you can before training begins tomorrow."

He turned and rapped on the door. The guard opened up and handed a couple of coarsely made sacks to Piso.

"Your evening meal!" Piso grinned and chucked one bag toward the Thracians and the other at Phyrus, who fumbled the catch. Pelleneus picked the bag up for him. "Good night, boys."

The door closed behind him, then the lock clanked. As Marcus followed the others to the stall Piso had indicated, he saw the other inmates eyeing them warily. There was no attempt to greet the new arrivals, no sign that they were regarded as comrades in any way. Just a sullen, brooding silence and empty expressions. Outside, the rain battered the tiles on the roof, and where it found a way through, it dripped onto the slaves in a steady, miserable rhythm. When they reached the stall allotted to them, Marcus and the others slumped down onto the straw. Pelleneus opened the bag and reached in to find several hunks of stale bread, hard and unappetizing. He shared them out, and then Marcus slumped back into the corner of the stall and chewed slowly as his teeth chattered and his wet body shivered uncontrollably.

He would have to get out of here, he resolved. There must be some way to escape, some way to get away from this dreadful place and continue his quest to reach Rome and find General Pompeius. Before it was too late to save his mother.

FIFTEEN

A HARSH CLATTERING SOUND shattered Marcus's sleep. He jerked upright and winced as he felt the stiffness in his limbs and neck. Blinking, he looked around and saw that his companions were also stirring.

"What in Hades is that racket?" Phyrus grumbled as he sat up, rubbing his face.

Marcus saw the other occupants of the building tumbling from their stalls and rushing to the main door. With a clank from the lock, the door groaned on its hinges as the guards outside opened it. One of them was holding up a metal chime and beating it with the flat of his sword.

"Move yourselves!" he bellowed. "Last man out gets a beating!"

"Come on!" Pelleneus leaped up, dragging Marcus to his feet behind him. "Hurry, Phyrus!"

They rushed out of the stall into the scrambling tide of bodies making for the door. Most of the other prisoners were men, but there were a few boys among them, Marcus's age and older. He saw the Thracians just ahead, thrusting through the crowd that was packed in around the door. Then they were lost amid the tall figures of adults pressing around him. Marcus felt a stab of fear. What if he fell over now? He was sure to be crushed underfoot. He grabbed Phyrus's tunic and pushed in beside his bulk.

"What the—?" Phyrus looked over his shoulder with a scowl. Then he saw Marcus and tucked his arm protectively around the boy's body. "Stay close, and keep on your feet," he growled as he edged forward. "I'll look out for you, lad."

Together they moved slowly toward the door. Packed close to the others, Marcus could smell their sweat and dirt, and he sensed their fear as they strove not to be the last man out the door. Then the timber frame loomed ahead, outlining the pale morning sky. There was only a handful of men behind them, and as Marcus passed through the door, he glanced back and saw the Spartan standing outside the stall, staring at the last of those struggling to get out. He had a contemptuous expression on his face as he slowly walked toward the door.

"Don't just stand there, lad!" Phyrus pushed him forward, and Marcus turned to see that the rest of the slaves were forming a line in front of the cellblock. A tall, severe-faced man with a lean, muscular build stood glaring at the slaves as they formed up. He wore a leather jerkin over a red tunic, leather armguards, and heavy military boots like those Marcus's father had favored. He carried a vine cane in one hand and tapped it against his heel as he stood and watched. Piso came trotting up with a large waxed tablet and stopped at the man's shoulder. Marcus looked at the man warily as he followed Phyrus into position alongside Pelleneus, and stood waiting as the last occupants hurried to join the end of the line. There was a brief pause before the Spartan emerged from the door and strolled calmly toward the line.

The man who had been watching them assemble came striding over with a furious expression. He stopped right in front of the Spartan and thrust his face forward so that they were almost nose to nose.

"What kind of a hurry do you call that?" he bellowed in Latin. "When the morning call is sounded, you run out here as fast as you can. Do you understand me?"

The Spartan just stared back without any sign of fear, or even interest.

The other man whirled around. "Piso! Over here, on the double!"

Piso scurried over. "Yes, Centurion Taurus?"

"Who is this 'orrible little man?" He jabbed his finger at the Spartan. "Is he one of the new batch Porcino brought in?"

"Yes, sir. They make up the last batch of the new intake. The master bought this one from an auction in Sparta. Name's Patroclus."

"Sparta, eh?" Taurus turned fully to the man and rested one hand on his hip as he clutched his cane tightly in the other. "Must think he's a hard man. Does he speak Latin?"

Piso nodded. "That was my understanding, sir. But he's barely spoken a word to me since the master bought him, and then only in Greek."

"I see." Taurus sneered at the Spartan. "So, I imagine you think you must be King-bloody-Leonidas reborn, the way you pranced out of the cellblock like that. Well?"

The Spartan stared straight ahead, in total silence. Taurus suddenly slammed the handle of his stick into the man's stomach. Patroclus doubled over with an explosive grunt.

"How dare you refuse to reply!" Taurus bellowed. "How

dare you walk out onto my training ground without a care in the world. It will not do!" He lashed out with his stick, striking the Spartan across the shoulders. Marcus flinched as he heard the crack of the blow just a few feet to the right of where he stood. He risked a glimpse sideways and saw that the Spartan was on his knees. Patroclus gritted his teeth and then rose slowly to his feet and faced his attacker again.

"Not had enough, then?" Taurus slapped his face with a vicious backhanded blow, and then followed it up with a forehand. Patroclus blinked, but his face remained impassive as he opened his mouth and spat out some blood.

"Bah!" Taurus snarled. "I'll break you down to size soon enough, my friend. You'll see. Now, then..." He took a pace back and ran his eyes along the line. Marcus was just too slow in looking away, and caught the man's eye. In an instant, Taurus sprang toward him and poked his vine stick into Marcus's chest, forcing him back a step.

"What's this?" He glanced around at Piso. "Is Porcino planning on a fight between Pygmies?"

Piso and the other guards laughed dutifully while Taurus turned his attention back to Marcus. "Name?"

"Marcus Cornelius, sir," he replied. Then, thinking quickly, he added, "Son of Centurion Titus Cornelius of the Sixteenth Legion."

Taurus frowned. "Your father was a soldier?"

"A centurion, sir."

"And now you're a slave, eh?" Taurus tutted. "The Gods will play their games. Tough luck, boy. From now on you are plain and simple Marcus. That is the only name you will have until we find a fighting name for you, if you live that long."

He was about to move on, and Marcus could not believe his chance to explain the injustice of his situation was slipping away.

"Wait!"

Taurus froze. "What? Did you say something?"

"I shouldn't be here," Marcus said quickly. "I was taken illegally and sold as a slave."

He never saw the blow, just felt his head snap to one side as Taurus struck him. He staggered back, dazed, as the man shouted into his face.

"Never, ever speak out of turn again, slave! You hear me? I don't give a cuss who your father is, or what your story may be. Got that? You are a slave, the scum of the earth, and I hate the very sight of you. Your only hope now is that I let you become a gladiator one day. Until then you are nothing. And you will call me master whenever you are called to speak. Understand?"

"Yes...master," Marcus blurted out. His head was still ringing and he felt dizzy enough to be sick. He fought the nausea off as he swayed on his feet.

"That's better." Taurus turned away and strode back to the center of the training ground to address the line of men. "Now that we are all here, the training can begin. I will start with some introductions....I am Aulus Tullius Taurus, your chief training instructor. I trained soldiers before I trained slaves, and before then I was busy killing barbarians for Rome. I will train you to become killers, eventually. Before then, you must become fit and fearless, so I will work you until you drop and I will beat anyone who complains or falls behind the others, like our foolish Spartan friend over there. From time to time we will be honored with the presence of Porcino, the lanista who owns this school. You will not address him unless he speaks to you first. And then you will call him master. Next, there is my assistant Piso. He is a slave, but unlike you lot, he has proved himself in the arena. Piso is in charge of issuing kit, rations, and rewards, so you will treat him well." Taurus turned to indicate four men standing to one side. "Those men are your drill instructors. Me, you call master. Piso and the drill instructors call me sir, and you call them sir in turn. If you fail to remember this simple rule, you will be beaten. There are only two other rules here. Do exactly what you are told, and do it at once. Disobedience or hesitation will be punished without mercy."

He paused to make sure that everyone had time to let his words sink in. "For the next four months, you will be trained to build your strength and fitness. After that, you will begin basic weapons training. I will be watching you closely, and in another four months I will choose your fighting speciality. Some of you will fight as heavy infantry. Some will be lightly armed. Others will be trained to fight animals. The youngest of you will be given kitchen and cleaning duties until I decide you are big enough to handle weapons. When you are ready for your first real fights, then you will be moved out of the recruits' barracks and into more comfortable quarters. To work, then." He finished abruptly and clicked his fingers to summon Piso to his side. "Time to assign the training groups."

"Yes, sir."

As Piso opened his wax slate and took out a brass stylus, the four drill instructors came trotting over and stood apart in front of the line of slaves. Marcus watched them blankly as his mind filled with sad memories of his life on the farm outside Nydri. Back then, he had been loved and looked after and was happy. Now he was subject to the cruel discipline of the gladiator school, and he wondered just how long he could endure his grim new life. Taurus and Piso paced over to the far end of the line and began making their way along. Taurus stopped in front of every man and boy, examined them briefly, and then told Piso which group to enter them into. As he reached the Thracians, Marcus saw him squeeze their shoulders and arms and then examine their hands and legs.

"Light group," he decided, and moved on to Phyrus.

"By the Gods, this one is built like a bear. Ever killed anyone with those great paws of yours?"

"No, master," Phyrus muttered.

"A shame. But you will before long. Heavy group, no question about it."

Taurus moved on to examine Pelleneus after a quick glance at the waxed slate Piso held out to him. The Athenian stood still as he was prodded, and then Taurus stepped back, glancing over him shrewdly as he scratched his chin. "Good muscle condition. As you would expect from a boxer. And you'll be light on your feet, I should imagine. Could equally make a good secutor or a retiarius. Hmmm. Put him down in the mixed group for now."

Piso nodded and made a quick note while Taurus moved on to Marcus. Marcus stared straight ahead, not daring to offer any defiance that might be rewarded with a further blow from the training instructor.

"Ah, here's the centurion's son again." Taurus leaned forward and squeezed Marcus's shoulder hard in his viselike fingers as he spoke in a mocking tone. "What to do? Make him a heavy fighter, perhaps? Except that he would collapse under the weight of the kit. A retiarius? No, he couldn't heft a trident and would only tangle his feet in the net. Well, then, put him in the youth group. That's all he's fit for right now."

"Yes, sir."

Marcus felt his face burn with embarrassment, and he would dearly have loved to tell Taurus where he could shove his opinions. But he kept his mouth tightly sealed and looked straight ahead as he controlled his anger.

When Taurus reached the end of the line, he took one quick glance at the Spartan and gave his verdict. "Mixed group. If he lives long enough, I doubt that this one will ever be good for anything but fighting animals."

"I will fight you, master," the Spartan replied coldly. "Now, if you are brave enough."

"Fight me?" Taurus looked amused. "I don't think so. If you were to so much as raise your hand toward me, I'd have you crucified within the hour. You'd best remember that." Taurus paused and raised his voice so that all of the new recruits to the gladiator school could hear him. "That goes for you all. The only fate waiting for any one of you who strikes me, or any member of my training staff, is a slow, agonizing death. There are no second chances for a gladiator. Remember that well, and you may live. Fail to, and you will surely die." He nodded somberly. "You are dismissed!"

SIXTEEN

THERE WERE TWENTY-THREE OTHER boys in the youth class under the command of a wizened old instructor named Amatus. Thin and sinewy, Amatus had fought as a retiarius for fifteen years. He had won most of his fights and been spared by the crowds in the handful that he had lost, but he had failed to distinguish himself sufficiently to win the favor and rewards that some of his contemporaries had achieved. So he was destined to live out the remainder of his days as a slave, instructing new recruits in the gladiator school of Porcino.

Marcus was one of the youngest in the class. He might have lacked the years, but having been brought up on a farm and encouraged to exercise regularly by his father, he was fit and strong for his age. The other boys had come from across the empire and had different-colored skins and features, and Marcus could only understand a handful of them who spoke either Latin or Greek. They had all arrived at the school within the last month, and a pecking order had already been established.

The self-appointed leader of the group was a large Celtic boy named Ferax, from one of the tribes that lived close to the Alps. He was three or four years older than Marcus, and much taller and broader. He spoke Latin with a coarse accent and walked with a pronounced swagger when he led the youths out onto parade each morning. From the outset, he had taken a dislike to Marcus, when they first spoke shortly after Marcus had arrived. He had finished using the latrine and was returning to his stall when Ferax and his four cronies blocked his path.

"Son of a Roman centurion, eh?" Ferax sneered. "You look more like the son of a sewer rat to me."

His companions laughed. Marcus glared back, bunching his hands into fists. He did not want to fight the larger boy, but at the same time he did not want to take his insults.

"In case you didn't know, my name is Ferax." The Celt thumbed his chest. "This is my gang. These two are Celts like me." He indicated the two tall blond-haired boys to one side, then nodded at the other two, swarthy and slim. "And these two were plucked from the slum of the Subura in Rome. Hard cases." He stepped forward and jutted his head out, face-to-face with Marcus. "Let me tell you my rules, sewer rat. My mates and I take the first share of the rations. Also, if I want, you and the others will do our duties for us once the day's training is done, such as fetching water or cleaning our kit."

"You can fetch your own water," Marcus replied.

"Oh!" Ferax chuckled. "We've got a tough one here, lads! I'd better warn you that the last lad who refused to do what I say got himself a good beating. Once word got 'round about what happened to him, all the other boys have been as good as gold. So, you do what I say and you won't have any trouble. Otherwise . . ." Ferax took a step back and clenched his fist in front of Marcus's face. "You'll be feeling this breaking your nose. Understand?"

Marcus stood quite still and stared back in silence. Ferax nodded, then turned to his cronies. "Right, the greeting's over. Let's leave him."

As they strode away, Marcus pressed his lips together. Ferax was a bully. He would have to be watched carefully and avoided as much as possible. Even so, Marcus felt a powerful urge to confront him.

But not yet. Later, when he had been toughened up and knew how to handle an opponent. Then he'd see just how tough the Celt really was.

While the men worked out all day, the youths were dismissed from the training ground during the afternoon and were sent to the kitchen to help prepare the evening meal and then serve it to the men in the cellblock and the gladiator quarters, when evening came. It was hard and demeaning work, but Marcus did it without any complaint, and all the time his mind remained fixed on the need to escape from the school and make his way to Rome. He also thought of his mother, condemned to toil on the estate of Decimus. It made his heart heavy to think of her, and he knew that she would be worrying about him in turn.

Not that she would easily recognize him anymore, he reflected ruefully. Like all the others who had been trooped out of the cellblock that first morning, Marcus had been issued two gray tunics and two pairs of boots, each one bearing an identifying numeral burned into the heel of each boot. All their existing clothing had been taken away—the best of it sold to a local merchant, the rest to be burned.

Marcus's head had been crudely shaved. Now all the trainees looked hard and brutal and difficult to distinguish from one another, like the chain gangs of convicted men sent to the mines. Marcus had hated having his head shaved. The slave who did it handled his cutting shears with little care, scraping his scalp in a number of places. But even that torment was nothing compared to what came next.

Once the boys emerged from the caged pen where they had been sheared, dazed and bleeding from the cuts and scrapes on their scalps, Amatus had led them into the forge in the corner of the compound. A dozen of the school's guards were waiting for them, and beyond stood a slave, sweat running down his face as he worked a small furnace, out of which a long iron handle extended.

"First boy, come forward," Amatus ordered, gesturing to one of the Nubians. The boy flinched, but before he could try to edge back into the ranks of his comrades, two of the guards grabbed his arms and pinned him between them. Then they dragged him toward the forge as he struggled wildly in their grasp. Amatus took a dampened rag and grasped the end of the iron handle. As he drew out the branding iron, the shaped symbol at the end—a large letter *P* above two crossed swords—glowed orange, and the heated air around it wavered. He approached the Nubian boy, who was now writhing desperately in the grip of the two guards.

"Hold him still," Amatus ordered, and the guards braced themselves and kept the boy from moving. Amatus pulled back the boy's tunic and pressed the branding iron onto his chest, just above the heart. The boy screamed as there came a sizzling noise, and the air filled with the pungent scent of burning flesh. A moment later it was over, and Amatus stepped back as the boy fell limp. The guards dragged him outside the forge and dropped him on the ground.

"Next one!" Amatus called out.

One by one, they were taken forward and branded with the symbol of Porcino's gladiator school. As they waited, the boys glanced at one another nervously, some shuffling away from the front of the crowd in a bid to put off the torment. But that was as far as they got, as the guards herded them back. Marcus's terror at the prospect of being branded was made worse by every cry of fear and scream of agony that came out of the forge. But he kept silent and did not attempt to move to the back of the group. He glanced around and met the gaze of Ferax.

The Celt stared back, and Marcus saw that he, too, was afraid. Ferax had been shaking as their eyes had met, and now he looked angry, glaring at Marcus. Taking a deep breath, he pushed through to the front of the crowd and stood as tall as he could. He crossed his arms and waited to be called forward. When the next victim had been carried out, Amatus thrust the iron back into the furnace to heat it again. Then he turned to the remaining boys. "Next!"

Ferax took a step forward, but then Marcus blurted out, "Me! I'll go next."

Amatus nodded, and the guards stepped forward to take Marcus's arms. He felt his heart pounding as he stepped toward the forge. He had no idea why he was doing this, other than it seemed to prove something to Ferax and the others, not to mention Amatus and the guards. As he approached the forge, he pulled his tunic down from the collar to expose his chest. Amatus nodded to the guards. "Hold him."

Marcus let them take his arms, but stood still, muscles tensed and teeth gritted so hard his jaw hurt. Amatus looked surprised and paused a moment before taking the brand out of the forge again.

"Well, looks like one of you at least has got some backbone." He smiled faintly at Marcus. "Brace yourself, lad, this is going to hurt like nothing you've ever known."

He raised the branding iron. Marcus's eyes widened as he beheld the shimmering white shape. The air around it rippled. Amatus placed his left hand on Marcus's chest to steady it and brought the branding iron up. At the last moment, Marcus clenched his eyes tightly shut. There was an instant when he felt the heat; then his world exploded in a torrent of burning agony and horror. It felt as if he had been struck by a ram, then a searing, stabbing shaft of anguish pierced his body. He smelled his flesh burning, sharp and acrid, making him feel dizzy and sick. He heard the hiss and sizzle as his flesh scorched. Then the pressure eased as Amatus drew back the brand. But the agony only increased. Tears pricked out in the corners of Marcus's eyes, and a keening moan forced its way between his clamped teeth.

"Easy with that one," he heard Amatus say. "The lad's got guts, I'll say that for him."

As they stepped out into the open, the guards eased Marcus down onto the ground and gently pushed him back against the plastered wall. He opened his eyes and stared around at the others. His heart was beating fast, and the pain consumed his mind as he sat stiffly and gritted his teeth. The cries and whimpers of the boys who had gone before him sounded in his ears. Marcus shifted his eyes to the side and saw Ferax looking at him. The Celt looked furious, and his lips curled into an expression of hatred. Then the guards took him and hauled him toward the forge as he began to struggle in their grip. Marcus did not watch—but he heard the animal groan of rage and pain as Amatus branded Ferax. Suddenly the pain was too much for Marcus and he just had time to lean to one side before he vomited. And again, until there was nothing in his stomach. Then he slumped back against the wall and passed out.

When he came to, he was lying on straw, staring up into the rafters of the cellblock. At once he felt the sharp sting of the burn on his chest, and groaned as he struggled to rise to his elbows.

"Easy there," a voice said comfortingly, and Pelleneus loomed over him. He had a wet rag in his hand and offered it to Marcus. "Try this. It helps ease the pain . . . a little."

Marcus took the rag and looked down. The burn was red and dotted with pale blisters that wept. He dabbed at the burn as gently as he could, and felt a fresh wave of pain. "Ahhhhhh . . ."

The dampened rag only seemed to make the pain worse, and he had to fight it off before he handed the rag back and forced himself to nod his thanks.

"Hurts like Hades, doesn't it?" Pelleneus said, and took a sharp breath.

"You too?" asked Marcus, gesturing toward the Athenian's breast.

"All of us. Though some went with a fight." He nodded toward Phyrus, who sat against the other side of the stall, glowering. Marcus could see that his face was bruised and one eye was badly swollen.

"It took six of us to hold him down." Pelleneus smiled faintly. "The lad doesn't know his own strength."

Marcus frowned. "You held him down? You helped them to brand Phyrus?"

"We had to. If it had been left to the guards and the instructors, then our boy here would have struck them down. You heard what they do to any of us trainees who turn on one of Porcino's staff. I'd sooner Phyrus knocked *me* out cold than one of them, and go and get himself crucified."

"I suppose so." Marcus shrugged. "Doesn't seem right, though."

"It was that, or watch him die," Pelleneus replied tersely. "What would you have done?"

Marcus wanted to say that he would have refused to help subdue Phyrus, that he would have fought at the giant's side to resist the agony and the shame of being branded as the property of Porcino. But however much he might want to fight back, he knew that Pelleneus was right. There was nothing he could have done. Nothing any of them could have done. He looked down at his lap in despair.

Pelleneus took pity on him. "Marcus, you're a slave now. You'd better get used to the idea as soon as you can. If you sit there dreaming of resistance and escape, then you will only make life ever more miserable for yourself. It will start to drive you mad." He paused for a moment. "That's what happened to me. I refused to accept slavery. I disobeyed my masters and even tried to run away once. They recaptured me a few days later and beat me black and blue. That's what resisting your master gets you—pain and more suffering. Take it from me, best thing you can do is accept that the past is dead to you. Look to the future. Stay alive and, one day, win your freedom. That's all that matters to you now."

Marcus nodded slowly, as if accepting the advice. But deep inside he could not do what Pelleneus told him to do. It went against every fiber of his being, and betrayed the memory of his father and the duty he owed his mother. Marcus silently swore an oath that he would never forget the past. Besides, it was the memory of all that he had lost, and all that he had to avenge, that filled him with the determination to endure the terrible situation he found himself in.

"Ah, so the centurion's brat is stirring at last!"

Marcus looked up and saw Ferax standing in the entrance to the stall. Behind him stood his cronies. All of them were stripped to the waist so that their chests were bared, exposing the blistered emblem of the school's brand. The Celt regarded Marcus with a sneer. "Last I saw of you was when you fainted outside the forge."

Marcus swallowed nervously and rose to his feet. "At least they didn't have to drag me in there."

"What?" Ferax frowned. "You calling me a coward? I took the branding like a man." He puffed up his chest and rested his hands on his hips. "I stood it like a warrior."

"Yes." Marcus smiled thinly. Even though Ferax was far bigger than him, and his heart was pounding in his chest, he recalled the fear he had seen in the Celt boy's face before he was branded, and it gave Marcus some courage. "I heard your, er, war cry. So did everyone else, I imagine. Still, it *was* quite painful."

"At least I didn't faint like some girl."

"No, you didn't," Marcus conceded. "You just sounded like one."

Ferax's nostrils flared. "You'll pay for that, you Roman runt." He balled his hands into fists and entered the stall. Marcus stood his ground, bracing his feet apart as he raised his hands and held them ready to grab his foe, or clench them to strike back. His face contorted into a snarl. Ferax paused to look at him and then laughed.

"By the Gods, just look at him. He must think he's Mars, the war god!"

His friends laughed with him, and then Ferax turned back to face Marcus, all trace of humor gone from his expression. All that Marcus could see there now was a cruel determination to cause him as much pain and humiliation as possible. He felt his guts turn to ice, but still stood his ground, prepared to take a beating long before he ever asked for mercy.

"I'm going to enjoy this," Ferax growled. "I'm going to tear you apart."

"Oh, no, you don't," a deep voice rumbled. Marcus turned in surprise and saw Phyrus rising to his feet. The giant stepped between the two boys and glared at Ferax. "If you hurt him, I hurt you. I hurt you bad. You and those others." Phyrus raised a huge fist and smacked it down into the palm of the other hand. "See?"

Ferax flinched at the sound. He stared at Phyrus with a mixture of awe and frustration, and then backed away to the entrance of the stall. There he turned his attention back to Marcus.

"You're safe for now, brat. But you'll have to fight your own battles sometime. When you do, I'll be there, waiting.

You hear? Come on, lads." He waved to his followers and moved away toward the other end of the cellblock.

Marcus relaxed as he watched them go. He nodded to Phyrus. "Thanks."

Phyrus shrugged and scratched his chin. "Don't like bullies. They're scum. Let me know if that boy gives you any more trouble."

He turned away and returned to his corner. Despite his gratitude, Marcus knew that Ferax was right. The Celt could afford to bide his time. Marcus could not escape, and the time would come when he must face Ferax on his own.

SEVENTEEN

THE LAST DAYS OF SUMMER PASSED in a relentless routine of training and kitchen duties. Marcus and the other boys were roused at first light, and they marched over to the kitchen block to help prepare the morning meal. Marcus was tasked with lighting the kitchen fires on the blackened iron grates below the cooking grills. A small brazier was kept permanently lit in one corner of the kitchen, and once Marcus had laid the kindling, he carefully carried over some of the glowing embers and inserted them into the fireplace. Then, puffing his cheeks, he gently blew to make the embers catch and to direct the small licks of flame into the kindling. There were three fires to be lit and maintained, and Marcus had to make sure that he kept an eye on each of them. Fresh wood had to be brought continually from the store outside the kitchen and laid by the hearth, ready for use.

The slave in charge of the kitchen was a former gladiator named Brixus, who had been crippled in a fight some years ago. The hamstring in his left leg had been almost severed by a sword blow. Although the crowd had spared him, it was the end of his career in the arena. Porcino had transferred him to the kitchen, where he might still be of some use to his owner. Brixus was solidly built and looked the same age as Marcus's father, except that his hair was thick and dark, with not a hint of gray in it. He made his way around his kitchen with a very pronounced limp that gave him a rolling gait.

Ferax and his friends made fun of him behind his back, silently gesturing to each other and doing quick imitations of his walk. When he glanced around, or turned suddenly, they would instantly return to their duties overseeing the large cauldrons of thick barley meal, which bubbled and hissed faintly as the boys stirred the steadily thickening breakfast with stout wooden paddles.

An hour after Marcus and the others had risen to prepare their meal, the new trainees trooped into the caged mess hall next to the kitchen. The men picked up their bowls and wooden spoons and then waited in line to be served from the steaming cauldrons. They sat on long benches in silence and ate from the bowls in their laps. The drill instructors slowly walked up and down the benches, ready to lash out with their vine canes at any man who talked. Only when the men had finished eating and been marched off to begin their morning training were the boys allowed to eat. Then they washed the bowls and spoons and waited for Amatus to lead them to the training ground.

The large open space in the center of the school was surrounded by a ten-foot-high timber stockade. Inside, the earth had been beaten flat and covered with dark sand from the shores of the Bay of Neapolis. It was here that the new intake of slaves began their training for the hard and dangerous life that lay ahead of them. The instructors bellowed their orders as each of the four groups took turns at running around the perimeter, lifting weights, and making their way through a simple obstacle course, all designed to increase their stamina, strength, and agility.

Amatus followed his class around the training ground, his vine cane ready to strike at any boy who lagged too far behind the rest, or did not put enough effort into lifting weights, or stumbled clumsily. Marcus was mindful that Amatus had admired his courage when he had been branded, and he did his best to keep the instructor's respect. No matter how hard his lungs burned with the effort of his exertions, or how leaden his limbs felt, Marcus drove himself on. Some of his companions were not so determined, and soon carried the bruises and welts from Amatus's cane. Only one other boy showed the same determination as Marcus, and that was Ferax. While Marcus had more stamina, Ferax had the strength, and they more or less matched each other in terms of agility.

Although the rivalry was unspoken during the training, Amatus was experienced enough to spot it at once, and he goaded them on gleefully.

"Come on, Ferax! That boy is half your size! What's the matter? Can't keep up with him? You will, my lad, or you'll feel the end of my vine stick! Move those legs, you lazy Celt swine!"

Or, when Marcus was grimacing as he struggled to raise one of the heaviest weights up to his chin, Amatus would come and stand by him and roar in his ear. "Call that a weight? I have seen maggots lift heavier rocks than those! How the hell do you expect to grow as big as Ferax if you don't work at it? Come on, Marcus, show that bloody Celt what a Roman can do!"

Marcus felt the gaze of the other boys on him and knew

that he must impress them if Ferax was not to win them over to his side. At the same time, he was aware of the simmering hatred the Celt directed at him. For a while there was nothing Ferax could do about it. The days were too strictly organized to find time to take out his wrath on Marcus, and by the time the boys retired to their stalls to sleep at night, they were too tired for anything but sleep. Marcus would curl up in the straw while Pelleneus and Phyrus would talk in low voices for a while before they, too, fell asleep. The Spartan still kept aloof, for the most part, but occasionally contributed a comment to the conversation if he felt it necessary to correct an opinion.

It was a month after Marcus arrived that Ferax found his opportunity. It was after the evening meal, and Marcus was the last to leave the kitchen and make his way back to the cellblock. On the way, he stopped, as usual, in the latrine that stood in the corner of the school wall. The season was turning and the evening air was chilly as the nights drew in. A single small brazier burned at the far end of the latrine block, and by its wan glow Marcus made his way to one of the holes in the two wooden benches opposite each other. There was only one other occupant, one of the Nubian boys who had finished his chores only a short time before Marcus. They nodded a casual greeting to each other since the Nubian could still speak only a handful of Latin words, though he understood a good deal more, thanks to Amatus's vine cane.

Marcus pulled up his tunic and sat down on the wooden bench, worn smooth by many years of use. The faint trickle of running water came up from the channel that carried the waste away, out under the wall into a small stream that passed close by the gladiator school. He had nearly finished his business when he heard the crunch of footsteps approaching the latrine entrance.

"Oi, Nubian, outside!" Ferax jerked his thumb over his shoulder. "I want a word with the centurion's son."

The Nubian nodded, then stood up and reached for the handle of the sponge stick in the nearest of the tubs of vinegar that stood between the two benches. He applied it quickly, then lowered his tunic and hurried from the latrine, casting a wary glance at Ferax as he dashed past.

Ferax sauntered slowly down the length of the latrine as he undid his belt. "Well now, boy, it's time to see just how brave you can be. You ready for it?"

Marcus felt his insides turn to ice as he hurriedly scrambled up and pulled his tunic down. He glanced around quickly, but all the windows were little more than slits high up on the wall, and there was only one doorway into the latrine. He was trapped. Marcus snatched up a sponge stick and held it ready in front of him. Ferax stared at him and then chuckled. "What, you think you're going to stop me with a *stick*?"

"Leave me alone," Marcus said as firmly as he could. "I won't warn you again."

"Oooh, you scare me." Ferax pretended to tremble. "You really do."

Marcus realized that there was no way out of the confrontation. There was nothing he could say to talk Ferax out of it. As he accepted this, Marcus felt a sense of calm in his mind and heart. He would fight and most likely lose. But he would hurt Ferax as much as possible in the process.

"Then I'm not the only thing that scares you," Marcus

responded. "I saw you when we were waiting to be branded. I saw how scared you were. I saw you shake like a coward. That's why you hate me, isn't it?"

Ferax stopped six feet from Marcus and snapped the belt out between his hands. "Does it matter why? The fact is I hate you and I want to hurt you, Roman." He began to wrap the belt around his right fist, ending with the buckle across his knuckles. Then he took a wary step toward Marcus, lowering his body as he prepared to spring. Marcus raised the sponge stick and leaped forward before his opponent could attack. The soiled stick, soaked in vinegar, struck Ferax on the cheek, and he let out a brief cry of surprise and pain as Marcus stabbed the stick at his face, aiming for the eyes. As Marcus had hoped, Ferax instinctively raised his hands to ward off the blow, and the Celt's fingers closed around the shaft of the stick, snatching it away. Marcus released his grip and threw himself forward into Ferax's body, punching into his stomach with all his weight.

"Ooof!" Ferax grunted as he bent over.

Marcus punched again and then changed his angle and slammed his fist into Ferax's nose. The older boy's surprise quickly passed, and now he let loose an animal growl, ignoring the blows Marcus rained on him. Ferax shoved Marcus back with his left hand and then slammed his right into Marcus's side. The blow was sharp and painful and took his breath away, but he knew that if he stopped fighting, Ferax would pulverize him. Ferax punched him in the side again, then aimed a blow at Marcus's head, catching him on the jaw. The buckle cut into his flesh, and Marcus saw a bright flash of white, then swirling sparks, as he staggered back a step. Ferax followed up and hit him again, close to the ear. Marcus felt his legs wobble, and he went down on one knee, instinctively raising his hands to protect his head. Ferax hit him again, and Marcus fell flat onto the paved floor with a gasp. Above him, the vicious expression of the Celt swam in the dim light cast by the brazier as he leaned over Marcus and punched him again, and again, until he lost consciousness.

EIGHTEEN

"You're late," Brixus said gruffly as he approached Marcus from behind, the following morning. "I'll give you a good hiding if you don't have those fires ready in time."

Marcus rose stiffly from where he was arranging the kindling in the hearths. He looked down at Brixus's boots as he nodded. "I'm sorry, Brixus. It won't happen again."

His voice was strained and muffled, and Brixus stepped up to him and lifted his chin to raise his face up, then caught his breath.

"Looks like you've been thoroughly worked over, my lad."

Marcus's left eye was swollen so much it was closed. His face was cut and bruised, and his lips were split and crusted with dried blood. He held one hand protectively over his ribs. Brixus puffed his cheeks out and steered Marcus toward a stool in the corner of the kitchen. "You sit there. I'll find something else for you to do."

"I'm all right," Marcus mumbled.

"No, you're not," Brixus replied with a wry smile. "You're a mess. Now, do as you are told and sit down." He pushed Marcus toward the stool, then turned and looked around the kitchen and clicked his fingers as he pointed at one of the other boys. "Bracus! You're on fire duty this morning. Get 'em laid and lit. And you, Acer, go and fetch Amatus."

"Amatus? The drill instructor?" The boy looked fearful.

Brixus cocked an eyebrow. "Do you know another Amatus? No? Then get to it!"

Marcus eased himself down onto the stool and winced as pain stabbed into his side. He breathed as gently as he could until the pain had gone away. Then his thoughts returned to the previous night. The last thing he could recall of the confrontation with Ferax was being beaten while he tried to curl into a protective ball on the ground. Then all was blank until he woke in the night to find Pelleneus mopping his face with a damp cloth, and Phyrus in the background, looking on anxiously. The faint glow of a torch lit the scene as Phyrus muttered, "It's my fault. I should have kept an eye out for him."

Pelleneus shook his head. "That's not possible. You couldn't have prevented this."

As Marcus stirred, and groaned in agony, Pelleneus leaned forward. "Who did this to you? Tell us, Marcus."

Marcus shook his head.

"It was the Celt, wasn't it?"

Marcus did not reply.

"I thought so." Pelleneus nodded. "Well, he's not going to get away with this. I'll see to him."

"No!" Marcus croaked. "Leave him to me. I'll have my own revenge."

"You think so?" Pelleneus glanced over his injuries. "Next time, he's going to kill you."

"I'll be better prepared," Marcus mumbled through his swollen lips.

"He's right," a voice interrupted, and they turned toward the Spartan, standing a short distance away. "The boy has to fight his own battles if he is to become a man."

Pelleneus glanced around. "Another fight will kill him, Spartan. So just leave the philosophy to us Athenians, eh?"

The Spartan shrugged. "The boy knows what I say is true. This is his fight, and you don't have the right to take it from him." He turned his dark, penetrating gaze on Marcus. "I know your mind, boy. You have the blood of a warrior in your veins. You must not shame yourself by avoiding this fight."

"I won't." Marcus nodded as he closed his eyes again. "I will beat him."

Pelleneus let out a sigh of frustration. "It's your funeral, Marcus. And thank you, Spartan. You are as helpful as ever...."

When dawn came, Marcus had taken a while to get back onto his feet. Every movement was agony as he made his way from the cellblock to the kitchen. Now he looked across the counters to where Ferax and his cronies were joking with each other as they filled the cauldrons with ground barley, oil, salt, and animal fat. He felt a yearning for revenge. Come what may, he would face Ferax again. But next time he would be prepared. He would be stronger and he would learn how to fight well. When he was ready, Marcus would teach the Celt a lesson he would never forget. At that moment, Ferax looked up and caught his eye. The two boys stared at each other, and then Ferax winked and pursed his lips in a mock expression of pity.

Marcus felt a dreadful wave of rage and hatred sweep through his body. The desire for revenge even eclipsed the feeling he had for Decimus, who had caused all this to happen in the first place.

Amatus entered the kitchen, looked around until he saw Brixus, then strode up to him. "You asked for me?"

"Yes, it's the boy there." Brixus nodded toward Marcus. "He's been beaten—badly. I doubt he will be able to train today, and I thought you should know."

"Beaten?" Amatus came over to Marcus and looked him over, noting the injuries. "Who did this to you, boy?"

"No one," Marcus said quietly, meeting Amatus's gaze defiantly. Out of the corner of his eye he was aware that Ferax was watching them closely. He cleared his throat and spoke as clearly as he could so that all in the kitchen would hear. "I slipped in the latrine."

"Is that so?" Amatus could not help smiling slightly. "How many times? I had no idea taking a dump was so dangerous. Look here, boy, there's no point in trying to pull the wool over my eyes. I've heard it all before. Someone attacked you. That's against the rules and they're going to have to be punished. Master Porcino does not take kindly to people mishandling his property. So tell me, who did this?"

"I told you, I was in the latrine block and I slipped, sir. That's all."

"And that's a lie, boy." Amatus frowned and poked his finger into Marcus's chest. "I don't like being lied to. Tell me, or it'll be you I punish."

"I slipped, sir," Marcus replied flatly.

"On your head be it, then." Amatus turned to the cook.

"Can't afford him to have any complications. He's off training for two days."

"No, I can still do it." Marcus struggled to his feet, only to have Amatus push him back down as he continued speaking to Brixus. "You've got yourself a full-time helper for a while. Make the most of it."

"There's plenty of work he can do here." Brixus nodded. "I'll keep him out of trouble."

"Better had." Amatus lowered his voice. "I can't let this sort of thing happen again. Next time there will be consequences for those involved." He turned back to Marcus. "As for you, since you have such a problem keeping on your feet in the latrine, then the latrine obviously needs a good clean. That'll be your job from now on. You're off the evening kitchen detail. Instead you'll scrub and wash down the latrine block each night. Maybe that'll teach you not to lie to me."

Amatus strode off, out of the kitchen and back toward the instructors' mess, to finish his morning meal. Once he had disappeared from view, Brixus looked around the kitchen and took a deep breath. "What are you all standing still for and gawping like fools? Get back to work!"

The boys instantly returned to their tasks, heads lowered as they avoided his gaze. Brixus stared at them a moment to ensure they were concentrating on their duties, and then returned to Marcus. "You ever polished brass before?"

Marcus recalled the medallions on his father's harness, each one awarded for an act of bravery. During the winter, the old centurion used to take out his kit and show Marcus how to keep it clean and gleaming through use of an abrasive powder mixed with olive oil, rubbed in with an old cloth before being wiped away and buffed until it glinted. Marcus looked up at Brixus. "I know how to polish."

"Good, because the master wants his table brass ready for a banquet in five days' time. You can help me with the job."

"Yes, sir. Thank you."

Once the men had eaten, and the boys had cleared and cleaned the kitchen before hurrying off to join them on the training ground, Brixus gestured to Marcus to follow him. They crossed the compound to the main gate, where one of the guards stepped into their path and raised his hand.

"Halt! What's your business here?"

Brixus limped to a stop and then fished inside his tunic and brought out a waxed slate. He flipped it open and pointed to the instructions etched into the wax, together with the impression of Porcino's seal ring. "There."

The guard glanced over the slate. "What about the boy?"

"He's my assistant."

The guard looked at Marcus and then stood aside as he nodded to the rest of the section guarding the main gate. "Open up."

The locking bar was removed, and the thick door opened just wide enough for Brixus and Marcus to pass through. It closed behind them with a deep thud as the guard waved them toward the villa.

"Come," said Brixus as he limped a short distance up the track before turning on to the drive that led to the villa of Porcino. After the recent days of minimal comfort in the school, Marcus saw that the owner lived very comfortably indeed. The drive to the house was lined with neatly trimmed bushes, and every so often a short pillar supported the bust of a man. Marcus thought he recognized some of the faces from the statues he had seen at Nydri and in the towns and ports he had passed through on the way to Capua.

"Who are they supposed to be?" he asked Brixus quietly.

"These?" Brixus gestured toward the busts. "They're the Roman quality, they are. Consuls, senators, high priests, and so on. Our master likes to impress his guests, and at the same time he's shrewd enough not to pick sides. See there? That's Marius, and directly opposite is Sulla. Bitter enemies in life, and their legacy still divides the people of Rome. But Porcino aims to keep both sides happy whenever their supporters happen to pay a visit to the school."

"Do they come often?"

"Often enough. There's always some politician wanting to buy up some gladiators and put on a show to impress the mob."

"What about General Pompeius?" Marcus asked, trying not to show his excitement. "Does he come here?"

"Not likely!" Brixus snorted. "He's far too grand to pay us a visit in person. But we've had one of his stewards here a while back. He bought four pairs of fighters for a private entertainment at Pompeius's palace outside Rome."

Marcus smiled to himself at the prospect, however slim, that such a fate might befall him one day. Perhaps Pelleneus was right. He should concentrate on staying alive long enough for such a chance to be placed before General Pompeius.

Porcino's villa, like most grand Roman villas, was built with a large courtyard in front, entered through an elaborately decorated arch. Beyond the courtyard lay the main house, built around a neatly kept garden, at the center of which lay a pond, where the water from a fountain tinkled lightly. There was a small door in one corner of the courtyard that led to the slaves' quarters. Here was the familiar grim plainness of the school. Bare walls and gloomy rooms with high, barred windows. Brixus continued down a short corridor into a storeroom. The shelves were stacked with brass and silver platters, bowls, and goblets. Elsewhere, there was a collection of fine Samian ware, glass jugs, and a few glass bowls. Brixus pulled up a couple of stools, and returned with a small box containing some rags, pots of abrasive powder, and a small jar of oil. He muttered as he brought down a stack of brass platters and set them down between the stools. Handing one to Marcus and taking one for himself, they set to work.

"So," Brixus said as he mixed some powder and oil in a small dish. "What's your story, young Marcus? How did you come to be a gladiator at the tender age of . . . what?"

"I'm eleven," Marcus replied.

"As old as that?" Brixus mused with a faintly mocking smile. "Almost a man, then?"

Marcus had grown used to the ironic banter of adults, and did not rise to the bait. "I was taken illegally. My mother was also kidnapped, and my father, a retired centurion, was killed."

"Ah, yes. I had heard that was your claim. Son of a centurion, eh?"

"It's true."

"If you say so." Brixus shrugged. "So what was your mother, an exotic eastern princess?"

"She was a slave," Marcus replied. "At least she was when

my father bought her after the slave revolt. But he freed her and they were married."

Brixus paused and glanced at Marcus, rag-wrapped finger poised over the brass platter in his other hand. "Your father took part in the campaign against Spartacus?"

Marcus nodded. "He was there at the final battle, where the slave army was crushed and Spartacus himself killed. My mother was one of the women captured when the legions sacked the slave camp."

"I see." Brixus looked down and continued rubbing the powder and oil into the brass platter. "I have to tell you, Marcus, I was there too, at the end of the great slave revolt. I was at that battle."

"You?" Now it was Marcus's turn to pause. "You may have known my father. Which legion did you serve with?"

"I didn't serve with the legions. I served Spartacus."

Marcus looked at him in surprise. Brixus returned his gaze with a cold, emotionless expression, and Marcus wondered if he was telling the truth. Perhaps this was another of the practical jokes the men in the school seemed so fond of.

"I thought all the slaves captured by General Pompeius were put to death."

"They were. The day before the battle, I injured my leg when my horse fell down a slope and rolled over me. I was forced to watch the battle from a wagon in the slave camp. Otherwise I would have shared the fate of all the men who were captured under arms. As it was, I was taken when the Romans entered the camp. I was sold to one of the slave dealers who were following the legions. He sold me to Porcino soon after."

"I see." Marcus dipped his rag in the mix and began

163

to polish the other half of the platter. "Did you ever meet Spartacus?"

"Oh yes, most of the army knew him. He always made a point of walking through the camp each night to talk to his followers." Brixus paused and glanced warily at Marcus. "I saw him on many occasions. Spoke to him too."

"What was he like?" Marcus asked eagerly.

"He was a man like me. There were no horns growing out of his head. No fire burning in his eyes, and he did not eat his prisoners, as you have no doubt been taught."

"But he must have been a great warrior. My father says the slaves fought like demons. Spartacus must have been a giant, like Phyrus."

Brixus shook his head. "Spartacus was not a big man. He was my height and my build. He had dark curly hair and piercing brown eyes, like you. When the revolt broke out, he had never killed a man. Never even fought in the arena. But he took to command like a fish to water. In days, he had organized us into a formidable fighting force. In months, he had gathered tens of thousands of followers, and captured enough weapons to equip us all. The other gladiators took on the job of training the slaves, and we did it well, as the departed spirits of many a Roman soldier will testify." Brixus gathered some more of the polish mixture and turned his attention to a new section of the platter. "Whenever we went into battle, Spartacus led the way, followed by the men of his personal bodyguard."

Brixus smiled fondly as he recalled the memory, and Marcus stopped polishing to stare at him, his mouth dropping open slightly.

"Were *you* in his bodyguard?"

Brixus frowned. "I did not say that. All I said was that I knew him, along with many who followed him. That's all. Now, ask me no more questions about Spartacus or you'll get us both into trouble."

"Trouble?"

Brixus lowered his platter and leaned closer to Marcus. "If your father was who you say he was, then you must know how much the Romans were terrified of Spartacus. They still are. They know that the spirit of Spartacus lives on in the hearts of every slave in Italia. Our masters want to make us forget. So you can imagine how angry Porcino might be if he overheard our conversation."

"But we're alone," Marcus protested. "No one can hear us."

"Walls have ears," Brixus replied. "I've said enough already. Now get back to work, boy, and no talking."

Marcus sighed, frustrated that he could not learn more about the great Spartacus. He raised his platter and began to rub the brass vigorously. All the same, he could not help wondering about Brixus. There was more to him than Marcus had thought. Much more. Despite his denial, clearly he had known Spartacus well. Well enough to put his life in danger if the truth became known. Marcus carefully looked up from under his eyebrows at the man. Come what may, he was determined to discover more about Spartacus.

NINETEEN

As soon as he had recovered from Ferax's beating, Marcus returned to training with the rest of the class. Autumn swept across the Campanian countryside, bringing with it wind and cold squalls of rain. Brown, crispy leaves from the trees outside the school swirled over the walls and collected against the sides of the buildings and in the corners. The change in the season had not the slightest effect on the daily routine, however. After breakfast, Marcus and the other boys marched out to the training ground, where Amatus instantly set them to work.

Every day it was the same set of exercises repeated over and over. The boys were exhausted, and having completed their duties for the day, collapsed onto the straw in their stalls and fell asleep at once. Marcus was the last to sleep, having been tasked with latrine-cleaning duties. Only when the wooden benches had been scrubbed, the vinegar tubs emptied and refilled, and the channels beneath the latrine benches sluiced clear, could he rest. It took weeks before the stiffness in his muscles wore off by the next morning. But as autumn gave way to winter, he began to feel stronger. He could lift far heavier weights than when he arrived. His stamina was also steadily increasing so that he no longer felt exhausted by the day's labor, and he rose each morning alert and without any stiffness in his muscles.

In the last month of the year, Amatus decided that the boys were ready to begin weapons training. As they marched into the training compound, they saw a small cart loaded with wooden swords and wicker shields. Marcus felt his pulse quicken at the sight. At last they were going to be taught how to fight! Even though he knew that this was another step on the way to the deadly combat of the arena, he was keen to learn the skills his father once had. He had already realized that there was little chance of escape while the guards watched the slaves closely from the towers. One day, perhaps soon, he would win his freedom, and he would be better able to find his mother and set her free and protect her.

"Right, you lot!" Amatus shouted as he stood by the cart. "Each boy take a sword and a shield and stand in a line in front of the training posts!"

Marcus joined his companions as they pressed close to the edge of the cart and waited their turn to be equipped. He felt a sharp poke in his side as Ferax leaned toward him. "Wooden swords for now. But let's see what damage they can do, eh?"

Marcus turned to look up at the Celt. "Wood or steel—either way, I will cut you down to size."

"Oho!" Ferax chuckled. "I can't wait."

"Silence there!" Amatus bellowed. "One more word from you, Ferax, and you're on latrine duty."

Ferax bowed his head quickly and pushed himself in front of Marcus and the others to take his training weapons from Amatus. When it was Marcus's turn, he was surprised by the weight of the shield and the sword. He experimented with a few loose swings as he made his way over to one of the training posts—stout lengths of wood standing as high as a man, battered and chipped from years of enduring blows from the gladiator school's students. When all the boys were in position, Amatus approached a post in the middle of the line. He turned to face them.

"I've spent the last months making you fit enough for what lies ahead. Now the real work begins. You will continue your exercises, carrying this kit. You will also be trained in basic fighting techniques. Today we will cover the absolute basics: the block, the thrust, and the recover. Watch me closely."

Amatus raised his shield and placed his left foot forward. "See this? You keep your weight evenly balanced and then lower your body so that you are ready to throw your weight forward or back as necessary. Always lead with your left foot and follow with your right. It's not like normal walking." He looked around at the boys. "Got that? I don't want to see any of you crossing your legs over. You do that in a real fight, and your opponent can catch you off balance and knock you down in a flash. Learn to move properly now, and it'll become second nature. Right, adopt the stance, and when I advance, you retreat, keeping the same distance between us. When I fall back, you follow up. Clear? Then into position."

Marcus advanced his leading foot, held his shield up, and glanced to either side to make sure he was in the correct posture. Amatus paced down the line, nodding approval and barking sharp criticism as he inspected his students. He paused in front of Marcus.

"What the hell are you doing with that sword? It's a *sword*, not a bloody walking stick! Hold it up, level with the ground, tip just in front of the shield! You have to be ready to strike or block at any moment."

"Yes, sir." Marcus did as he was told.

"That's better." Amatus moved on.

When he was satisfied that everyone was ready, Amatus began to drill them in movement, gradually increasing the pace and testing their reactions with occasional swift advances and retreats. Those who were slow to react were bawled at and made to run around the training compound before rejoining their comrades. As the hours passed, the weight of the equipment began to tell, and Marcus felt his muscles burning under the strain. But he gritted his teeth and continued, watching Amatus closely and matching his movements as swiftly as he could.

At length, Amatus straightened up and lowered his shield. He looked over the class with a slight sneer. "That . . . was . . . pathetic. I've never seen such a bunch of losers in all my born days. So, we'll just have to keep at it, until you thick-headed farmboys get it. Take position! Begin!"

The movement drill continued for the rest of the day and the next morning. Only then was Amatus satisfied enough to teach them the basics of fighting: the block, the thrust, and the recover. Then he built these into the drill, letting out a deafening "HA!" each time that his right hand punched forward. The boys responded by raising their shields and swords, ready to parry direct attacks, as well as overhead blows and slashes from the side. When Amatus drew back and lowered his sword, they made their thrusts at an imagined foe and let out their own shrill cry of "HA!"

"What the hell was that?" Amatus responded furiously to their first effort. "You trying to make me laugh? When you strike, you give me a roar like a lion. There's more to winning than using a blade well. You have to scare your opponent. You have to make 'em think you're some wild barbarian warrior whose blood is on the boil. Make 'em fear you and the fight's half won. Let's try it again."

He dropped into a crouch, paused, stepped back twice, and pointed his sword toward the sand to signal his students to attack. Marcus thrust out his wooden sword with all his weight, at the same time that a cry ripped out of him from the bottom of his lungs, adding to the din of the rest of the students.

Amatus pursed his lips and nodded. "Better, but you still don't scare me. Work on it."

For the next few days they continued the drills. Then Amatus moved them on to the basic sword strokes, and they spent hours thrusting and cutting at the training posts, the air filled with the sharp crack of wood on wood and the yells as each boy struck.

All the time, Marcus eyed Ferax closely, watching out in case he tried anything while Amatus was not looking their way. For his part, the Celt regarded Marcus with contempt and let it be known that he had beaten Marcus up. Now the other boys regarded Ferax in fear and did all that they could to avoid his attention. So none of them befriended Marcus, nor even spoke to him. He tried not to care, as he still had the two Athenians for company, as well as Brixus, who treated him well and saved some extra scraps of food for him at the end of most days. However, Marcus felt the despair slowly building in his heart. He was no closer to finding General Pompeius and regaining his freedom and that of his mother. Nor would he ever have his revenge on Decimus while he was imprisoned in this gladiator school.

His misery was compounded by the cruel tricks that Ferax played on him whenever Amatus had his back turned. Some days he would deliberately position himself close to Marcus and then trip him as they were running circuits of the training ground. Or he would shove Marcus when they were using weights, causing Marcus to drop them on the sand, and Amatus would spin around and bellow abuse into his face and strike him with his cane. Marcus bore it all with a grim determination, to bide his time, build his strength, and wait for the day when he was ready to turn on his tormentor.

The year drew to an end, and still no opportunity for escape presented itself, as the slaves were kept inside the walls. The gladiator school began to make preparations for the annual festival of Saturnalia. One morning, wagons trundled into the school laden with jars of wine, fine bread, haunches of cured meat, and baskets of pastries. They were unloaded by Marcus and the others under the watchful gaze of Amatus and a section of the school's guards, to prevent anyone stealing anything. Once the supplies for the feast had been placed in one of the storerooms, Amatus locked the door and took the key to Taurus.

While they waited for Amatus to return, Ferax stepped toward the door and sniffed. "Smell that, boys? Smell all that good food? In two days we'll be eating our way through it."

One of the guards laughed. "You'll get what's left over after the men have finished eating, my lad. That's what you'll be feasting on."

Ferax scowled. "That ain't fair. We've just as much right to it."

"You're just a kid. Right at the bottom of the pecking order." The guard cuffed Ferax on the ear. "And you call me master when you address me."

"Yes, master." Ferax bowed his head. He saw Marcus and grinned. "But you're wrong about one thing, master. I ain't at the bottom of the pecking order. He is, that one there." His lips twisted into a sneer. "The son of a centurion."

Marcus stood still and concealed his feelings of hatred and anger as Ferax continued in a louder voice, addressing the rest of the class. "When Saturnalia comes, I get first choice from the table. Then my friends, then you lot, and lastly him." He stabbed his finger at Marcus. "If anyone tries to jump the line, then they'll have me to answer to, and you all know what happens to those who try to defy me...."

Hardly any of the boys dared meet his eye, and a few glanced nervously at Marcus as they remembered his fate.

"I'm not afraid of you," Marcus said firmly, though inside, his stomach knotted with anxiety.

"No? Well, you should be." Ferax glared at him and slowly shook his head. "Not that you'll be around to fear me for much longer."

Marcus frowned. "What do you mean?"

Before Ferax could respond, a voice cut through the air.

"What's all this?" Amatus bellowed as he strode back toward them. "Hanging around like a bunch of farmhands." He shook his cane. "Get in line, damn you! Or you'll feel my cane across your backs!"

At once, the boys rushed into formation, and Amatus led them off to the training ground, where he drilled them hard for the rest of the morning and into the afternoon. Once the boys were dismissed and made their way to the kitchen, they talked in excited tones about the coming festival. Marcus knew about Saturnalia from his days on the farm. As the year came to an end, the house would be decorated with garlands made from the branches of pine trees. In the kitchen, his mother would labor over special treats. On the day of the festival, Marcus's father, as head of the household, would act as the host for his family and slaves alike, serving at the table where they would gather to eat. Afterward, Aristides would take out his flute and play music for a while, before someone else would tell a story or put on a mime. Then, as night closed in, Marcus would ask Titus to tell them a tale of his days in the legions, of the sights that he had seen as General Pompeius's legions had marched across the known world. Marcus sighed. That was in the days when the farm had been making money and Titus had owned several more slaves. When his fortune had turned, the slaves were sold off one by one and the celebration of Saturnalia became a very quiet affair.

Marcus smiled as he recalled the happier days that were almost like a dream to him now. A suddenly painful dream. He wondered what form the festival would take in the gladiator school. Would Porcino himself come to serve his slaves? It hardly seemed possible. At least there would be a brief break from the usual exhausting daily routine. That was something at least, he reflected, and he kept his mind full of the promise of a stomach filled with good food for the rest of the day's training session.

Afterward, as he helped in the kitchen, Marcus noticed that Brixus was watching him carefully, as if sizing him up.

When the evening meal was over and Marcus was about to set off to the latrine to finish his duties for the day, Brixus took his arm.

"Marcus." Brixus spoke quietly. "Do you still want to know more about Spartacus?"

He nodded.

"Then come back here once you have finished in the latrine."

"All right. I will."

Brixus released his grip and Marcus hurried off. As he scrubbed the benches, he could not help wondering at Brixus's change of heart. When they last spoke of the rebellion, Brixus had ended the discussion abruptly, the moment that he had felt he had said more than he should. Although he was tempted to rush the cleaning of the latrine, Marcus did not dare to let Taurus find fault with his work, so he refilled the tubs and carefully sluiced the channels as always, then put the brushes and buckets away in the cupboard by the door before leaving. The night was dark, and a chilly wind blew across the gladiator school.

Brixus was sitting at one of the tables in the kitchen when Marcus returned. The room was lit by a single oil lamp at the end of the table. A small jar of wine sat in front of Brixus, and he was pouring himself a full cup as Marcus entered. Brixus looked around quickly, and then relaxed when he saw Marcus.

"Ah, good. Come and sit down, boy." He nodded to the stool on the other side of the table, and Marcus did as he was told, noticing that there were two cups on the table. Brixus filled the spare cup and pushed it carefully toward Marcus.

"There, drink it. Helps to keep the cold out."

"Thanks." Marcus nodded as he took the cup, a plain clay vessel with a chipped rim. He had drunk wine before, heavily watered down by his mother, but the rough flavor of the drink Brixus had poured for him took him by surprise.

"Not the best stuff." Brixus smiled. "But wine isn't so easy to come by in here. I bought this one from the guards."

"You have money?" Marcus said in surprise. Most slaves he knew of were not allowed to keep money.

"Yes, of course. Porcino allows his most trusted slaves to earn and save money. After all, one day we might have enough to buy our freedom, and he'll make a tidy sum out of it, as well as not having to feed and house us as we grow old. Anyway..." He took a quick sip and narrowed his eyes a little as he looked across the table at Marcus. "You want to know about Spartacus."

"Yes."

"All right, but first let me put things straight between us. I imagine you haven't forgotten that day when we were polishing brass for the master at his house."

"I remember it."

"Yes. And you will also remember that I said I knew Spartacus."

Marcus nodded. "You said that you knew him very well."

"So, you went away with the impression that I was perhaps a friend of his?"

Marcus did not know what to say, and instead took another sip of the fiery liquid as he waited for Brixus to continue.

"Whatever the truth of it is, young Marcus, I think you must know how dangerous it would be if people got the impression that I was close to Spartacus. Romans have long memories, and they are not a forgiving people. I know that you are a Roman, but I also sense that you have a good heart. You are not like some of the boys who pass through the school. Crafty little thieves and bullies, some of them. Especially lads like that Ferax and his thugs. You are not like them. So I trust you, and now I have to know *how far* I can trust you." He stared at Marcus for a moment. "You must not breathe a word of what I say to you, understand?"

"Yes."

"Good." Brixus sighed with relief. "Now that I have your word, what can I tell you about Spartacus?"

Marcus looked at him eagerly. "Were you one of his bodyguards?"

"No, I was more than that. I was one of his lieutenants. I commanded his scouts." Brixus smiled sadly as he gestured to the plain plaster walls surrounding them. "This is all that is left to me. I used to be a fine gladiator, then a leader in Spartacus's army. Now I am just a humble slave."

"If my father told me the truth, then you are not humble. You fought well. You won your glory."

Brixus shook his head. "There was no glory in that last battle, Marcus. It was a bloody massacre. We had been on the run for months, always just a few steps ahead of the pursuing legions of Crassus, who defeated us in several battles and skirmishes. Then Pompeius arrived and we were caught between the two armies. We had no choice but to turn and fight. By then we had lost many thousands to sickness and injury, and there were barely five thousand men who could still hold a sword or spear. Most of them were cut down in the first charge. But Spartacus and his bodyguards cut their way deep into the Roman lines before they were halted, surrounded, and cut down. It was all over in less than an hour."

Marcus stared at him. "But that's not what my father said. That's not what people say."

"Of course not. Too many men had reputations to build for it to be anything other than a great victory against a dangerous enemy. Crassus claimed that he had beaten us, but Pompeius—the great Pompeius—reported back to Rome that it was really he who had overcome the slave horde. When I was held prisoner in his camp, I heard him making speeches to his men, telling them what heroes they were. He was very generous with his awards and praise, and I daresay your father was one of those who did very well out of it. Small wonder he was content to stick with his general's version of events."

Marcus felt a sour taste in his mouth. He did not want to believe what Brixus was telling him.

"Of course, the one thing that Pompeius could not destroy or corrupt was the inspiration that Spartacus gave to us. Even though the rebellion was crushed and Spartacus was killed, his example lives on. Ask almost any slave. He is our secret hero. We live for the day when another Spartacus will rise up and shatter our chains. And perhaps the next time it is we who will be victorious and Rome that will be humbled."

He drained his cup and looked directly at Marcus. "There. You wanted to know more, and now I have said my piece. What I need to know is that you will keep it secret."

Marcus nodded slowly. "I will. I swear it, on my mother's life."

Brixus watched him closely for a moment. "That is good enough for me. Give me your hand, young Marcus."

Leaning across the table, Marcus reached out and felt Brixus's weathered palm close round his hand. They shook briefly, then Brixus released his grip.

"That's all for tonight. You must be tired."

"Very." Marcus slid off his stool. "Thank you for the wine."

Brixus smiled and waved a hand toward the door.

Outside, Marcus hunched his head down into his tunic and marched quickly up the short path from the kitchen to the cellblock. The guards passed him inside and locked the door behind him. When he reached his stall in the gloom, Marcus slipped off his boots and crawled onto his pile of straw, pulling his spare tunic over him to keep warm. Sleep came easily, despite thoughts of what Brixus had told him swimming around in his head. The sleep was deep and dreamless.

Until he was kicked sharply in the ribs. "Get up! Get up, you thief."

Marcus stirred, his mind drowsy. He squinted up as a torch blazed over him. The man who had shaken him now wrenched him up onto his feet. Marcus could see that it was Amatus who was holding the torch, and the man who had kicked him painfully was Taurus, the chief instructor of the school.

"What have you done with it, thief?"

Marcus blinked and shook his head. "Done? Done with what, master?"

"The venison joint you stole from the storeroom."

"What?" Marcus glanced from one man to the other. "What venison, master? I swear I haven't taken anything."

"Liar!" Taurus held up a boot. The ties had snapped, and the leather uppers flapped as he shook it. "This is yours."

Marcus stared at it and shook his head. "My boots are over there, master. At the entrance to the stall."

"Three of them are. This one was found, a short while ago, when the watch was changed. Guess you must have abandoned it in your rush to escape before you were seen, eh? It was found in the storeroom used for the festival of Saturnalia. The lock had been smashed. Some wine had been drunk and the venison stolen." He frowned and sniffed Marcus suddenly. "You smell of wine!"

Marcus felt a ripple of icy terror sweep down his spine. "It wasn't me! That's not my boot. I swear it."

"Shut your mouth, thief!" Taurus held the sandal up to the torch, revealing its marking: LVIII. "See it? Fifty-eight. That's one of a pair issued to you. So, no more lies, thief. You'll pay for this. Do you know what we do to thieves?" He bunched Marcus's tunic in his fist. "Well?"

"N—no, master."

"We get them to run the gauntlet." His lips twisted into a cruel smile. "Your comrades will form two lines. Each slave has a club, and when the word is given, the thief has to run down the entire length of the gauntlet, being beaten as he goes." Taurus chuckled. "The thing is, I've rarely ever known a slave to survive long enough to reach the end."

Marcus felt his stomach churn. He wanted to deny it, to claim his innocence, but from the look on Taurus's face, the man would never want to hear a word of it. The raised voices had woken some of the others, and by the dim light of the brazier at the end of the barracks, Marcus could see their faces peering at him over the sides of the stalls. He saw Ferax, and their eyes locked on each other as a crafty smile slowly formed on the Celt's lips.

TWENTY

In the pale light of dawn, Marcus was dragged out of the windowless cell that Taurus had thrown him into the previous night. The air was cold and he fought down the instinct to shiver. He was determined not to let anyone see that he was afraid. More afraid than he had ever been in his life. The fear was not just for himself but also for his mother, and he cursed himself for failing her. Amatus fastened his hand around Marcus's arm in a powerful grip and led him past the barracks and through the gate into the training compound. Taurus stood waiting for him.

"Still say you're innocent, boy?"

Marcus nodded. "I stole nothing, master. It was someone else who made it look as if it was me. I swear it, by all the Gods."

Taurus frowned. "Careful, lad. The Gods are not inclined to show much mercy to those who swear falsely."

"I know, master."

"Whatever the Gods think, you're in my hands now, and you'll take your punishment. Understand?"

Marcus hesitated before he gave a resigned shrug. "Yes, master."

There was a brief silence and then Taurus spoke again. "Look here, Marcus, if it wasn't you who stole the meat, then who was it, eh?"

Marcus had a clear idea of who had framed him. If anyone was behind this, it had to be Ferax. But Marcus had no evidence to support any accusation against Ferax, and in any case, with the discovery of his boot, and the smell of Brixus's wine on his breath, it was natural for Taurus to assume that he was guilty. All that Marcus could do was to resolve that he would have his revenge on Ferax, if he survived his punishment. He looked up bleakly and met the gaze of the chief trainer. "I can't say who it was. Only that it was not me, master."

"Then you leave me no choice." Taurus straightened up and switched his steely gaze to Amatus. "Summon every slave to bear witness."

"Yes, master." Amatus released his grip, bowed his head curtly, and turned to hurry back toward the barracks. Marcus stood stiffly and stared straight ahead as Taurus tapped the tip of his vine cane against the side of his boot. A short time later, the first of the gladiators trooped through the gate and formed a line opposite Marcus. The men barely cast a glance over the young boy as they stood waiting. Once the last of them had arrived, next came the boys from Marcus's group. Most were curious, some seemed to regard him with dread as they imagined themselves in his place. Ferax and his cronies regarded him with faint mocking smiles as they strode by, and Marcus felt his rage flare up inside him. Last of all came the serving slaves of the gladiator school, Brixus among them. There was a surprised expression on his face when he saw Marcus. Then he and the others hurriedly formed up to one side.

When the last of them was in place, Taurus took a deep breath as he paced to the middle of the training ground. "For those who don't yet know, you have been summoned here to bear witness to the punishment of this thief. The boy stole food from the kitchen last night. Thanks to his foolishness, he was caught. By now you should all know the punishment for theft. Let this morning be a warning to you all." He turned to Amatus. "Bring your class forward. Two lines across the center of the training ground!"

Amatus bellowed at the boys, who quickly trotted forward and formed an avenue in front of Marcus. It stretched the length of the training ground, nearly to the stockade, fifty paces away. The boys stood facing each other in two lines six feet apart. Once they were in place, Amatus strolled to the side, where a wicker basket contained a stack of stout wooden staves. He took up a large bundle, holding the staves up against his chest, and then returned to his waiting class.

"Take one each!" he ordered, stopping in front of each boy as they armed themselves. Ferax hefted his staff and gave it a vicious experimental swing, which thudded down into the gravel in front of him. Then he glanced at Marcus and winked. When the last staff had been issued, Amatus took up a position at the far end of the gauntlet.

Taurus turned to Marcus. "Take off your tunic."

Marcus faced the man, with his back to Brixus and the other slaves, and then reached down and pulled the hem of his tunic up over his waist, before shuffling it over his shoulders. Taurus took the tunic away from him, and Marcus stood in his boots and loincloth. There was a faint gasp of surprise, and Marcus glanced around to see Brixus staring at him, wide-eyed.

"Quiet, there!" Taurus roared. "Those on the gauntlet make ready! I don't want to see anyone slacking off. As the boy passes in front of you, you will do your utmost to strike him, hard. Anyone who fails to land a blow, or strikes too softly, will be the next one to pass through the gauntlet. Is that clear?" He grasped Marcus by the shoulder and steered him toward the pair of boys at the head of the gauntlet. "When I give the word, you begin." He lowered his voice to a whisper. "Best to run like hell. Keep your arms up to protect your head. Don't hesitate and don't fall down. If you do, then you're dead. Understand?"

Marcus nodded, his body trembling in the grip of naked terror.

"Then get ready. On the count of three. One... Two..."

"Stop!"

Taurus spun around with a furious expression. "Who said that?"

Marcus looked over his shoulder and saw the slaves glancing at Brixus. The old cook swallowed nervously and then shuffled forward a pace. "It was me, master."

"Brixus? How dare you? How dare you intervene?" Taurus bunched his fist around the head of his vine cane as he strode up to the cook, his expression as black as night. "What is the meaning of this?"

Brixus rose to his full height and faced the drillmaster squarely. "The boy is innocent, master. I know him. Marcus is not the thief."

"Really?" Taurus snarled. "What makes you think that? Unless you were there and saw the thief in person. Well?"

Brixus's eyes briefly met those of Marcus. Then Taurus rammed his cane into the cook's stomach, and he folded over with a groan, slumping to his knees. Taurus leaned over him menacingly. "Well?"

"It was . . . me." Brixus gasped for breath. "I stole the meat."

Taurus froze. "What's that? You? I don't believe it!"

"It's true, master." Brixus fought for breath. "I did it. The boy is innocent."

Marcus shook his head in bewilderment. Brixus was the thief? A cold chill of doubt gripped his heart as he wondered why Brixus had spoken up. Was it guilt, perhaps, for Marcus's taking the blame for the stolen venison? Every face on the drill exercise ground was turned toward the two men, and there was a long silence before Taurus straightened up and placed his hands on his hips. "All right, then. If it was you, why confess now, when you could have got away with it, eh?"

Brixus caught his breath and looked up. "I'll not have some boy take his strokes on my behalf, master."

"Why not?"

"I have my pride. I may be a slave, but I still have some sense of honor."

"Honor?" Taurus barked out a laugh. "Honor! Wonders will never cease! Honor is for free men, Brixus. It's a luxury no slave can afford."

"Though I am a slave, I am still a man, master."

Taurus took a step back. "All right, on your feet, then. Let's see how your sense of honor copes with a good hiding." He turned to Marcus. "You, boy! Get your tunic and stand to the side."

Marcus hesitated, too surprised to move. Taurus raised his vine cane threateningly, and Marcus snatched up his tunic and trotted over to the slaves. As he pulled it back over his head, he heard the drillmaster order Brixus to strip and take up his position at the start of the gauntlet. Marcus shuffled his head through the top of his tunic and saw the cook limp toward the waiting lines of boys. Taurus stood just behind him, waited for complete stillness and silence, and then called out.

"Make ready! One... Two... Three. Off you go, Brixus!"

The cook ducked his head down and raised his arms to each side to protect his skull from the blows to come. Then, with a swift lurch forward, he entered the gauntlet. Marcus caught his breath as the first pair of boys struck out with their makeshift clubs. Brixus was moving faster than they had anticipated, and they had little time to prepare their strikes. One staff deflected off his side and the other glanced off his shoulder as he ran in a low crouch. The second pair of boys were more prepared, and their blows landed solidly against Brixus's back with thuds that carried clearly across the training ground. He took his blows and scurried on, dodging unevenly from side to side to put off the aim of his assailants. Marcus watched his progress, stomach knotted in anxiety.

"Come on, Brixus," he muttered. "You can do it."

Brixus was over halfway through the gauntlet, and his combination of speed and erratic movements had managed to save him from the full force of the blows aimed at him. There were only another twenty or so paces to go now, but near the end of the gauntlet, Marcus could see Ferax raising his club, edging forward into the path of Brixus. The cook had his head bowed down slightly and did not see the danger until the last moment, as he sensed the presence of someone directly ahead of him. With a savage shout of triumph, Ferax swung his club down and it glanced off the side of Brixus's head. His legs gave way underneath him and he sagged onto his knees, his torso swaying, as if he were drunk. Ferax hefted his club, standing over the helpless cook.

"No," Marcus muttered desperately. "No...NO!"

He sprang forward, sprinting diagonally across the training ground. Ferax was turned slightly to one side and could not see him approaching. His attention was fixed on his victim, and he grasped the stave in both hands and began to raise it high above his head. Marcus threw himself across the hard-packed gravel, desperate to save his friend.

"Hey, you!" Taurus bellowed. "Where the hell do you think you're going?"

Marcus ignored him, concentrating all his attention on Ferax. The Celt's shoulder and arm muscles tightened as he made to swing his club, and Marcus launched himself forward, grabbing frantically at the bigger boy's wrists an instant before his full weight smashed into Ferax's side. The breath was driven from their bodies as both crashed onto the ground to one side of Brixus. Ferax was momentarily too surprised to react. Marcus used the advantage. He aimed several blows into Ferax's stomach, winding him so that the Celt lay gasping on his side. Marcus quickly rolled away and rose into a crouch, ready to continue his attack. But for the moment, Ferax could not fight back. Taking his chance, Marcus scrabbled over to Brixus.

"Get up! Come on, Brixus, on your feet."

Brixus rolled his head to one side, dazed. "I...I can't."

"You must! Or die here!" Marcus grabbed him, gritting his teeth as he strained to help the man onto his feet. Then, taking one arm across his shoulder, he struggled forward.

Ahead lay the last two boys, Ferax's companions. They looked from their leader to Marcus uncertainly.

Marcus was overcome by fury.

"You even touch Brixus, and I swear I'll kill you...." he hissed through clenched teeth. The boys kept hold of their staves but made no moves toward Marcus as he staggered by with Brixus and collapsed at the end of the gauntlet. His chest was heaving from the exertion as he forced himself to his feet and stood over Brixus protectively.

"Well, well!" Taurus laughed as he strode over to them. He looked at Marcus with an amused expression. "You're skin and bone and with just scraps of muscle on you, but by the Gods, you have the heart of a lion! I may make a gladiator of you yet, young'un."

"No! Not if I can help it!" Ferax growled, trying to get back on his feet, one hand stretching toward the wooden club he had dropped. His fingers closed around the haft, and then he let out a sharp cry of pain as Taurus stepped down on his fingers with his nailed boots.

"Let go of it, lad! You had your chance. Next time you'd better not hesitate. Consider it a lesson learned."

Ferax glared up at him.

"I said, let go. I won't say it again."

After a moment's hesitation, Ferax loosened his grip and shuffled back. He turned his attention to Marcus and muttered, "You're dead. I swear it, by all that's sacred. You will die by my hand."

TWENTY-ONE

Brixus winced as he struggled to ease himself up on the bedroll. He leaned back against the plaster wall of the infirmary and breathed carefully for a moment, in order to not make the pain from his cracked ribs any worse. Aside from the strips of cloth tied firmly about his body, and one forearm bound with splints, his body was covered with livid purple bruises and dark scabs where his skin had been grazed or cut. Marcus felt sick with horror at the severe beating the cook had taken for him.

"Come now." Brixus forced a smile. "I don't look that bad."

Marcus shook his head. "You're a mess."

"Thanks. If that's what I get for saving your hide, then next time I won't bother." He pretended to look hurt and disappointed for a moment before his smile returned. "Anyway, it's been two days since it happened, and I haven't seen you since."

"Taurus has been keeping me busy. He said that I should take on most of your duties until you recover. When I've not been training, I've been kept busy in the kitchen. Taurus has been watching over the place like a hawk. I think he's making sure that there's no further trouble between me and Ferax."

"Some chance," Brixus snorted. "I know his type. Ferax will not rest until he has destroyed you."

"I know," Marcus replied quietly. He cleared his throat and continued. "Anyway, how are you feeling today?"

"It hurts all over, but the surgeon says that there's no permanent damage. It'll be a while before my arm is better. So, you'd better do a good job of looking after my kitchen, young Marcus, or Ferax won't be the only one out for your blood!"

Brixus paused and stared intently at Marcus. "I understand you stepped in to save me. I still can't remember much about what happened. After the first blow to my head, things went a bit hazy. Taurus told me about it."

"Taurus?" Marcus was surprised.

"Yes. He's given orders that I'm to be well looked after. Of course he said that he was only doing it to make sure that Porcino didn't lose a slave, and that I needed to recover as soon as possible to resume my duties in the kitchen. But he wasn't fooling me. I could see that he was impressed by both of us."

"Oh?"

"Surely. Me for taking the blame, and you for rushing to defend me. Taurus may be a hard-bitten old brute, as so many legionary veterans are, but he's fair-minded and knows a good quality when he sees it."

Marcus nodded, but he was not interested in Taurus. Only the question that had been fixed in his head ever since Brixus had saved him from the gauntlet.

"Why did you do it? Why did you save me?"

Brixus stared at him a moment, all trace of humor drained from his face. Then he shrugged faintly. "I don't believe you stole the meat. In all likelihood, it was that thug, Ferax. He saw a way to lay the blame on you and have you disposed of in a way that was sure to increase his hold over the other boys. I couldn't stand by and let that happen, Marcus. That's why."

Marcus was not so sure. He wanted to believe the cook. Brixus had proved to be one of the few people he counted among his friends in the gladiator school. However, it was hard to accept that someone should risk such danger for the sake of a few months of friendship. Not unless there was some other reason. But what could that be?

"I thank you for my life, Brixus," Marcus said awkwardly. "It was not just my life at stake, but my mother's as well."

"I know. You told me all about her. About what had happened to your family." Brixus fell silent again, chewing on his lip as he stared intently at Marcus. Then he gestured to the floor beside his mattress. "Sit down. I want to talk about something."

Marcus did as he was told, settling onto the flagstones, legs crossed.

"That's better," said Brixus. "I don't have to strain my neck to look up at you this way. Now, Marcus, I need to ask you a few questions."

"What questions?"

"About your family... About that mark on your shoulder."

Marcus raised his eyebrows in surprise. "You mean that scar?"

"Scar? I suppose it could be called a scar."

"How do you know about it?"

"I saw, when Taurus told you to remove your tunic before the gauntlet," Brixus explained. "When did you get the scar?"

Marcus shrugged. "It's always been there, as long as I can recall."

"I see. Do you know how it happened?"

Marcus shook his head. "It must have been when I was an infant. Why do you ask?"

"Just curious." Brixus pursed his lips before he continued. "Do you mind if I see it again?"

Marcus was puzzled by the request. "What's so special about the scar?"

"Let me see it."

There was a strange gleam in the man's eyes, and Marcus felt nervous. He hesitated a moment and then eased the shoulder of the tunic down to expose the puckered flesh of the mark on his skin. It felt strange to him that he had never been able to see it for himself and had only ever been able to trace his fingers over the peculiar shape. He half turned to show his shoulder to Brixus. The cook stared at the mark in silence. Then he coughed. "Thank you."

Marcus pulled his tunic back into place and shuffled back to face the man. Brixus was looking at him with an intense expression. "Do you know what the mark on your shoulder is?"

"No. I've never been able to see it properly."

"It's not a scar, Marcus, nor any kind of birthmark. You've been branded. Just as I thought when I saw it for the first time, two days ago."

"Branded?" Marcus shivered at the idea. "Why would anyone brand me when I was a baby? Anyway, what kind of a brand is it?"

"A wolf's head mounted on the tip of a sword."

Marcus could not help a quick laugh. "What is that supposed to mean?"

"I can't say for sure, not yet," Brixus replied quietly, glancing over the boy's shoulder toward the door of the cell. Then he continued in a low voice, scarcely more than a whisper. "Tell me about your family again. You say your father was a centurion."

"That's right."

"What about your mother? Where did she come from? How did she meet your father?"

"She was a slave," Marcus replied. "She was involved in the revolt led by Spartacus and was bought by my father when the rebels were crushed. He set her free and married her."

"And then you were born," Brixus mused. "Tell me, what does your mother look like? Describe her to me."

As Marcus concentrated and painfully recalled as much about his mother's features as he could, Brixus listened closely all the while, nodding from time to time as if to encourage him to continue. When Marcus had finished, Brixus frowned and shook his head as he muttered to himself. "She must have taken the branding iron with her. . . ."

Marcus leaned closer. "What are you talking about? You're not making any sense. Brixus, tell me what this is about. Tell me!"

"I . . . I'm not certain, Marcus. My mind has been greatly troubled ever since I saw that brand of yours. It may mean something, it may not. But I cannot tell you any more until I have proof. Then I can tell you what I know. Until then you must say nothing of this to anyone." He suddenly gripped

Marcus tightly by the wrist and drew him closer. "Not a word to *anyone*, do you understand?"

"Why? What's the secret?" Marcus asked in frustration. "What are you hiding from me?"

"It is better that you do not know. Not yet." Brixus relaxed his grip and slumped back with a grimace, his breathing coming in sharp snatches. He waved a hand toward the door. "I am tired now. I need rest. Taurus will be wanting you back at the kitchen, I'll wager. Best get yourself over there if you want to avoid a thrashing."

"No," Marcus said firmly. "Tell me what you know."

Brixus shook his head. "It is too early for that, and too dangerous. I will tell you all I know when the time is right. Trust me. Now, go!" He reached out and thrust Marcus toward the door, forcing him to scrabble around to keep his balance. With a dark frown, Marcus stood up and angrily balled his hands into fists. Brixus turned his face away and did not speak anymore. Marcus left the cell and strode out of the infirmary, hurriedly making his way back to the kitchen, filled with frustration.

The Saturnalia was celebrated on a cold, windy day. While the wind and rain lashed across the gladiator school, rattling on the tiles and howling around the walls, the slaves, the drill instructors, the clerks, and even Porcino himself were all gathered in the largest of the barrack blocks. This year the lanista had decided to have all his slaves fed at the same time, without regard to age. Tables and benches had been carried through from the kitchen and set up down the length of the building. Then, once the slaves had taken their places, Porcino and his freedmen entered carrying trays laden with food and drink. Today, for once, there was no training, and the men and boys gazed with unrestrained delight at the food set before them. Fresh loaves of bread, cured joints of meat, cheeses, jars of garum sauce, and heavily spiced sausages. Marcus was sitting beside Pelleneus. Opposite sat Phyrus and the Spartan. Phyrus leaned forward and grasped one of the loaves, tearing out a large mouthful and chewing furiously.

"Easy there, my friend"—Pelleneus laughed—"or there'll be none left for the rest of us!"

"Too right," Phyrus mumbled, spitting crumbs. "Mmm, it's got sesame seeds."

Beside him, the Spartan brushed away some of the crumbs that had fallen on the sleeve of his tunic, then reached for the smallest of the sausages and bit off the end, eating with studied indifference.

Marcus waited until the men had filled their wooden platters before tentatively reaching for some meat himself. Pelleneus nudged him.

"There's no pecking order at Saturnalia. Eat up."

As Marcus helped himself, Phyrus leaned over the table and hurriedly swallowed before he spoke. "How's the cook doing? I heard you had been visiting him."

"Brixus is recovering well. Should be returning to duties any day now."

"Just as well," the Spartan commented. "He's about the only slave who knows how to cook."

Marcus flushed. "The other boys and I do our best."

The Spartan shrugged. "Well, I hope you learn to fight better than you cook, young Marcus. If you want to live."

"Tshh, ignore him," said Pelleneus. "Enjoy the day."

Marcus nodded happily. Despite everything that had happened to him, he had taken comfort from his three companions and had grown to regard them almost as if they were older brothers. No, not brothers, he thought. More like uncles.

"Ah, here comes the wine." Pelleneus nodded toward the door, and Marcus saw the drill instructors returning to the barracks laden with jars of wine and baskets filled with wooden cups. Taurus approached them and set a jar into the iron holder on the table, and then set down four cups in a succession of sharp raps.

"I'm not so sure if I really care to patronize this establishment," the Spartan commented drily. "This serving man seems far too surly."

"Make the most of it," Taurus grunted. "Tomorrow you're all mine again."

As the drill master moved on, Marcus exchanged a glance with the other three, and they burst into laughter.

The feasting continued through the day and in the evening. After the remains of the banquet were cleared away, the tables were pushed aside and Porcino ushered a troupe of entertainers into the barracks. Torches were lit and placed in the wall brackets, and by their light the entertainers provided some acrobatics before moving on to a repertoire of crude mimes that soon had the gladiators, most of whom were drunk by this time, in hysterical bouts of laughter. Marcus, who had only had one cup of wine, felt pleasantly dizzy as he leaned against the side of the pen and watched the performance with a bleary smile. But then his mood darkened again, because he knew the morning would mark a return to the hard training regime of Amatus.

When the performers had finished their acts and left the barracks, Porcino climbed onto a table at one end of the room and raised his hands to attract the slaves' attention.

"Quiet! Quiet, there!"

Slowly, the conversation died away and all eyes turned toward the owner of the gladiator school. Porcino waited until he had silence and everyone's attention was turned on him. Then he drew a breath and addressed them.

"Gladiators, you have earned your celebration of Saturnalia! It has been my pleasure to reward you for the effort you have put into your training. I have never seen such a fine intake of men, and boys. You do honor to my gladiator school, and you do honor to the tradition of those fighting men who have gone before you. Gladiators, I salute you!"

Around Marcus, the men and boys cheered lustily for a while. All except the Spartan, who gazed at his fellow slaves with thinly concealed contempt. Gradually, the cheering died away and Porcino continued.

"You are indeed as fine a body of fighters as I have ever trained. I am proud of you. In a few days I will be even more proud of you. We are to be honored with a party from Rome's finest families. They are coming to my school to be entertained by some of you. I expect those who are chosen to fight well and uphold their honor, and mine. For those that distinguish themselves, I can tell you that great fame and fortune will await you in Rome. For surely, once the Roman lords see you in action, they will want to show you off to their friends and the people of the greatest city in the world. Think on that, my gladiators! Greatness beckons. You have but to answer with a full heart and all the skills you have been taught," he concluded.

There were muted cheers from a handful of the men in the barracks, too drunk to fully understand the words of their master. Most were sober enough to understand the import of Porcino's words. Glancing around, Marcus could sense the sudden change in the atmosphere. The mood of revelry had drained from the barracks, and it felt as if a cold, dark shadow had fallen across the room. Pelleneus lowered the cup from his lips and tossed it to one side with a bitter curse.

"I bid you good night!" Porcino called out. He was about to climb down from the table when the door to the barracks opened and a sentry entered, clutching his spear. He paused in front of the lanista and bowed his head.

"Master, I beg to report that one of the slaves has gone."

"Gone?"

The guard swallowed nervously. "Escaped, master."

The barracks fell silent as the men and boys strained their ears to catch what was being said. Porcino glared at the sentry. "Escaped? How? They were all supposed to be in here tonight. How could the fugitive get past you and your men?"

"Master, the slave was not in here. He was in the infirmary."

Marcus felt his heart quicken.

"Which slave is this? What is his name?"

"Brixus, sir."

TWENTY-TWO

Porcino IMMEDIATELY GAVE THE order for his guards and the drill instructors to search for Brixus. The slaves were locked into the barracks, and Marcus hurried to one of the narrow ventilation slits that overlooked the interior of the gladiator school. Looking out through the drafty opening, he could see the flare of torches in the stiff breeze, and the dark shapes of men scouring the other buildings for any sign of Brixus. The voices of Porcino and Taurus echoed from the walls as they led the hunt.

"So much for the seasonal spirit," a voice muttered beside Marcus, and he turned to see that the Spartan had joined him. "Funny how our master's goodwill vanishes the instant his property is at stake, and here we are again, slaves locked in our prison. Oh well." He smiled humorlessly.

Marcus turned back to the slit as a party of men rushed by. He had been shocked by the announcement of Brixus's escape. The cook had given him no indication of his plans, and Marcus felt hurt that his friend had not trusted him enough to tell him. He was also furious that he had missed the chance to join Brixus in his escape. He could have been on his way to find General Pompeius right now, rather than indulging himself with the other slaves.

"Do you think he will get away?" Marcus asked.

"How should I know?" The Spartan shrugged. "I can see only as much as you. But, for my money, Brixus is a fool to attempt it."

"Why do you say that?"

"Why? The man is lame. Even if he has managed to escape over the walls, he cannot hope to outpace his pursuers. Come the morning, they will search the countryside for him. His only hope is that this rain washes away any tracks that he might have left. With his limp, Brixus is going to stand out." The Spartan was silent for a moment and then clicked his tongue. "I'd be surprised if they didn't recapture him before nightfall tomorrow."

"And if he is taken, Porcino will punish him," Marcus mused.

"Yes."

Both of them stared out into the night before Marcus cleared his throat. "What do you think Porcino will do to him?"

"He will want to make an example of Brixus in order to discourage the rest of us from thinking about trying to escape. That will be weighed against Brixus's value. Quite a dilemma for our master, eh? A struggle between his desire for discipline and his greed."

"If discipline wins, then what?"

The Spartan turned to Marcus. "Porcino will have him crucified in front of us, and leave him there to die, and then leave him there for a while longer to make certain we learn the lesson."

Marcus felt his blood go cold. "Do you really think so?"

The Spartan nodded, then eased himself back from the ventilation slit and yawned. "Nothing we can do about it, boy. Best you get some rest. You'll need it when you go back to training in the morning."

Marcus glanced at him and nodded, but stayed by the opening, watching as the hunt inside the compound came to an end and Porcino ordered his men to start searching outside the walls. The Spartan cracked his shoulder muscles and turned back toward the stall as he muttered, "Anyway, happy Saturnalia, boy."

But Marcus could not reply. He was too caught up in thoughts of what would happen to his friend if they found him.

For the next few days, Marcus lived in dread of hearing the news that Brixus had been recaptured. He and the other boys continued with their training. The winter was cold and the boys shivered each morning as they rose with the dawn to carry out their duties in the kitchen before Amatus led them out to the training ground. As the new year began, he introduced his students to new techniques in swordplay, and then had them practice against the posts until he was satisfied that they were ready for the next stage.

It was a cold, bleak morning as Marcus and the others collected their training weapons and formed up in two lines, waiting for Amatus to begin the day's lesson. He stood before them, examining the slaves with a hard stare. Then he spoke.

"Today we put your training to the test for the first time. You're all a lot fitter, tougher, and stronger than you were when you arrived here. You also know how to handle a sword and shield. However, it's one thing to practice against a post. Quite another to be faced by a real opponent. And that's what you will be doing from now on."

Marcus felt his pulse quicken, and the boys on either side of him stirred with a mixture of excitement and anxiety.

"Today you will begin sparring with your comrades. The rules are simple. You will fight when I give the command, and you will stop the moment I give the order 'cease.' I want you to fight like you mean it. Like your life depended on it, because it will one day. You will do yourselves no favors by pulling your blows. I know some of you may be friends, but know this: a gladiator cannot afford to have true friends. A true friend you might give your life for. That is not the concern of a gladiator. Anyone you call a friend today may well be matched against you in the arena tomorrow. And then where will your friendship get you? Killed." He paused to let his hard words sink in. "Now, you need to know where to strike. Ferax!"

"Yes, sir!"

"Step forward, here!" Amatus pointed to the spot in front of his students. He turned Ferax around to face the other boys. "Watch carefully. Lower your shield, Ferax."

With the Celt standing before them unprotected, Amatus swiftly raised his training sword and pointed it at Ferax's face. The Celt flinched slightly.

"A thrust here may kill your opponent if it breaks through his skull. At the very least it will cripple him. However, it's a difficult blow to strike. But you can use it to distract him while you go for another target." He lowered the tip of his sword. "Like the throat, for instance. A good strike here will get you a kill. Lower down we have the chest. Best to avoid this area since many opponents will have armor, a shield, or both. You need to be very close and ram the blade home, if you are going to get through the ribs to the heart. Better to aim lower. As we say in the business, the best way to a man's heart is through his stomach. A good thrust here has a chance of striking an organ, or if you rip the blade out violently enough, you may disembowel him." Amatus tapped the tip of the wooden sword against Ferax's thighs and arms. "The limbs make good targets, and you should try to cut tendons to cripple your opponent. They won't bleed out, but at least they won't move, or strike as fast, and you can pick 'em off at your leisure." He lowered his sword. "There's no point in showing you targets to strike on the rear of your opponent, since no gladiator worth his salt will ever turn and run from you. If he does that, then he's as good as lost the fight already. Is that clear to you all?"

"Yes, sir!" the boys called back. Marcus joined them, even though he was unnerved by the cold-blooded advice that Amatus had just presented to them. It was the first time that the real purpose of all their training had been brought home to them so directly. Marcus wondered how the other boys were reacting to the possibility of one day having to try to kill someone they had trained alongside. He glanced to either side and noted the intent expressions on their faces as some exchanged brief looks with their companions.

"Very well." Amatus nodded to Ferax. "Back to your position."

Once Ferax had rejoined the others, Amatus pointed to the line of posts. "When I give the order, you will wait over there. I'll call you out two at a time. The rest of you will watch closely. Learn from their mistakes. Go!"

They hefted their shields and quickly trotted over to the stakes. Amatus waited until they were still, and then pointed to one of the Nubian boys. "You!" Then he pointed out one of Ferax's companions, a heavyset Celt with a spotty complexion. "And you! Step forward."

The two boys emerged uncertainly from the ranks, and Amatus clapped his hands together. "Quickly! Out here and face each other, ten paces apart."

They trotted forward to take up their positions, and Amatus stood slightly to one side, sword in hand. "Make ready!"

The two boys lowered themselves into a crouch, shields raised and swords advanced, slightly to one side.

"Begin!"

At once they closed on each other, halting just beyond reach, as each sized the other up. The Celt moved first, stepping forward and lunging with a loud cry. The Nubian easily retreated and knocked the blow aside. They both drew off for a moment, and then the Celt struck again, running forward and battering the other boy's shield. The Nubian took the blows, holding his ground, and then, just as the other began to draw back to catch his breath, the Nubian struck. He lashed out at the sword arm, a savage numbing blow that almost caused the Celt to drop his weapon. As he cried out in pain and surprise, the Nubian struck at his knee and then crashed forward, throwing his full weight behind his shield. The blow knocked the Celt back. He stumbled, then tripped and toppled onto his back with a thud and an explosive gasp of breath. The Nubian sprang forward, teeth flashing with a triumphant grin. He stood astride his opponent, sword raised, and then looked toward Amatus for confirmation of his victory. On the ground, the Celt seized his chance and kicked up into the Nubian's groin. With an agonized groan, the Nubian doubled up and staggered aside. The Celt scrambled to his feet and punched the other boy in the head, and again, until the Nubian's legs gave way and he fell to his knees. The Celt grasped the wooden sword and ripped it from the boy's grasp. He didn't spare the trainer a glance as he whacked the Nubian on the side of the head, sending him sprawling and dazed on the sand. Just as he went to strike again, Amatus intervened.

"Cease!"

The Celt drew back. Amatus ignored the boy on the ground as he stared around at his students. "Lesson one: the fight is not over until you are certain the other man is down and out." He turned to the Celt. "Help him up, and get back over there. Next bout: Petronius and Democrites."

The sparring went on for the next hour, and Marcus watched the fighters closely, noting their mistakes and where they achieved success. He felt increasingly anxious as he waited for his name to be called out, particularly as Ferax had not yet been picked either.

Several bouts had been fought when the gate to the training ground was opened by a guard and two men entered: Porcino and a stranger wearing an embroidered red tunic and fine leather boots that stretched up his calves. As soon as he saw them, Amatus called his class to stand at attention and ordered them to bow their heads.

"This is Amatus." Porcino casually indicated the trainer. "Breaking in the youth class, as you can see, my lord."

Marcus pricked up his ears as he heard the deferential tone in the lanista's voice. Clearly his companion was someone of note.

"Ah, good! Weapons training," said the stranger. "This is precisely what I want to see. Gives me a chance to buy the best for my friend's party. Please tell them to carry on. We can watch from the bench over there."

Porcino nodded. "As you wish. Shall I send for refreshments?"

"No. Later, perhaps, when we discuss the details."

Porcino nodded to Amatus. "Carry on."

As the two spectators watched, the bouts continued. Amatus observed his students closely, threatening to strike those who were slow to close on each other, shouting instructions and stepping in to stop the fights the moment it was clear that one of the boys had been defeated. As the last four stood waiting, Amatus called out two names, leaving Marcus and Ferax for the last bout.

Marcus felt his heart quicken as he glanced at Ferax. The other boy smirked.

"Oh, I'm going to enjoy this," Ferax said softly so that only Marcus could hear. "You can be sure that I won't be pulling any blows for you, my friend."

Marcus swallowed and turned away, tightening his grip on his wooden sword and wicker shield. He watched the fight but did not take in any of the details, as if the last but one of the sparring pairs were just two shadows dancing around each other. His mind was racing as he tried to recall all that he had been taught and all that he knew about Ferax. He must think of a way to beat his opponent. He had to make a plan.

"Cease!"

Marcus was shocked to find that the fight was over. He saw the winner helping the other boy back onto his feet, and the pair joined those who had already fought.

"Last pair!" Amatus beckoned to them. Marcus swallowed and did his best to look calm and fearless as he strode out and took up his position, turning to face Ferax.

"This fight's been a long time coming," Amatus announced in a faintly amused tone. "So let's see what you two can do, eh?" He lowered his voice as he continued. "I know you hate each other's guts, but keep it under control, and when I tell you to stop, you do so at once. Either of you try anything underhanded, I'll give you a hiding. Ready!"

Marcus lowered himself into a crouch, eyes fixed on his enemy. Inside his chest, his heart beat like a drum, and all his senses were strained to a fine pitch. All traces of a smile or cruel amusement had drained from Ferax's face, and he returned Marcus's stare with an intense expression.

"Begin!"

With a roar that strained his throat, Marcus charged forward. Ferax's eyes widened in shock, and at the last moment he hurriedly threw up his shield. There was a thud as they collided. Marcus struck out with his sword, thrusting past the shield and glancing off his opponent's shoulder. Ferax grunted in pain, and he retreated as quickly as he could, opening the gap so that he could use his sword more effectively. Now he could block Marcus's blows. After a sharp clatter of wood, their swords parted company, and each boy paused to eye the other warily.

Unlike in the other bouts, Amatus did nothing to urge them to close on each other. Instead he watched eagerly. The other boys were still and silent, too, keen to see how well the two foes acquitted themselves in an open fight. The excitement seemed to communicate itself to Porcino and his guest as well, and they leaned forward to watch.

Raising the blunt tip of his sword, Ferax paced forward, then with a sudden movement, he kicked up some sand, and Marcus instinctively blinked as a spray of grit stung his neck and chin. At once, Ferax sprang forward with a deafening bellow and savagely hammered his sword down on Marcus's raised shield, driving his arm down with every blow. Marcus ignored the jarring sensation in his left arm and concentrated on fending the attacks away from his head. Then he dropped down onto one knee, thrusting his shield up as he swung his sword in a cut to the Celt's thigh. The blow went home with a sharp thwack. Ferax roared again—in pain this time—and surged forward, pushing Marcus back. He tried to brace his boots into the sand to hold his ground, but the pressure was relentless and irresistible, and he was forced to give way.

Sensing victory, Ferax pressed on, swinging at Marcus as hard as he could. Then, with a quick switch in direction, his wooden sword swept around the edge of the shield and struck Marcus's left arm with a numbing slap. The blow was painful and deadened the senses in his arm so that his grip on the handle of the shield momentarily loosened. Two more blows on the wicker, and his fingers lost their hold —the shield slipping from Marcus's grasp. He let it fall and scurried back, remaining in a crouch as Ferax snarled triumphantly.

"There! Now, to finish the job!"

He approached steadily, raising his shield to use as a ram to bludgeon Marcus down. There was too little time to think, and as Ferax drew close, Marcus sucked in a breath and launched himself forward. At the last moment, he ducked down, rolling under the vicious slice that hissed over his head. In return, he hacked at Ferax's ankle, and felt the impact of the blow shoot up his arms as the Celt bellowed in pain and abruptly halted. Ferax's teeth were gritted, and he winced the instant he tried to put any weight on the smarting ankle. Marcus darted around his side, forcing his foe to pivot painfully. The smaller boy moved in quickly and thrust the point into the Celt's side and then scuttled back out of range.

"I'll get you," Ferax growled. "And I'll gut you."

Marcus kept moving, working around his opponent and forcing Ferax to keep putting weight on his injured ankle. At length, Ferax slumped down onto his knee and raised his shield, desperately blocking Marcus's attacks. Unable to find a way past the Celt's defences, Marcus withdrew five paces and steadily circled his foe, noting that although Ferax could no longer launch an attack, neither could Marcus get close enough to strike the decisive blow.

"A standoff!" Amatus announced. "Cease!"

"No!" Ferax shouted. "I can finish him. We fight on!"

"Suits me," Marcus replied coldly.

Amatus stepped in between them with an enraged expression. "You dare disobey my order? I'll see you both flogged for this. Cease, I said. Do it—now!"

Marcus did not respond as he sprang forward again, stabbing at Ferax's side. Once again, the wicker shield took the blow, and Ferax desperately slashed at Marcus's shin, just missing it as he fell back.

"CEASE!" Amatus yelled at the top of his lungs.

This time, Marcus reluctantly stepped back to a safe

distance and lowered his sword. Amatus stepped up to him, wrenched the training weapon from his hand, and turned to Ferax. "Drop your kit. You two are in the deepest trouble there ever was. I swear it! I'll beat you both black and blue. Right here! Right now! Damn you."

"That's enough!" Porcino interrupted as he and the other man strode up. "Leave them be, Amatus."

The instructor clamped his mouth shut, bowed his head, and backed away with as much respect as he could manage to retrieve from his sizzling anger. Marcus stood, chest heaving, blood pulsing through his head, and hands balled into fists.

"By the Gods," Porcino's companion marveled. "This boy is a fire-eater, make no mistake. And he is well matched by that young bull. Oh, yes! These two will do nicely." He turned to Porcino. "I'll have them too."

"These?" Porcino looked surprised as he dismissively waved a hand at Marcus and Ferax. "Why, they are still in training, my lord."

"Their technique is crude, but they have something else. A vital, raw hatred of each other. I can see that clear as day. Yes. They will do very nicely. A superb display for Varinius's son."

Porcino opened his mouth to protest, but the other man cut him short.

"Naturally, I will pay handsomely for them, on my friend's behalf."

Porcino made a quick calculation and responded with a cool smile. "I have to say that I have had my eye on these two. Most promising recruits I've had in a long time. They're sure to have fine fighting careers ahead of them. I would be losing quite an investment if they were forced to fight."

"Then be sure to ask a fair price of me when we settle our business in your office."

Porcino nodded, then inclined his head and gestured toward the gate. "If you would go ahead of me, most noble Marcus Antonius, I must speak briefly to their trainer."

"Very well," the man said, with a faint flicker of frustration flashing over his expression. "But be quick."

He turned away and strode casually toward the gate. Porcino approached Amatus. "Have them taken to one side. Find another trainer for the rest of your students. I want you to concentrate on these two. Drill them as thoroughly as you can. They must be ready to fight in five days' time."

"Yes, master."

Porcino turned to examine Marcus and Ferax. There was a sad expression on his face. Then the sentiment faded as his voice hardened. "They are to be kept with the other pairs selected for the event."

"Yes, master. A real fight is just what these two need. Will it be a display of fighting skills, master?"

Porcino shook his head.

"First blood, then?"

"No." Porcino shrugged. "My customer wants a very special entertainment. He is acting for someone in Rome who wants to celebrate a family birthday. Only the most lavish entertainment will do. When these two go out into the arena, it will be a fight to the death."

TWENTY-THREE

THE ARRIVAL OF THE PARTY FROM Rome was marked by a whirl of preparations. Porcino ordered in fine delicacies, wines, and the best food of the region, as well as hiring a celebrated cook owned by a wealthy merchant in Herculaneum to prepare a banquet for his guests. The arena attached to the gladiator school had a grandstand to one side, where spectators had a good view across the sand-covered oval. In the days before the guests arrived, Porcino's slaves repainted the woodwork and erected a goatskin awning over the structure to provide shelter from any rain, or from sunshine that might dazzle the spectators as they tried to follow the fight. The best couches from Porcino's villa were carefully carried across to the grandstand and arranged in a shallow curve facing the sand. The couches were covered with fine rugs and cushions; then the dining tables were laid out before them.

Marcus saw some of the preparations when he was marched over to the arena for training each morning in the lead-up to the event. As soon as Porcino's visitor had paid the fee for the two boys to fight, they were immediately separated from the other slaves and moved into a small block of individual cells that backed onto the guards' quarters. These cells were for those who were being made ready for a fight. Their food was carefully prepared to build up their strength: a thick meaty broth, boiled eggs, cured sausage with a high concentration of garlic, and watered wine. The food was good, but Marcus had little appetite and had to force himself to eat, mechanically chewing each mouthful and not savoring the flavor. His mind was filled with a growing sense of dread as each day passed.

The men and boys picked to entertain the Romans were kept isolated from the other gladiators, and were kept apart when not training. No talking was permitted in the cells, as each fighter mentally readied himself, forgetting his former companions and focusing his mind on the need to win, and live. Each morning, Marcus was roused from his cell by Amatus and taken to the arena to be personally drilled in the use of the weapons he would wield in the bout with Ferax. Porcino's customer had decided that they would fight with short swords and bucklers, with studded leather breastplates to protect their bodies. Marcus found the armor heavy and uncomfortable, and it took a while before he got used to it. Amatus concentrated Marcus's efforts on sword technique, adding a repertoire of new attacks and defenses.

Another instructor was preparing Ferax, working on his fitness in the training ground. At noon, the two pairs swapped places and Marcus put aside his sword and shield, as he was ordered to run around the boundary, stopping every so often to lift weights. After that, Amatus moved him on to the agility training, making Marcus duck and jump as he swiped a long cane at the boy's arms and head, or his legs. Marcus had to be alert to dodge the blows, but sometimes he was too slow, and winced whenever a stinging blow connected.

"Let that happen in the arena and you're dead," Amatus warned him.

Marcus nodded and hurriedly poised himself for his trainer to begin again, concentrating hard to avoid the next blows. Once Amatus was done with that exercise, he allowed Marcus a brief rest before he took up his weapons and moved on to the training posts to practice his sword strokes. As Marcus sat on the ground, wearily hugging his knees, he looked up at the trainer and asked, "Do you think I can beat Ferax?"

Amatus stared at him for a moment before he replied. "The odds are against you, young Marcus. Your opponent is bigger and stronger. If he can bring his weight to bear and knock you down, then you will be at his mercy." He paused, scratched his chin, and continued in a more kindly tone. "But there's always a chance, no matter what the odds. I've seen far more unevenly balanced fights yield a surprise result. The trick of it is not to get too close to him. Avoid direct contact and don't let him use his size against you. You're small and fast. Wear him down. A small cut here and there and you might bleed him enough to slow him down for a kill."

Marcus felt a shiver go down his spine at the mention of the word. Even though a deep hatred of Ferax burned in his heart, he still felt that he was not sure that he could kill the Celt if the time came. He cleared his throat and spoke.

"I've heard some of the veterans say that if a gladiator fights well enough, then even if he loses, he is spared by the crowd."

"Fat chance," Amatus snorted. "Not with the lot you will be fighting in front of."

Marcus frowned. "Why?"

"They've paid for eight of Porcino's best men, some of his animals, and you two boys. A small fortune. You can be sure that they will want value for money. It's not the same as a fight in a public arena. The mob are happy to watch a good fight, and generous to a man who puts up a decent struggle before he loses. That's because they haven't paid for it. With aristocrats it's different. They part with a fortune and aren't happy unless blood is shed. If they have paid for a fight to the death, then that is what they expect." Amatus leaned forward and punched Marcus lightly on the shoulder. "So, when you get in that arena with Ferax, only one of you is coming out of it alive. Get that fixed in your head. Clear?"

Marcus nodded.

"Then on your feet. There's work to do."

Marcus did not sleep the night before the fight. He sat propped up against the cold wall in his cell. Occasionally, he could hear a sound from one of the other cells as a man shifted on his straw-filled mattress, or muttered in his sleep. Once he could hear the sound of crying and a thin keening whine, before a guard strode down the corridor in front of the cells and bawled at the man to be quiet. Marcus had never felt so lonely or afraid, even through all he had endured since the day that a happy life had been murderously stolen from him and his mother. He tried to force all such thoughts aside and concentrate on the coming fight. Amatus was right—his opponent would try to rush him and use his superior momentum to defeat him. He would need to focus all his wits and be poised to evade Ferax's attacks. At the same time, he could not afford to get close enough to strike a killing blow. After a while, Marcus found himself wondering about Ferax. What would the Celt be thinking? Was he awake as well, planning his fight, tormented by fear and utterly unable to sleep?

At last, the thin light of the coming dawn filled the barred window high on the wall, casting a weak beam on the door to the cell. As the shadows of the window bars grew more distinct and the room became brighter, Marcus rose from his bedroll and stretched himself, easing the stiffness out of his muscles. He felt tired, but knew that the months of grueling training, and the advice that Amatus had given him in the past few days, meant that he was no longer the small, innocent child that had run through the olive groves of his father's farm. He was a fighter. Today he would put all his skills to the test. If he was killed, then all was lost. His mother would die alone and forgotten. If he won, then there was hope for them both.

There was a clank as the door at the end of the corridor was opened, and then the sound of feet shuffling along as each cell door was opened and closed. A short while later, the bolt on the outside of Marcus's door grated and the door swung open. A guard entered, carrying a bowl of porridge and a jug of water. He set them down beside Marcus's bed and paused a moment.

"Best get that inside you." He smiled gently. "You'll need all your strength today."

Marcus reluctantly reached down for the bowl. "Thank you."

Once the guard had left the cell and the bolt had been thrust back into place, Marcus gazed at the glutinous gray mass in the bowl, picked up the spoon, and forced himself to eat. The porridge was thick and salty, but he relished the feeling of warmth it left in his stomach and soon finished it.

An hour after dawn, the door to the cell opened again and Amatus ducked his head in. "On your feet. Time for you to kit up."

Marcus felt his body tremble as he followed the trainer out of the cell, down the corridor, and outside. The other gladiators were waiting for him in a line. Eight well-built men in plain tunics and sandals, and Ferax. None met his eye as they stared ahead. Taurus stood to one side, tapping his vine staff into the palm of his hand.

"Last boy! In place, quickly!"

Marcus hurried to the end of the line and stood as tall as he could. He stared fixedly at the wall in front of him. Taurus strode along the line, scrutinizing those chosen to fight. Satisfied that they were not showing any obvious signs of fear, he nodded to himself and began to address them in his customary parade-ground bellow.

"The master's guests have already arrived at the villa. Porcino is treating them to a light meal while he briefs them on each of you, giving details of your strengths and weaknesses for when they bet among one another. For those of you unlucky enough to be the favorites, I have a few words of advice: don't lose. They'll not thank you for it and will be sure to turn down any appeal for mercy. The first bout will take place at the fourth hour, with an interval of half an hour to permit the guests to eat and talk between fights. The boys will fight last. There'll be a few animal fights afterward to end the day." He paused to stare hard at them. "Porcino's customers have paid for a good show. I don't want to see any kid gloves stuff. Nor do I want to see any quick kills. Show them some sword skills first. Give them some drama before you make it serious, understand? Right, that's it. You know what you have to do. Time to sort out the kit. Follow me!"

Taurus abruptly turned and marched toward the armory as the gladiators and Amatus followed on behind. The weapons and armor were kept in a securely locked building with small windows, each containing a solid iron grille. Inside there were racks of spears, tridents, swords, and knives, as well as helmets, body armor, arm padding, shin guards, and the weighted nets used by those gladiators training to become retiarians. Marcus looked at the weapons as he tried to suppress a shudder. Taurus ordered them to form a line in front of a sturdy table while he and Amatus issued the kit.

"First man, Hermon!"

A tall Nubian at the head of the line stepped forward. Taurus scrutinized him briefly. "You'll fight as a secutor. Helmet, large breastplate, shield, right shin guard, and short sword."

Amatus nodded and selected the weapons and armor from where they were stored, and brought them back to the table. While the Nubian began to fasten the straps of his armor, Marcus glanced at his opponent. Ferax stood rigidly, facing forward. Although Ferax seemed perfectly still and in control of himself, Marcus saw a bead of sweat trickle down the Celt's neck. The fingers of his left hand twitched slightly, and his legs trembled. So, Marcus thought, his opponent was just as scared as he was. That might even things up.

One by one, the fighters stepped forward to receive their equipment, and the quiet in the room was broken only by the curt commands of Taurus, the clink of metal, and lighter fumbling as the men adjusted their buckles. As soon as the gladiators had put on their armor, they found some space to heft their swords, carefully noting how well the weapons were balanced.

Ferax took his kit, and then it was Marcus's turn. He took the pile of arms and armor, noting the cuts in the leather breastplate and surface of the shield. Moving to one of the benches lining the wall, Marcus set his equipment down, and after a short pause, he lifted the breast and back plates and began to buckle them around his body. Amatus watched him with a critical eye, sighed, and stepped over to him.

"That won't do." He tugged the breastplate. "Too loose, Marcus."

While Amatus adjusted the buckle and tested the fit, Ferax snorted with derision. Marcus tried to ignore him, and nodded to his trainer. "Thanks."

Amatus shrugged. "Just do as you were taught, lad. If I had caught you making such a slovenly job of it on the training ground, I'd have boxed your ears. Make sure you do it properly next time." He paused and smiled faintly. "Assuming there is one."

"Yes, sir."

Marcus took up his buckler and tested the weight. The small shield was light, and the metal of the boss was thick enough to protect his hand from any blows. The sword was lighter than those he had used in training, and the edge had been honed to a lethal sharpness. He grasped the hilt tightly and experimented with a few quick thrusts and cuts, feeling the weight and balance.

Once the gladiators had finished arming themselves, Taurus rapped his vine cane on the table. "Sit down! Each pair on opposite sides!"

The fighters did as they were told, taking their places on either side of the armory, sitting on the benches in silence. Taurus nodded to the other trainer.

"Stay here and watch this lot. There's no ceremony today; the guests just want the fights. I'll send for these men when the show begins."

Once Taurus had gone, Marcus and the others sat still, waiting, not making a sound. He looked sidelong at the other fighters, wondering how they could look so composed in the face of death. Opposite him, Ferax glared back, eyes wide and boring into Marcus. After a while, Marcus looked away, fixing his stare on a helmet on the shelf above his foe. A shaft of light from outside caught the bronze cheek guard, and it blazed with color.

A long hour passed, and then Marcus could make out the sounds of light laughter and excited chatter, and he guessed that the spectators were taking their places in the stand above the arena. Sure enough, Taurus returned soon after and stood in the door of the armory. "First two pairs! Follow me!"

The four rose up; two heavily armed secutors and two Thracians, the latter armed with vicious-looking curved blades. They strode out of the armory and Marcus heard their boots crunching down the gravel that lined the tunnel to the arena. Then all was quiet for a while before the cry of the gladiators reached his ears.

"We who are about to die salute you!"

There was the faint clatter and clash of metal and some cries of support. It continued for a while, and then there was a disappointed groan from the spectators, followed by silence. There were none of the usual sounds of the school. Because a fight was on, the rest of the gladiators were locked into their barracks so as not to distract the spectators from their entertainment.

"Next pair!" Taurus called through the door.

It was nearly midday when Marcus and Ferax were called for. Taking up their weapons, they followed Taurus into the covered way that led from the school a short distance to a stout iron cage beside the arena. The last pair of men were sitting on benches on either side, their shields, swords, and helmets close by. Two guards armed with spears stood outside the cage, ready to operate the sliding door that led into the arena. As Marcus and Ferax entered the cage and sat down, Marcus heard a low growl and glanced around to see that there was another cage slightly hidden by the curve of the arena's stockade. Inside, there was a blur of fur, and he heard another growl. Wolves, he realized. Ready for the last act of the show. The sounds of the spectator party carried clearly to his ears. The lower tones of adults talking, pierced by the shrill chatter of children.

The four fighters waited, under Taurus's stern gaze. Then Porcino's voice called down from the spectator stand. "Next!"

"Up!" Taurus ordered the two men, and they hurriedly rose to their feet, pulling on their helmets and buckling the chin straps. Then they picked up their shields and swords and stood ready. Taurus grasped the edge of the sliding door with his hand and pushed it open. Through the opening, Marcus could see the arena, with dark stains in the sand. Beyond lay the audience. Six adults—four men and two women—and three children. Marcus did not have time to register the details of their faces before the two gladiators had entered the arena and the door slid back into place.

"We who are about to die salute you!" the gladiators chanted.

There was a pause, then the shrill cry of a whistle, and the bout began. The clang of sword on sword made Marcus flinch, and he shuffled to the edge of the bench so that he could see into the arena through the gaps in the stockade. The forms of the gladiators were hard to make out, only as partial fleeting glimpses. Aside from the exchange of blows, delivered with grunts, there was little noise. The audience was watching the fight in rapt attention. Marcus turned away, feeling sick. Any moment it would be his turn, and he was seized by a sudden conviction that he would lose the fight and die on the sand. Slowly, if Ferax had his way.

There was a hurried scramble of blows, and a crash as a body slammed into the stockade right in front of the cage. The man's body blocked the light passing through the gaps, and Marcus almost jumped from the bench as the bloodied tip of a sword burst between two of the stockade's posts. The body sagged a little, then there was a deep groan as the blade withdrew, and a soft thud as the dead man fell to the sand.

A moment later, the door to the cage opened and the survivor stumbled through in a daze. There was a deep cut on his thigh, and he left a trail of spots behind him as he passed between the two boys and walked down the covered way toward the camp. Through the opening, Marcus saw two slaves approach the body of the gladiator, with hooks on the end of long sticks. They stopped, hooked through the flesh under his shoulders, and then they turned and dragged the body across the arena to a small gate set to the side of the viewing stand.

Taurus waited until the body was out of sight before he turned to Marcus and Ferax and gestured toward the arena. "It's your time! Out there, now!"

TWENTY-FOUR

Marcus took a deep breath, and then he and Ferax intoned: "We who are about to die salute you!"

They stood erect before the spectators, sword arms raised toward the party of richly dressed Romans. Marcus could see that two of the men were seated with the women. One of the others he recognized as the man who had watched the gladiators at Porcino's side some days earlier. The fourth man was a tall and broad-shouldered with dark, receding hair. He sat in the place of honor, in the middle of the couches arranged to look out over the sand. He was appraising the boy fighters with a cold expression. Then his attention was broken as one of the children, a girl roughly the same age as Marcus, sat on the couch beside him.

"Careful, Portia!" the man called out. "You'll tip my wine over!"

"Sorry, uncle. I just wanted to thank you for bringing me with you." She leaned forward and planted a kiss on his cheek, then rose quickly and rejoined the two boys, who were noisily discussing which of the lads in the arena would win the last fight.

"It has to be the Celt. Look at the size of him!"

"To be sure—he'll pulverize the other boy."

"He's much more powerfully built."

"What odds will you offer on the small one?"

"Five to one. But you'll be wasting your stake. Take my word for it."

Marcus and Ferax were still standing with swords raised, and Porcino glanced at his customers, waiting for the signal to begin. However, the man seated in the center of the stand was talking in low tones to one of his companions. Porcino frowned slightly and then cleared his throat. The man looked up, glanced at the two boys in the arena, and gave Porcino a curt nod.

The lanista took a deep breath and called out, "Fighters! To your places!"

Marcus lowered his sword and turned to Ferax. He backed away until they were ten paces apart. There was a sudden movement at one of the entrances as two guards emerged and trotted around to each side of the arena where the wooden handles of branding rods protruded from small braziers. The guards took up the rods and raised the glowing tips as they stood by the wooden posts, ready to use the heated irons to spur the boys on if they looked reluctant to lock swords.

"I won't need a rod to make me fight." Ferax spoke in a low voice as he readied himself in a crouch, sword and buckler raised. "But you might."

Marcus gritted his teeth and stood balanced, waiting for the signal to begin.

"The final bout of the day!" Porcino announced. "The Celt Ferax versus Marcus, from our Greek territories."

For a flickering instant, Marcus wondered if he should

turn to the spectators and claim that he was a Roman citizen. He could make his appeal for justice, before the fight began. He might be saved, and maybe freed. Before Marcus's thoughts ran any further, Porcino raised the whistle to his mouth and blew a sharp note, then called out, "Fight!"

With a roar, Ferax rushed forward, sprinting across the sand. Marcus braced his boots and held up his buckler. At the last moment he skipped to one side and Ferax hurtled past. Marcus slashed desperately at his arm, but the tip of the blade hissed through the air without striking. At once, Marcus spun around to face his opponent, stepping forward as he had been trained. Ferax scrambled around just in time to parry a blow aimed at his shoulder. For a moment the two exchanged a series of sword blows with a sharp ringing clatter, and then Ferax backed off. They stood, poised, staring at each other. Marcus felt his heart pounding against his ribs, and there was a peculiar sense of elation in his mind.

"I told you!" The man who had chosen them for the fight gripped the arm of the commanding figure in the middle seat. "I knew that these two would provide good sport, Julius!"

The other man stroked his chin and then responded. "What odds will you give me on the smaller one?"

"Him...? Let's see. Seven to one."

"Done! I'll wager fifty gold pieces."

"Fifty? Very well."

Their voices were lost as Ferax let out another bellow and strode toward Marcus, watching him carefully. As Marcus feinted to one side, Ferax moved to cut off his escape, then corrected himself as Marcus dodged back in the other direction.

"Oh no you don't," Ferax growled. "I'll have you this time, you little runt."

"I don't think so," Marcus replied, forcing a sneer onto his lips. "You're too clumsy, Ferax. Too stupid."

The bigger boy's face went white with rage, and he snarled for a moment before he stopped and laughed. "Think you can trick me into losing it? Think again."

He stepped forward and unleashed a series of blows that Marcus had to desperately block with his sword and buckler. There was no chance to strike back, as Ferax had a longer reach. Steadily, Marcus was forced to give ground, edging back toward one of the guards holding a red-hot branding iron. Ferax grinned as he deliberately drove Marcus toward the danger. At the last moment, when he was sure he could sense the burning heat, Marcus threw himself to one side and rolled across the ground before scrambling back onto his feet.

"Oh! That's good!" the man called Julius cried out. "Now, don't give any more ground, boy! Hold fast and outfight him!"

As he heard the encouragement, Ferax's expression darkened, and once again he closed menacingly on Marcus, raining a savage series of blows upon him. As he blocked and deflected each one with his buckler, the shock of the impact jarred his arm painfully, and Marcus winced. He knew that his shoulder would soon go numb under the onslaught, and there was danger that he would let go of the buckler.

Ferax drew off, breathing heavily. "Not...long now, Roman. Want to beg me to make the end quick?"

Marcus shook his head. "I want to take my time killing you."

"Don't even try to sound hard." Ferax sneered. "Mommy's boy. That's what you are, aren't you? That's what I heard. Puny little weed, too weak to save his mother from slavery."

Marcus stood quite still, staring back at his tormentor. Inside he felt his blood turn cold. He stopped thinking about how to win the fight. He stopped thinking at all. The only thing that remained was a murderous rage. Before he was aware of what he was doing, he flew at Ferax. A strange howl tore from his throat as he struck again and again, smashing his blade down on the other boy's buckler and hammering away at his sword as Ferax stumbled back, his expression stricken with surprise and fear.

Only desire and animal instinct guided Marcus as he hacked and slashed. He heard a cry as the blade bit into the bicep of Ferax's shield arm. The shield dipped, and Marcus struck again, glancing off its rim and laying open his opponent's forearm. The buckler thudded onto the sand as drops of blood pattered beside it. Ferax turned sideways, struggling to defend himself with just his sword now. Marcus struck hard, letting Ferax parry the blade wide. As the swords moved to the side, Marcus punched his buckler into the other boy's face. There was a crunch as Ferax's nose was crushed, and he groaned in pain as he staggered back, blood pouring across his lips and chin. Marcus punched again, and Ferax threw his sword arm up to block the blow. As he did so, Marcus ducked down and stabbed the Celt's thigh, ripping the tip free in a fresh welter of blood. In a last, desperate attempt to save his own life, Ferax leaped at Marcus, crashing into him, and they both tumbled into the sand. Marcus saw the sky briefly, clear and blue, then he rolled over, away from Ferax. His sword was caught under his body and was wrenched from his fingers as he rolled.

Marcus leaped at Ferax, who was still dazed as he tried to rise up on his knees. Marcus's shield smashed the blade from the Celt's hand; then he hit him again on the side of the head, and again, before Ferax toppled onto his back and lay still, head lolling from side to side as his eyes fluttered.

Marcus struggled to his feet, swaying from the nervous exertion of his attack. Now that Ferax lay helpless before him, the fighting rage fell away, and reason returned to his mind. Marcus looked around, saw his sword, and moved to snatch it up. As he returned to Ferax, he realized that his left arm was badly cut below the elbow, even though he could not recall the blow that had caused the wound. A searing jolt of pain ran up it as Marcus waggled his fingers. Then he dropped onto his knees beside Ferax's head, raised his blade over his opponent's bared throat, and hesitated. Ferax stared up at him, confused and helpless. Marcus brought the edge of the sword to an inch from the Celt's throat and glanced at Taurus. The head trainer made a quick slicing gesture with his hand and nodded at Marcus. *Do it.*

Marcus took a deep breath and tried to steel his heart, but still he could not cut Ferax's throat. Instead he looked up at the stand, toward those watching expectantly. The man in the center seemed surprised.

"What are you waiting for?" asked his companion. "Finish him!"

"Finish him!" the others echoed, except for the man, and the girl, Portia.

Marcus shook his head and pointed to the leader of the Roman party. "Sir, what do you say?"

The man was still for a moment, his brows knitted as he thought. Then he shrugged. "I say... kill him."

For a moment all was still, then Marcus rose to his feet and tossed his sword aside.

"What do you think you are doing?" Taurus blazed from the sidelines of the arena. "Pick that bloody sword up and kill him!"

"No," Marcus answered firmly. "I won't."

"You will, and you'll do it now. Or, by the Gods, I will kill him myself, and then you."

Marcus shrugged wearily. His body felt cold, and his arm hurt terribly as the blood trickled down to the end of his fingertips and dripped onto the sand.

Taurus strode over to Marcus's sword and scooped it up before he turned toward Ferax. Standing over the dazed Celt, he raised the sword, ready to plunge it into the boy's throat.

"Stop!" the man called out, his voice carrying clearly across the arena. "The boy lives. His fate has been decided by the victor. So it shall be. However"—he smiled faintly— "I will not tolerate any act of defiance by a slave. Porcino, have your men take the Celt away. The other one, from Graecia, stays here."

Porcino looked puzzled. "Stays? Why?"

The man shot him an irritated look. "Because Gaius Julius Caesar says so. That is why. He stays, and he fights those wolves you have been keeping for the final act. If he loses, then that is the price he pays for defying us. If he lives, then he is favored by the Gods and I shall not defy their will. Bring on your wolves, Porcino."

TWENTY-FIVE

THE OWNER OF THE GLADIATOR SCHOOL opened his mouth to protest; then, wary of angering his influential guest, he nodded. "As you wish."

He turned toward the arena. "Taurus! Remove the Celt and the guards. Marcus stays where he is. Let him have a sword and—"

"No," Caesar interrupted. "He shall fight with a dagger. If I am to put it to the test, then I want the Gods to work to save this one."

"Yes, sir. A dagger it is. Taurus, give him yours."

The chief instructor did as he was ordered, muttering to Marcus, "Look after it. Cost me a fortune. Anything happens to it and I'll hold you responsible."

"If anything happens to it, then it's likely that something would have happened to me, master," Marcus replied grimly. "Any words of advice on how to fight wolves?"

"Yes." Taurus cracked a rare smile as he ruffled Marcus's hair. "Stay out of their jaws."

He turned and walked out of the arena, closing the door to the gladiator cage behind him. A moment later he reappeared above the gates leading to the animal pens. A

231

rope was attached to the top of each gate, rising up to a pulley suspended from a frame. He paused and looked down at Marcus. "Ready?"

Marcus glanced around the arena. There were dark patches in the sand where blood had soaked in. Other than the braziers, there was nothing else in the arena but himself. The bleeding from the wound on his left arm had slowed and was already congealing over the torn flesh. But it hurt every time he tried to move it, and would be no use to him. He would have to make do with the dagger. Marcus took a deep breath and looked up. "Ready."

Taurus took hold of the rope on one of the gates and hauled it in. The pulley squealed under the load, and the bottom of the gate slowly lifted clear of the sand. At once, Marcus saw the paws and black snout of a wolf thrusting to get out of the cage. The gate had barely risen knee-high before the wolf squirmed under it and into the arena. It rose into a crouch, head lowered and cold eyes fixed on Marcus. Up until now, Marcus's mind had been reeling with the relief of having defeated Ferax, the pain of his wound, and the hope that he might survive to save his mother. The thought of taking on a pair of wolves had not made him afraid. If they were anything like the wolves he had known in the hills above the farm, then they would be pitiful creatures, afraid of their own shadows.

But the wolf that faced him now was something altogether different. It was much larger and had a shaggier coat. It had also been starved and goaded, as the burn marks on the pelt clearly showed. As it watched Marcus, the wolf's flesh on each side of its muzzle crinkled, revealing fangs. The wolf snarled. Marcus realized it would show no mercy.

When the time was right, it would pounce and tear his throat out. It was this prospect that unleashed the flood of terror that swept through his body. His legs trembled.

Taurus released the rope and the gate thudded down. Moving over to the next rope, he hauled on that one, raising the gate and letting out the second wolf. The animals turned to face each other and snarled. For a moment, Marcus hoped that they might turn on each other, but the bond of their nature, the scent of blood, and the prospect of the hunt instinctively united them. The first wolf padded out along the perimeter of the arena, eyes fixed on Marcus. It paused at a patch of bloodstained sand to sniff and then lick the surface. Marcus watched it in fascinated horror, and so missed the movement of the other wolf as it crept closer, almost on its belly. When Marcus turned back toward it, he saw, with a start, that it was no more than fifteen feet away. He stepped back, and a snarl behind him made him glance over his shoulder. The other beast had also moved closer.

Looking from wolf to wolf, Marcus backed away, edging toward the side of the arena below the spectators. His skin had grown cold with sweat, and he dared not blink as he moved slowly and steadily, crouching low and holding out the blade as he moved. Every so often, one of the wolves would rise slightly, make a short run toward him, and stop. Soon, Marcus sensed the palisade close behind him, and halted, knowing that they would spring on him at any moment.

"He's afraid!" A young boy's voice called down, close by.

"Of course he is," replied the girl. "I think you would be too, if you were in his boots."

Marcus glanced up briefly and met the girl's eyes, and saw pity there.

"What's there to be afraid of?" said the boy. "They're only like dogs. You have only to speak commandingly, and those wolves would roll over like puppies."

"I don't think so," a man's voice responded, and Marcus recognized it as the leader of the party. The man who called himself Caesar. "They're quite wild. Quite lethal."

"I can't see properly!" the boy's voice piped up. "Tell him to move out where we can see him, Uncle Julius."

The man ignored the boy, and there was silence as the spectators lined the rail and leaned forward to view the boy facing the two wolves. Marcus could only wait for them to make a move. All was still and silent, except for the pounding of blood in his ears. Then there was a blur of motion as one of the wolves bounded forward. It leaped at him. Marcus ducked down as the creature slammed into the palisade and twisted to snap at him, its claws gouging. He cried out as his wounded arm burned in agony, and thrust out with his dagger. He missed, struck out again, and was rewarded with a yelp. Far from discouraging the wolf, the wound only seemed to enrage the beast, and it lunged, clamping its teeth around the leather armor covering Marcus's shoulders. It began to crush the joint between its powerful jaws.

Marcus stabbed again and again, feeling a warm gush over his hand. Still, the wolf held his shoulder, shaking and worrying it, as the other wolf braced itself to leap at Marcus from the other side.

There was a gasp from above, then the girl cried out, "They're going to eat him! Someone help! Please!"

"Portia! Get back from the rail!"

Marcus heard a shrill cry, and then the girl's body tumbled onto the sand beside him. In an instant, the other wolf swerved toward her. Portia threw up her arm. The wolf's jaws opened and snapped around her elbow. She screamed in pain.

Marcus had to help her. He stabbed and stabbed in a blind frenzy at the wolf that was still attacking his shoulder. Finally, with a gurgling growl, it released its grip on him and collapsed, dragging the knife from Marcus's hand. Without thinking, Marcus sprang toward the other wolf, clamping his hands around the beast's throat, crushing his fingers into the windpipe. The wolf snarled and shook its head, causing the girl to scream in agony as the teeth tore into her flesh. Marcus released his grip, balled a hand into a fist, and struck the animal's snout as hard as he could. The wolf released Portia and backed off a few paces before turning and bracing its powerful legs for another attack.

"Behind me!" Marcus shouted, thrusting himself between the girl and the wolf. "Stay behind me."

As he stared at the wolf, time seemed to slow, and Marcus was aware of many things at once. The panicked cries from the spectators. Taurus clambering down from the stockade wall. Porcino standing frozen in horror. The agony in his arm and the terror in his heart. The wolf readying itself to leap. And the glint of the dagger in the sand, no more than six feet to his right. Marcus braced his legs, raised his hands, and as the wolf came toward him, he jumped to his right, colliding with it in midair and knocking them both to the ground. There was a writhing mass of fur, claws, and teeth snapping viciously, right in front of his face. Wincing, Marcus grabbed the wolf's lower jaw with his left hand and thrust it up, away, with all his might. At the same time, his right hand groped frantically across the sand. His fingers grazed the blade of the dagger, groped for the handle, and closed around it, just as the wolf tore free of his left hand. The shaggy head drew back, the jaws opened, hot breath closed over his face like a warm cloth, and the wolf lunged for his throat.

The blade flashed through the air, the point smashing into the wolf's ear, shattering the skull and piercing the animal's brain. Its body jerked, and it collapsed on top of Marcus, where it trembled for a moment before it was still. The hot musky smell of the animal filled his nostrils as the fur smothered his face. He struggled to free himself, but the pain in his left arm was unbearable and the loss of blood was making him feel dizzy. Hands pulled the dead wolf away, and several faces swam overhead.

"The—the girl—is she safe?" Marcus muttered.

Then he passed out.

TWENTY-SIX

MARCUS DREAMED HE WAS at home on the farm. It was a bright day in late spring, the land was alive with the fresh buds of flowers, and leaves gleamed on the trees. The sun bathed him in its warm embrace, and butterflies flitted through the air as other insects buzzed drowsily. He had been out hunting but had failed to catch anything. Nevertheless, he was happy and filled with contentment as he started down the track between the olive groves that led to the gate. His heart lifted as he saw his mother and father waiting for him there, smiling as they beckoned to him. Marcus broke into a run as he went toward them, arms outstretched.

Then, when he was no more than twenty paces from them, his parents began to fade away, to become like shadows.

"No..." Marcus moaned, shifting.

As they faded into nothing, the farm, too, began to disappear, and darkness thickened in the air around him, blotting out the landscape. He cried out in despair, "Mother, Father! Don't leave me!"

Then there was a sharp pain that burned down his side, and his eyes opened a crack as he woke. He was in a plain, whitewashed room. A door opened onto a colonnade, over-looking a neat courtyard garden. He recognized it at once and realized that he was in Porcino's villa. There was a scrape close to his side, and he turned his head to see a man sitting on a stool.

"I am not your father, alas," the man said, and smiled. "Although I have known a few women in my time, and it's possible."

He laughed. A warm, hearty laugh.

Marcus stared at him. "I know you. I think. I recognize your face." Then it struck him. This was the leader of the party who had come to see the gladiator show.

"We haven't been formally introduced, my boy. My name is Gaius Julius Caesar." He spoke as though the name should mean something to Marcus, and his smile faded a little when his name provoked no reaction. "Anyway, I wanted to be here when you regained consciousness. I wanted to thank you for saving the life of my niece, Portia."

Marcus closed his eyes briefly and forced himself to concentrate. "The girl who fell into the arena?"

"Yes."

"She's unhurt?"

"Yes. Quite safe. Porcino's surgeon has dressed her wound and says she will recover well enough. Thanks to you." Caesar leaned forward and rested his elbows on his thighs. He was wearing a richly embroidered red tunic. "This time it was an accident." He mused. "Next time, who knows?"

"Next time?"

Caesar stared at Marcus for a moment in silence. "I think I may have stayed away from Rome too long. You don't seem to have heard of me, young man."

"No, sir," Marcus admitted. A thought struck him, and he felt a sudden surge of hope. "Do you know General Pompeius?"

"How could one not know Pompeius? The greatest man in Rome?"

"Is he a friend of yours?"

"Pompeius the Great?" Caesar thought a moment and shrugged. "I doubt whether any truly great man can ever have real friends. Enemies, yes."

Marcus felt the hope drain from his body. "Then you are his enemy."

"No. It's just that I do not aspire to be the friend of so great a man. Not yet." Caesar eased himself back and sat erect, as if seated on a throne. "You have done me a great service, Marcus. Yet, I have more use for you. Though you have not heard of me, I have some influence in Rome, and soon I will have far more power. Naturally, that will ensure that I will have a growing number of enemies—I, and my family. Today's events have helped me to make a decision. I need a bodyguard for Portia. Someone tough, skilled with weapons, and brave—and someone unobtrusive. It would not do to show my enemies that I am afraid of them. No one will pay much attention to a boy your age. That's why I have decided to make you Portia's bodyguard. That will be your job, from now on, or until I find other duties for you."

Marcus's eyes widened. "Me? But, sir, I already have a master. I am owned by Porcino."

"Not anymore. I bought you this afternoon, while you were asleep. I paid Porcino as good a price as he would get for a fully trained gladiator, so he's more than happy with the deal. Oh, and from now on, you will call me master and not sir. Understand?"

"Yes . . . master."

"Good!" Caesar clapped his hands together. "That's dealt with, then. You will rest here until your wounds are better healed, and then one of Porcino's men will escort you to join my household in Rome. Your duties will be explained to you then. How does that sound, Marcus?"

Marcus lowered his gaze from the man and thought for a moment. He would be leaving few friends behind. The three men in his stall were the closest of his companions, and he would miss them, but that was a small price to pay for being brought much closer to Pompeius and what he hoped to be the end of his quest. Marcus looked up at Caesar and nodded. "I am honored, master."

The man rose to his feet and his expression hardened. "I have stated my thanks to you. That is enough. We will not mention the matter again. From this moment, never forget that I am your master and you are my slave. Is that clear?"

"Yes, master."

"When we next meet, it will be in Rome. I wish you a swift recovery."

Without waiting for a reply, Caesar turned and walked out of the room, leaving Marcus to his thoughts. The footsteps receded into the distance, and there was silence, apart from the birdsong from the nearby vegetable garden. Marcus was alone. He stared up at the ceiling and felt more hopeful than he had for a long time. Only that morning he had been afraid that he would not live to see another day. Even though he had defeated Ferax, he would have been condemned to continue training as a gladiator, facing the peril of many more fights before he had the chance to win his freedom. Now he would be the guardian of a pampered Roman aristocrat, living in the heart of Rome, with good prospects of finding General Pompeius and presenting his case to him. Yes. He sighed peacefully. Life had taken a turn for the better.

"I'm not disturbing you, am I?"

Marcus quickly turned his head toward the voice and winced as a burning twinge shot through his shoulder.

"Oh!" Portia looked at him anxiously from just inside the doorway. "I didn't mean to surprise you. I'm sorry, I should have knocked. Only I didn't because I didn't think I should be here. Father would disapprove. He's a friend of Uncle Julius's and spends most of his time worrying about how things should appear."

As Marcus gritted his teeth and waited for the pain to subside, Portia came to the side of his bed and stared down at him. "You look...dreadful. All covered with bruises and cuts, and your arm in bandages."

Marcus raised his right hand and gestured toward her. "You don't look too good yourself."

Besides the dressing on her elbow, she had some scratches and grazes on her pale cheeks.

Portia ignored the comment and frowned slightly. "Does it hurt much?"

"Yes."

"I see." She looked beyond him and then met his gaze again. "I wish I hadn't fallen over the rail. I wish that you didn't have to get hurt on my account. I'm sorry."

"I would have had to fight the wolves in any case." Marcus smiled faintly. "I was bound to get injured. In fact, I'm lucky to be alive."

"You were very brave," she said quietly.

"I did what I had to."

"Yes, I suppose." She cocked her head slightly to one side. "Do you mind if I ask you something?"

Marcus pursed his lips. "No. What is it?"

"I was wondering, why didn't you kill that other boy when you had the chance? I could see he hated you. He would not have spared you if the positions had been reversed."

"That's true enough," Marcus reflected.

"So why didn't you do it?"

"He was beaten. There was no sense to it. The fight was over. It seemed like a waste to kill him...." Marcus tried to remember the moment more clearly. "I don't know. I can't recall it very well. It just didn't seem ... right."

Portia stared at him and then laughed. "You don't sound like any gladiator I have ever met."

"And you've met quite a few, then?" Marcus responded drily.

She stopped laughing. "Yes, actually."

There was a difficult silence, and then she continued in a more even tone. "It seems that you are to be my bodyguard. My uncle Julius thinks you will be quite formidable. For my part, I have only one question to ask of you. Are you prepared to kill anyone who endangers me?"

Marcus thought a moment and nodded. "If I have to."

"Very well. Then I shall see you later, in Rome, Marcus." A smile flickered on her lips as she spoke his name. Then she patted his good arm and hurried to the door. With a furtive look both ways, she stealthily emerged from the room and crept away.

Marcus fell asleep soon after, and woke the next morning with his muscles feeling stiff and bruised. The wound to his arm and the crushing bite from the wolf caused him a great deal of pain, and he cried out as he tried to get out of bed. A moment later the gladiator school's surgeon, Apocrites, hurried into the room.

"What do you think you are doing? Lie back down, at once, before you reopen those wounds."

Marcus did as he was told, and the surgeon quickly inspected his wounds and changed the dressing on his arm. He left the bites and minor cuts uncovered.

"Best let some fresh air get to them. They'll heal quickly enough. The arm will take a bit longer. I've stitched the wound together. In eight to ten days the stitches can be extracted. Tell that to the surgeon in your new master's household, assuming there is a surgeon, that is."

Marcus nodded, then cleared his throat. "How is Ferax?"

"The other boy? He'll recover. You knocked him silly, of course, and he's still a bit dazed. That thick Celtic skull of his saved his head from being caved in. I understand he's something of a laughingstock among the rest of his class. He's even got a new nickname. They're calling him 'Mouse-bait.' You, on the other hand, are something of a hero."

"A hero?" Marcus shook his head. "I've never been more scared in my life."

"Oh, and what did you expect?" Apocrites sighed wearily. "That's what it is to be a gladiator. Always. Anyway, that's all behind you now. You're off to Rome, I hear."

"I'm to be a bodyguard to Caesar's niece."

"Well, that should be safe enough. I doubt you'll ever have to do anything more dangerous than prevent your charge from choking on some sweet delicacy."

"I hope you're right." Marcus eased himself into a more comfortable position. "When will I be ready to travel?"

Apocrites straightened up and scratched his cheek. "Two, maybe three days from now. The master is sending one of his carts to Rome to collect some armor he has ordered. You're to travel in the cart. Just think, boy—in a few days you'll be in Rome. That'll be quite an experience." Apocrites's eyes glittered.

"Yes. I hope it will," Marcus agreed. He was already thinking of how he would set about finding General Pompeius.

TWENTY-SEVEN

Marcus's wounded arm was in a sling, and he supported it as carefully as he could as the cart lumbered up to a hole in the road and lurched to one side. Ahead lay the small town of Sinuessa, where they were to stop for the night in one of the inns. With winter over and the first days of spring imminent, the roads were busy with traders and other travelers making use of the good weather. There were carts piled with all kinds of goods heading in both directions, and groups of people on foot, as well as a handful of loners. As the cart trundled past a chain gang heading in the opposite direction, Marcus regarded them with pity. Most were barefoot and in ragged tunics, and their sullen downcast expressions told of their inner despair as they dwelled on the prospect of a life of slavery. Marcus turned around to watch them for a moment, angered. To see such abject creatures cut him deeply. Yet, he reminded himself, there had been slaves on his father's farm. Marcus had accepted the fact as he had grown up alongside them, and had been inclined to see them as family and friends, and assumed that they were content with their lot. Now he knew different. He had lived as a slave and carried the burden of that condition with him every day. He longed to taste freedom again, and to be master of his own destiny.

He watched the chain gang for a moment longer as it passed a single figure in a long hooded cloak, making for Sinuessa, fifty or so paces behind the wagon. The man had a staff and a begging bowl, and he paused to request a few coins from the guard in charge of the chain gang. The guard cuffed the man aside and strode on. Perhaps there were worse things than being a slave, Marcus thought as he turned away. But, unlike slaves, even beggars could choose their path in life.

The cart driver clicked his tongue and flicked the reins, urging the mule team on. Marcus shot him an irritated look. The bouncing of the cart made his arm hurt badly enough as it was without going any faster. However, he stilled his tongue. Brutus, the driver, was a heavily built freedman who begrudged the fact that he was as poor free as he had been as a slave. They had hardly exchanged a word since leaving the gladiator school, and Marcus was not looking forward to spending several more days in the man's company while they traveled to Rome.

The traffic slowed as it reached the gates of Sinuessa, and those passing into the town paid their toll to enter. The rest detoured around the town to pick up the road again on the far side. Brutus sat impatiently, clicking his tongue and muttering, "Come on, come on. Haven't got all bloody day..."

At length, the leader of the mule train in front of them paid over his coins and passed through the gate; then it was the turn of Brutus and Marcus. The toll collector strode over and glanced at the cart. "The cart's empty. You have no goods apart from the vehicle?"

"Well spotted," Brutus grumbled. "Just me, the boy, and the cart."

"Is the boy yours?"

"He's a slave. I'm delivering him to some patrician in Rome."

"Ah, well then, you'll have to pay a toll for him as well as the cart."

"What?" Brutus's heavy brows knitted together. "What nonsense is this? Since when has Sinuessa charged for slaves?"

"Look there." The toll collector pointed to the placard of rates mounted above the gate. A new entry had been painted at the bottom. "New ordinance passed by the town fathers last month. Slaves are now included as goods on which duty is payable. I'm sorry, sir," he apologized unconvincingly. "But you'll have to pay for the boy."

Brutus turned to glare at Marcus. "I'd better not end up out-of-pocket on this. Your new master will have to cover my costs when we reach Rome."

Marcus shrugged. "You'll have to take it up with him, then. It's nothing to do with me. I'm just a slave."

"And don't you forget it," Brutus growled. "Any more back talk and I'll give you a hiding, y'hear?"

Turning back to the toll collector, Brutus took out his purse and counted over the toll. "There! And you tell the town fathers from me that they're a bunch of bloody crooks."

"Thank you, sir." The man smiled. "I'll be sure to pass on the customer feedback. Now, move on."

Brutus cracked his reins and yelled to the mules, "Yah! Move, you dumb brutes!"

The cart rumbled through the arch and into the town. The smell of rotting vegetables, sewage, and a musty dampness filled the air, and Marcus's nose wrinkled. Brutus drove with seemingly little concern for the other people in the wide thoroughfare, and they were obliged to hurry out of his way, and then he hurled insults after him. He turned off the main street and entered the yard of an inn, hauling back on his reins to halt the mules.

"Down you go. Hold the traces while I deal with the cart."

Marcus climbed down one-handed and then went forward to take the lead mule's traces. Brutus called over one of the stablemen, and they unhitched the polearm and heaved the cart over against the wall. Once that was done, Brutus took the traces to lead his team off to the stables. He nodded toward the cart.

"Find yourself some straw for bedding. You sleep in the cart."

"What about you?" Marcus asked.

"Me? I'll get myself a bunk in the inn. After I've had a drink, or two. You stay here. Don't leave the yard."

"What shall I eat?" Marcus was getting cross with the driver. "I've not had anything all day. You can't let me starve."

"You're a slave. I can do what I like."

"Yes, but I'm not *your* slave. You were told to look after me until we reach Rome."

Brutus sniffed, and then cuffed his nose. "All right," he replied sourly. "I'll send some food out to you, if I remember." Without another word, he strolled away and entered the low door into the inn.

Marcus glared after him briefly and then went to help himself to some straw from the stables, and carried it back to the cart. Once he covered the floor of the cart, he eased himself up and leaned back against the side.

"Still a slave," he muttered.

For a while he just sat and listened to the hubbub of the surrounding streets, pierced by the occasional braying of a mule, or a shout, or shriek of drunken laughter from the inn. As he was about to close his eyes and rest, he saw a man cautiously enter the yard. He wore a long cloak, and held out a bowl. A faint chink of coins carried to Marcus as the man shook the bowl. Marcus remembered the beggar he had seen earlier on the road. He kept quiet as the beggar lowered the bowl, once he saw that no one seemed to be about. Creeping into the middle of the yard, the man glanced around. Marcus could only see his chin, since the hood covered the rest of his features. The hidden face turned toward him, and the beggar paused briefly before approaching the cart.

"You're wasting your time," Marcus spoke out. "I don't have any money to give you."

"Money?" the beggar said quietly. "I don't want money from you, Marcus."

Marcus started. "How do you know my name?"

"I know you well enough," the beggar replied. "Perhaps better than you know yourself."

He approached the end of the cart, limping slightly, and, passing his staff across to his bowl hand, he drew back his hood to reveal his face.

"Brixus..." Marcus shook his head in wonder. "By the Gods, I hoped you had gotten away. What are you doing here?"

"I've been waiting to speak with you, Marcus. I followed you all the way from Capua." Brixus looked around to make sure that they had the yard to themselves, and then he climbed in and eased himself down opposite Marcus. "There's something I need to tell you. Something very important. I had to speak with some others before I could tell you. Now they know what I know, and they agree that I should tell it all to you. It is your right. Your heritage."

Marcus was still getting over the shock of seeing his friend, and shook his head in bewilderment. "What are you talking about?"

Brixus stared at him with an intense expression. "There's no easy way to tell you what I know, and some of what I have guessed. I must be quick, since I don't know how much time I have before anyone comes."

"Brixus, you must go!" Marcus replied in alarm. "If you are seen and recognized, then you'll be caught. You won't escape with that leg."

Brixus smiled craftily. "It's not as bad as it appears. I'll be fine. Now, you just listen."

Marcus opened his mouth to protest, but Brixus held up a hand to silence him, and Marcus nodded. Brixus tapped Marcus's right shoulder.

"It's about that brand I saw. I recognized it at once, but it made no sense. Not at first, not until you told me about your mother. You said she was a slave, a follower of Spartacus."

"That's right. Until she was captured and my father bought her."

"Marcus, I have to tell you: your mother was not a follower of Spartacus."

"Then what?" Marcus leaned closer to Brixus. "Why would she say so? Why lie to me?"

"It was not a lie. In some ways she *was* a follower. But she was more than that, far more. She was his wife, insofar as a slave can have a wife."

"Wife?" Marcus felt his blood chill. "My mother . . . and Spartacus?"

"Yes."

"How do you know this?" Marcus asked suspiciously.

"Because I was one of his chosen band. There were twenty of us, sworn to protect the life of Spartacus. We were marked, as he was, by a special brand. When one of us died, another was chosen, and branded. Only we knew about the mark: the wolf of Rome impaled on the sword of a gladiator; no, *the* gladiator—Spartacus. It was he who designed the brand and had it made, he who first bore the brand, and who in turn branded us. We were a brotherhood, Marcus. Your father and the rest of us. Only his woman shared in the knowledge of the secret symbol."

Marcus swallowed nervously. "And it's the same mark as I have on my shoulder?"

"Yes. And mine. Look here."

Brixus pulled the shoulder of his cloak and tunic down and twisted toward Marcus. A thin white line of scar tissue depicted the wolf's head and the sword. Brixus pulled his clothes back into place.

Marcus shook his head. "It can't be right. It has to be a coincidence."

"Well, then you can imagine how surprised I was to see the brand on you. That's why I had to discover more about it. That's why I had to spare you from the gauntlet." Brixus paused and rubbed his forehead thoughtfully. "You see, after the final battle, when Spartacus was killed and his army defeated, his woman, Amaratis, disappeared. She was with child, and Spartacus had ordered her to escape if the battle was lost. But there was no escape. The armies of Crassus and Pompeius had us trapped. As you know, I was lying injured in the camp during the battle. I saw Amaratis. She told me she was taking all that was valuable to her and would try to find a way home to her people. That was the last time we spoke. I'm guessing now that she took the branding iron with her. She must have still had it when she was captured, and when the centurion became her master. And when her child was born, she branded him." Brixus gripped Marcus's arm gently. "When she branded you."

"But why?"

"Because she wanted you to carry the sign of the rebellion with you. One day, I imagine, she intended to tell you the truth. The whole truth."

"What truth?" asked Marcus, feeling a growing sense of nausea fill the pit of his stomach. "What truth?"

"That you are not the centurion's son. That she was expecting a child when she was taken, and the father of that child was Spartacus himself."

"No...NO!" Marcus shook his head. "It's not true. I know who my father was. He was a centurion. A hero. I loved him." He felt his throat tighten as all the feelings he had ever had for the man who had raised him as a son rose up. Marcus felt his heart swell with longing and grief.

"Hush!" Brixus urged him, glancing around anxiously. "Marcus, it's a hard truth, but it *is* the truth. Believe me."

"No. I won't." Marcus brushed back the first tears. "It's a lie."

"Then how do you explain the mark?"

"I—I can't."

"Think, Marcus. Think back to your childhood. You must know that your mother was keeping something back. From you and your father."

Marcus tried to clear his mind and remember. Almost unwillingly, he recalled his life on the farm, his mother and Titus, and the oddly formal nature of their relationship at times. And also how his mother had always told him that he would be more than the son of a farmer one day, far more.

"Marcus, I don't have much time. Listen to me. I don't expect you to understand all this at once. You are the son of Spartacus. That means you are an enemy of slavery, and that means you are an enemy of Rome. If they ever discovered your true identity, you would be in grave danger. Never tell another soul what I have told you. But there's more to this than you know. The spirit of Spartacus survived his defeat. He lives on in the hearts of slaves across the Roman empire. If ever there was another rebellion, there would be thousands who would flock to join the banner of his son. That day may never come. But if it does, then it is your destiny to strive to complete your father's work. Do you understand?"

"Destiny?" Marcus felt his mind reeling. He shook his head. "No! My destiny is to win my freedom and save my mother from slavery. That's all."

"For now, perhaps. But it does not change who you are and what you stand for. In time you will accept that." Brixus leaned back. "I have told others what I know. That is why I escaped, to pass the word on to other slaves who still remember Spartacus. Even now they are whispering that his son lives."

Marcus glared at him. "Then you put my life at risk."

"No. All that is known is that you live, and that you are a gladiator like your father before you."

"That is already too much knowledge," Marcus said bitterly. "If those who control Rome get to hear of this, they will stop at nothing to find me."

"Then you had better do your best not to arouse suspicion," Brixus suggested. "Marcus, I know it is a dangerous secret, and I surely feel sorry that the burden is laid on such young shoulders, but you are your father's son. If ever there comes a time for the slaves to rise up against their masters again, they will need a figurehead. They will need *you*." Brixus looked around again, shuffled over to the edge of the cart, and lowered his legs to the ground. "I must go. I have already seen a wanted sign with my description on it near the inn."

"Where will you go?" Marcus did not want him to leave. Not when one question after another was building up inside.

"I will remain at liberty for as long as I can. I will travel wherever there are slaves and tell them that the Great Revolt is not finished. Hope lives. Wherever you see a master beating a slave, look for me, Marcus, and I will be there. And so will the spirit of Spartacus, and that of his son."

He leaned forward and grasped Marcus by the hands. "Look after yourself. You are as a son to me."

Then he turned and hurried away, through the gateway of the yard and into the street. Marcus was tempted to run after him, but then he recalled his mother and he knew that he must remain in the cart. He must go to Rome and do all that he could to reverse the great wrong that had been done to his family....

He paused and smiled bitterly to himself. His family was a lie. Titus did not share his blood and was not his to avenge.

As he sat and waited for Brutus to send him some scraps of food, Marcus felt a vague sense of purpose stirring inside him. He had never been a free Roman. Not really. It was slave blood that ran in his veins, and always had. His bond was with slaves, not the free. He had started this quest to right the wrong that had been done to his mother and him. Now there was a far greater injustice looming over him, and soon he must decide what he could do about it. He could choose to follow the path Brixus had laid out for him, or he could create his own destiny. Either way, he must go to Rome. He reached over his shoulder, his fingertips brushing along the scar tissue of the brand, and he whispered softly to himself.

"Father..."

MARCUS KNEW HE HAD MADE a fatal mistake the moment he backed into the corner of the yard. He felt the heel of his sandal scrape against the cracked plaster of the wall and instinctively took a half step forward to win a small space in which to move. It was what he had been trained to do at Porcino's gladiator school—always give yourself room to move in a fight, otherwise you surrendered the initiative to your opponent and put yourself at their mercy. It was a lesson that Taurus, the stern and cruel chief trainer, had beaten into the trainee gladiators.

At eleven years old Marcus was tall for his age, and the hard training had made him strong and tough and had given him some skill with a sword. Even so, he knew the odds were against him as he faced his opponent, a wiry man in his thirties, fast on his feet and with a keen eye that anticipated almost every move that Marcus made in their fight.

Blinking away a bead of sweat, Marcus thrust aside his anxiety. He knew his only hope was to do the unexpected—something his opponent had not been trained to deal with. From the way the man moved and handled his short sword, it was clear that he'd been trained as a soldier, perhaps even a gladiator. When the man had drawn his sword on the boy he had begun with a few lazy thrusts and feints. The initial sneer on his face had quickly faded as Marcus confidently parried his sword blows aside. There had been a brief pause as the man withdrew a few paces to cast a fresh look at his young foe.

"Not so wet behind the ears then," he growled. "Still, you're just a little whelp in need of a good hiding. And that's what I'll give you." Then he closed in on Marcus in earnest, and the clatter of their sword blows echoed off the walls of the courtyard. Outside, in the Rome backstreet that passed behind the yard, the hubbub of voices dimly carried to Marcus's ears, muffled by the blood pounding through his head. He paid them no attention and concentrated on his opponent, watching for any flicker of movement that would indicate the next attack.

The man was good. He wouldn't have lasted more than a few heartbeats against an expert like Taurus, but it was only a question of time before he defeated Marcus. Despite the boy's quick, darting movements, the man soon edged Marcus into the corner, trapping him against the walls.

For an instant Marcus surrendered to the fear that the man would win and cursed himself for letting it happen. Forcing the thought from his mind, he settled into a crouch on the beaten earth and cobbles of the yard. He moved his weight slightly forward so that he was poised on the balls of his feet, ready to spring forward, or aside, in an instant. His sword was held level, a short distance from his side, where it could lash out to attack, or block any strike the man threw at him. His left hand reached out to keep him balanced.

There was a brief pause as they stared at each other.

Marcus was aware of movement behind the man as the figure watching from the doorway on the far side of the yard shifted his position.

As his gaze flickered aside the attack came. With a roar, the man sprang forward and slashed his sword at Marcus's head. The boy ducked to one side as the tip of the blade hissed through the air a few inches from his face. At once he made a cut toward his opponent's sword arm and sensed a faint jarring as the edge of the sword nicked the man's skin.

With a curse, the man fell back and raised his arm to look at the wound. It was only a shallow scratch, but the blood flowed freely, the droplets scoring jagged crimson lines down the man's forearm as he stared at the cut flesh. He fixed Marcus with an icy stare.

"That is going to cost you, boy. Cost you dearly."

Marcus's blood went cold at the menacing threat, but he kept his eyes on his opponent.

The man lowered his arm, tightening his grip in case the blood flowed into his palm and caused the weapon to slip. He strode deliberately toward Marcus, lips curled back in a vicious snarl. There was no attempt to pull back his blows this time. The clash of blades rang loudly in Marcus's ears as he was beaten back against the wall. The tip of the sword struck the plaster to one side of his head, and chips exploded off the wall. The blade ripped back, high, ready to strike down on Marcus's head.

"Stop that!" a deep voice called across the yard.

But the man's blood was up, and he aimed another blow at Marcus. At the last moment, Marcus desperately leaped forward, inside the arc of the blade. He went low, throwing his full weight into his attack as he punched with the guard of his sword between the man's legs, into his groin. There was a deep groan, and the man stumbled back with an agonized expression. He let out a cry of pain and rage, balling his left hand in a fist as he swung it hard. Marcus tried to duck the blow, but it glanced off his skull, and the impact snapped his head to the side. Bright white sparks filled Marcus's vision as his body flew through the air. Then he landed heavily, and the breath was driven from his lungs. He rolled onto his back, gasping, as the walls and sky spun around above him. The man lurched into view, groaning as he doubled over. Then Marcus felt the tip of a sword touch the bony notch at the base of his throat.

The man's eyes narrowed, and Marcus feared the man would thrust the weapon home to cut Marcus's throat as the tip tore through the top of his spine. He would die, and his heart was flooded with regret and shame that he had failed to win his freedom and find his mother. She had been enslaved at the same time as Marcus and taken to a farming estate somewhere in Greece, and if he died, she was doomed to end her days there. Clenching his eyes shut, Marcus prayed to the gods that he might yet be spared.

"Festus! That's enough!" the voice called out again. "Cut the boy, and I'll have you crucified before the day's out."

There was a slight pause before the light pressure of the sword tip eased, and Marcus dared to blink his eyes open. He was cold with shock, and his limbs trembled as he lay sprawled on his back in the corner of the yard. Above him he saw Festus gritting his teeth in frustration and, beyond, the smoke-smeared sky. Even though it was late in the spring, clouds hung low over Rome and threatened rain. Festus straightened up, reversed his sword, and snapped it back into his scabbard before turning toward the doorway to bow his head. Marcus scrambled to his feet, breathing hard, and stood apart from Festus as he bowed too.

When he straightened up, he saw the other man striding across the yard toward them, a thin smile on his lips. He stopped in front of Marcus and looked down, appraising him, and then turned to Festus, his chief bodyguard.

"Well? What do you think of him?"

Festus paused before replying cautiously. "He is fast, and skilled with a blade, master, but the boy still has much to learn."

"Of course he does. But can you teach him?"

"If it is your wish, master."

"It is." The man smiled swiftly. "It is settled. The boy is in your charge. You will train him to fight. He must learn how to use other weapons beside the sword. He must be able to use the dagger, throwing knife, staves, and his bare hands." The man looked at Marcus again. There was no hint of good humor in those cold eyes as he continued. "One day young Marcus may become a fine gladiator in the arena. Until then, I want you to continue the training he began at Porcino's school. But you must also teach him the ways of the street if he is to be an effective bodyguard for my niece."

"Yes, master," Festus nodded.

"Then you may leave us. Take the boy's sword with you. Then find my steward and tell him I want my finest toga cleaned and scented for tomorrow. The mob will expect nothing less from one of their consuls," he mused. "I want to look good when I stand beside that fat fool, Bibulus."

"Yes, master." Festus bowed again, then hurried across the yard back into the house. When he had gone, the man turned his full attention on Marcus.

"You know that I have many enemies here in Rome, young Marcus. Enemies who would harm my family as gladly as they would dare to harm me, Caius Julius Caesar. That is why I need someone I can trust to protect Portia."

"I will do my best, master."

"I want more than your best, boy," Caesar said firmly. "You must live to protect Portia. Every waking moment your eyes and ears must be open to every detail of your surroundings, if you are to detect threats before they can cause harm. And not just your eyes and ears. You must use your brain. I know you have quick wits. You proved that back in Capua."

He leaned forward and tapped Marcus lightly on the chest. "I may be consul, one of the two most powerful men in Rome, but even I can bleed just as easily as the next man. I have men who protect me, and men who spy for me; yet somehow I sense that you may prove to be one of my most useful servants. For now, you will guard Portia, but I may have other uses for you."